"*Like a River Glorious* rises a level above, touching on fine literature. If I were to write a Victorian romance, I'd call myself a roaring success for writing one like this! Blackwell puts it all together: fast-moving plot, excellent character development, outstanding background—all form a finely worked novel with a message of hope."
Gilbert Morris, best-selling author

"If you've ever wanted to live for a while in Victorian England, this is your chance! Blackwell's characters are as finely crafted as Venetian glass."
Bobby Funderburk, author

Like a River Glorious

LAWANA BLACKWELL

Tyndale House Publishers, Inc.
WHEATON, ILLINOIS

Library of Congress Cataloging-in-Publication Data

Blackwell, Lawana, date
  Like a river glorious / Lawana Blackwell.
    p. cm. — (Victorian serenade)
   ISBN 0-8423-7954-1 (alk. paper)
    1. Man-woman relationships—England—Fiction.   2. Swindlers and swindling—
England—Fiction.   I. Title.   II. Series: Blackwell, Lawana, 1952- Victorian serenade ; 1.
PS3552.L3429L54   1995
813'.54—dc20   95-14548

Printed in the United States of America

00	99	98	97	96	95	94
7	6	5	4	3	2	1

To Buddy, my husband and best friend—
and a godly example to our children.
Your constant, loving encouragement
has given all of us the confidence
to pursue our dreams.

With special appreciation to Gilbert Morris,
my writing mentor and friend.

Like a River Glorious

Like a river glorious is God's
   perfect peace,
Over all victorious in its bright
   increase;
Perfect, yet it floweth
Fuller every day,
Perfect, yet it groweth
Deeper all the way.

Frances R. Havergal

Prologue

September 8, 1855
Hospital tent outside Sevastopol, Crimea

Captain Adam Burke awoke from merciful oblivion into a pain-racked darkness filled with the scurrying figures of demons and ghouls. In shocked disbelief he listened as two demons just a few feet away chattered about the rumored likelihood of a Russian surrender while they sawed off the leg of a screaming boy.

Dear God . . . I'm in hell! He was sure of it, for he could recall the instant of his death. It had come when the cannon had exploded, tearing his head from his body.

Somehow, in this terrible place, his head had been reattached, and the pain pushed him to the edge of insanity. Adam watched the young man on the pallet next to his quiver and lie silent, and tears welled up in the one eye that was not matted shut.

Then to Adam's ultimate horror, Satan—covered with blood and holding a knife—turned in his direction and motioned to his demons. Adam let out a scream, but still they came toward him. His arms and legs were seized roughly, and his body was swung through the air to a table.

Blackness again swirled up to engulf him. As he gladly gave himself up to the comforting nothingness, his mind registered astonishment that Satan would speak the Queen's English and wear a British army uniform.

1

"WELL, how do I look?"

Turning in front of her dressing-table mirror, Corrine Hammond batted her long charcoal lashes and arranged her lips into a simpering smile.

"Why, you're the picture of virtue," mocked the man leaning against the wall with his arms folded. "Even Queen Victoria herself would be proud of you. Where in the world did you get such a . . . hideously modest frock?"

Corrine laughed, her small hands fingering the lace at the severe collar of her lavender chambray gown. "Madame Jollisaint went pale when I told her the designs I wanted. When I insisted, she finally gave the job to one of her assistants." She inflected her voice with a heavy French accent. "'Je ne sais quoi! Zee woman's body is to be displayed, like a magnificent painting. Why, now, do you want to dress like a nun?'"

Narrowing his heavy-lidded eyes, Gerald Moore gave her a knowing smile. "Yet you still couldn't resist having it tight around your little waist, could you?"

With a flounce of her skirt, Corrine turned back to the mirror. "Adam Burke may be a Methodist do-gooder, but he's still a man—at least I *assume* he is." She piled her raven hair to the top of her head, then angled her face slightly to study the contour of her delicately clefted chin. "While I'm appealing to his more noble instincts, why not get the attention of his baser ones as well?"

Gerald shook his head. "The poor bloke hasn't got a chance. Might as well send for the engravers to start on your engagement announcements."

"That might be rushing things a bit, wouldn't you say?" She let her hair loose to fall in glossy tendrils down her back, then took a seat on the cushioned bench in front of her dressing table, picked up a brush, and began pulling it through her hair. "I haven't even made his acquaintance yet."

"A minor detail that will soon be taken care of, I presume? After all, we've been here four weeks now."

"You should know by now that these things take time."

"Of course they do." His voice took on an impatient edge. "But never *this* much time. After all the research I did to pick this poor devil, I should have thought you would have played your hand weeks ago."

Corrine's anger flared. "That's just the problem . . . you didn't pick a *poor devil* this time, did you? I had to have a complete new wardrobe made up . . . unless you prefer that I call on him while I'm wearing my green silk. Or perhaps that red sateen you like so much."

Sighing, Gerald walked over to stand behind her, putting both hands on her shoulders. Thirty-eight years of age, his handsome blond features were marred only by anemic blue eyes and lips that were much too thin. "I'm sorry, darling—I shouldn't be pressuring you. It's just that we're close to being broke again, and we can't keep up the rent on this place for too long if nothing happens."

"Really?" As she watched his reflection from behind her in

2

the mirror, the fire in her eyes turned to ice. "I'm glad to hear you're worried enough about our finances to give up *gambling.*" Her voice dripped with sarcasm.

Gerald gripped Corrine's shoulders so hard that his knuckles turned white.

"Gerald, you're hurting me!" she hissed, reaching up to push at his hands.

He immediately loosened his grip, then crouched down on one knee behind her, peering over her shoulder at their reflections in the mirror. "Just remember who you were before *I* found you and taught you how to get what you want. Would you rather be back milking cows in Leawick again, living in a broken-down hut with a whining brat and that drunken sot of a husband?"

~

The mention of her former life was enough to send a chill down Corrine's spine. Growing up as the eldest of nine siblings, she'd shared a corn-shuck mattress with two other sisters in a crumbling stone cottage, where there never seemed to be enough room to breathe—let alone have any privacy. At fifteen, she married Thomas Hammond, a quiet charcoal burner in his twenties . . . and the first man who asked her. How he'd managed even to muster enough courage to propose was beyond her comprehension, for he could barely speak to her without stuttering—even after they'd wed.

The privacy Corrine had left her father's house to find was at last realized, for a charcoal burner's calling was a solitary one. For days at a time, Thomas slept and ate in a temporary shelter deep in the woods, by the side of the pit in which his logs were stacked.

On his rare homecomings, it didn't take Thomas long to realize that his beautiful wife had no interest in anything he had to say, stutter or not. By the time their baby was born a year later, he had discovered that a numbing solace could be found in pints of strong, black English stout.

The baby, a girl, was a disappointment to Corrine. Born with her father's sparse, fawn-colored hair and evidence of what might someday be the same weak chin, she was scrawny from the beginning and cried incessantly to be fed. Corrine resented these demands for nourishment, for they intruded upon her newfound solitude. The child was only a year old when Corrine turned her over to a younger sister during the day and found employment at a neighboring dairy farm.

Several months later she met Gerald Moore. He was on his way to Liverpool and was procuring lodging for the night at Leawick's Gaston House Inn when Corrine showed up with a delivery of cheese and butter. The next morning she went back, but this time with no deliveries. She left with him that very day.

They had been together for over eight years. He had taught her how to dress, how to talk, and how to carry herself around genteel people with a self-confidence just short of arrogance. She owed Gerald everything. She knew it, and he knew it, too.

~

Gerald saw her lips tighten as she regarded him in her mirror. "I'll *never* go back. Even if I have to go it without you."

"Without me?" A ghost of a smile flitted across his thin lips. "Then perhaps you should, dear. Your sense of gratitude has been sadly lacking of late." He reached out a hand to touch her cheek, then stood and headed for the door.

"Oh, come now, silly!" she said with a little laugh. She turned her face to watch him. "You don't have to be so dramatic."

The only sound was the squeak of the doorknob in Gerald's hand.

"Well, go then." She lifted her chin and began brushing her hair again. "You'll be back before nightfall."

"Not a chance, Corrine. I've had enough of waiting on Your Majesty." He pulled the door open and took a step toward the hall.

"Gerald!" Corrine slammed her brush down on the table and shot up to her feet, toppling over the bench behind her. "Gerald . . . don't go!"

His back was to her as he stood with his hand still on the doorknob. Tilting his head, he waited.

She was next to him in an instant, throwing her arms around his waist. "Don't leave me, Gerald!" she cried. "I didn't mean the horrible things I said!"

He turned to face her. "I think you did," he said quietly. "I think it's time to go our separate—"

"No!" She pressed against him so forcefully that he had to take a step backwards. "I love you, Gerald. . . . I'll *die* if you leave me!"

Slowly he brought his arms up around her as she leaned her head against his shoulder and wept. "There, there," Gerald whispered, trying to mask the satisfaction he felt. Looking over her shoulder, he caught the gaze of nineteen-year-old Rachel Jones, Corrine's maid, standing near the bureau with another gown in her arms.

"Leave us now," he told her.

Her eyes downcast and cheeks flaming, the girl was on her way to hang the gown in the wardrobe when Gerald spoke again. "Just put it across a chair or something and go!"

~

Thirty minutes later, Rachel's cheeks were still burning as she knelt to polish the sideboard in the dining room. *I wish they wouldn't treat me like part of the furniture!* she thought, scrubbing furiously at the rosewood carvings with a wool cloth. It was awful when they fought—and worse when they made up!

She wondered about this Mr. Adam Burke, who was to be their next target. Was he married, like that nice Squire Nowells? Corrine and Gerald had quarreled about him, too, after Squire Nowells had shot himself and they had to leave York in a hurry.

Setting the dusting cloth on the carpet for a moment, she reached up to tuck some stray wisps of hair back into the lace cap on her head. Poor Mrs. Nowells . . . and her family. Even though she'd heard the children were all grown and married, it still had to hurt, losing their father like that. And the terrible scandal!

Sometimes she thought it would have been better if Corrine and Gerald had left her at the Freeman's Charity for Foundling Children in Liverpool, which had been her home from her earliest memories. Posing as a married couple, they had shown up at the orphanage six years ago, offering to give employment to an older girl. They couldn't pay much, they had explained in front of Rachel to Mrs. Dawson, the proprietress, but they could provide a decent home and adequate meals.

They had seemed like angels from heaven back then, for

Rachel was on the threshold of her thirteenth birthday, when her stay at the overcrowded institution would have been terminated. Where would she have gone then? To the workhouse? She shuddered. The orphanage had been bad enough, but she'd heard many a horror story about the workhouses.

Several times lately she had considered seeking other employment. But how would she find another position without references? Corrine had made it clear, that day she'd come upon Rachel in the kitchen reading the advertisements for domestic agencies in the *East London Observer,* that she wouldn't be given any references if she left. "You leave us, Rachel . . . and I'll find out where you're working and tell your new employers that I discharged you because you're a thief!"

Still, she had mustered up the courage to answer a couple of the advertisements on the sly—on her way to the market just a few weeks ago, when they'd first moved to London. After being told icily at two different agencies that references were of supreme necessity, Rachel had given up any hope of finding a better job.

She didn't mind the hard work. Even at the orphanage, she had spent the better part of her childhood scrubbing, polishing, and dusting. Physical labor had become as natural to her as breathing. It was just so painful to see the Missus and him go about hurting people for money's sake!

She had another reason for wanting to leave—she didn't like the way Gerald had been looking at her lately. Just last week, when she was serving their dinner, he had let his hand linger on hers too long when she handed him a pewter salt cellar. And to top that off, he had turned to Corrine and said, "I believe our Rachel has blossomed into quite a comely young lady this past year. Those emerald eyes are going to melt some man's heart one day." Corrine clearly didn't appreciate his observation.

She caught her reflection in the gilt mirror above the sideboard. A pair of serious green eyes stared back at her, huge and thickly lashed, and set over a straight freckled nose and full lips. Of medium height, she carried herself erect and was careful to keep her shoulders squared. She had seen too many servants with rounded shoulders from bending and scrubbing.

Many times Rachel had daydreamed about some decent man telling her she was pretty, but it had made her insides grow cold to hear such flattery coming from Gerald Moore. That's when she had taken to locking her door at night.

~

Early the next morning, Rachel was reaching up for her market basket from a hook on the kitchen wall when Corrine appeared at the foot of the staircase, her hair in disarray around her shoulders. "What do we have to eat in here?" she mumbled, tying the sash of her silk wrapper at her waist.

Startled, Rachel stepped across the stone-flagged floor to the kitchen worktable and pulled out a chair. "Here, Missus," she said.

When Corrine had taken a seat, Rachel glanced helplessly back at the open cupboard. Her mistress usually didn't appear before noon, and the marketing hadn't yet been done. "The bread's stale and we're out of cheese, but I could cook up some eggs for you."

Corrine's yawn emphasized the fine lines that were beginning to show up around her eyes. "Never mind, just fix me some tea. And bring back some of those little seed cakes from Karina's when you go out."

That was the only secret the two of them shared—Corrine's sweet tooth. Gerald disapproved of her partaking of any foods that might cause her figure, and thus their fortunes, to change. As tiny as she was, she had a tendency to gain weight, so Gerald inspected her plate at every meal. The pastries and candies that Rachel brought back from marketing were slipped into a covered earthen crock in the cupboard and spoken of no more.

"When you get back," Corrine was saying while Rachel pumped water into a copper teakettle, "I've got an errand for you to run."

Biting her lip, Rachel leaned against the cast-iron range where she had set the kettle. It was starting again. . . .

"Rachel?" Corrine's voice came from behind her.

"Yes'm?"

"I want you to take a message to a Mr. Adam Burke for me, inviting him over for tea tomorrow afternoon."

She says it so easily, like she really believes she's just being sociable by having that poor man over, thought Rachel. With trembling fingers, she lit the gas jet with a lucifer match. *As if she doesn't even remember I was in the same room last night when they talked about him!*

"Rachel!" Corrine exclaimed irritably. "Did you hear what I said?"

"Oh . . . yes, Missus." Turning her head, she gave the woman at the table a halfhearted nod.

"So don't dillydally around with the shopping."

~

Basket in hand, Rachel hurried down the stone path leading to the front of the house. Corrine, a stickler for English tradition, made her use the back door exclusively, as befitting her station.

Gerald also used the servants' entrance, coming and going only under the cover of darkness, but for different reasons. All of this subterfuge was probably unnecessary, because he always made sure they rented a house a good distance from their prey. He was careful, nonetheless. Neighbors were sure to be interested in the activities of a supposedly unmarried woman of Corrine's beauty—and you could never tell who might be an acquaintance of whom.

The fact that the gin palaces and card rooms didn't come fully alive until well after the sun had set also had something to do with his nocturnal habits, Rachel suspected.

When she reached the road, Rachel looked back fondly at the house, an early Georgian building of red brick. Four white sash windows graced the narrow two-story exterior, and two dormer attic windows were set in a high-pitched roof. A trellised front porch, also white, gave character to the front.

She liked this house. While it was one of the smallest they had stayed in—Corrine and Gerald hadn't gotten nearly as much from Squire Nowells as they had hoped—the inside walls were papered in crimsons and golds, blues and browns. Most of the floors were white-veined marble—a burden to polish but, oh, so beautiful! Fireplaces were at each end, and even her attic room had vented floors that let in adequate warmth.

As special as the house was, the location was even more attractive. The East India Dock Road was a pleasant vista, lined with ancient houses with neat terraces and carriage drives. One had only to walk another block east to come upon the River Lea, where the masts and sails of hundreds of ships created a pretty picture.

But it was a melancholy joy that Rachel received from the house and its leafy avenue. She knew that in all probability they would leave London within a year—two years at the most.

She boarded an omnibus at Commercial Road, took a seat on the lower level, and settled in for the two-mile ride west to the dockside market at Wapping. Clutching her basket in her lap, Rachel watched pedestrians and other vehicles make their way through the fog-shrouded streets. She wished she could ride forever . . . or at least until she were miles and miles from her master and mistress.

Rachel sighed. Surely somewhere in England there was a place where people treated their servants with kindness and dignity and where men's faithfulness to their wives, or at least to their principles, made them immune to Corrine's seductive ways.

~

The noises and commotion of the open-air market that flanked the London Dock warehouses were almost overpowering. For a square block, the whole ground was covered with handbarrows, some laden with baskets, others with sacks. Over the chatter of housewives and servants rose the hoarse shouts of costermongers and the shrill cries of fishwives. The smell of turbot, flounders, cockles, red herrings, and sprats permeated the air and settled into the clothing of everyone in the immediate area. Rachel bought some salmon for tonight's supper, then moved on to the vegetable stands for potatoes and onions and to the fruit vendors for oranges and hothouse strawberries.

Don't dillydally around! Corrine's words came back to her as Rachel stood at the crossroads of Ratcliff Highway and Wapping High Street, her back to the market.

She had shopped as quickly as she could, but it took so long to find oranges that weren't soft. A morning breeze, full of April chill and dampness, pressed against her thin muslin dress and stirred the fringes of the gray wool shawl around her shoulders. Drawing the shawl tighter, she thought longingly of the quaint little shops lining Cable Street, just a block to the north. After a moment, she gave a sigh and pointed the toes of her leather slippers in the opposite direction.

She had only taken a couple of steps when an idea occurred to her. *The seed cakes!* Karina's Baked Goods had been out of the cakes already when she had stopped by, so Rachel had purchased a few slices of chocolate torte for Corrine instead.

But she really wanted seed cakes! There was a bakery down Cable Street—Nellford Brothers'. Surely some of the little pastries would be there. And how much longer could it take to pop into Solomon's and look at the paintings?

~

The bell attached to the transom jingled as Rachel opened the door and stepped into the art shop. The interior of the store was as cool as the morning air outside. Immediately an elderly man with wire spectacles looked up from behind a table in the far right corner.

"Ah, my good friend Miss Rachel Jones," he said, a smile lighting up his face through his white whiskers. "You haff come back to see me."

Surprised that the proprietor had remembered her name, Rachel timidly returned his smile. "I can only stay for a minute." She walked past rows of baize-covered screens displaying various works of art to his paint-spotted worktable.

"I haff to keep the windows open when I do this," Mr. Solomon explained, nodding towards the linseed oil he was rubbing on a wooden frame. "The odor makes my head ache. Do you find it cold in here?"

"I didn't even notice." Rachel turned to look at the paneled wall to her right, where an assortment of canvases covered almost every inch. She paused when she came to an empty space. "Did you sell the portrait of the lady?"

"Ah, you mean the Gainsborough. Last week . . . to an American. He paid the full price, too."

Suddenly remembering she had been told to hurry, Rachel set her basket down on the floor and pulled open the drawstring to her beaded purse, one of Corrine's castoffs. "May I buy two pencils?"

Mr. Solomon looked up from his work, his old eyes amused behind their spectacles. "So, the little lady is an artist? No wonder you're so interested in the paintings in my shop."

She looked down at her hands. "No, I just . . ."

In a flash, the amusement on the man's face turned to alarm. "I haff embarrassed you?" Setting aside the cloth, he came around the table and was at her side. "My wife tells me all the time that I speak without thinking . . . and she is right!"

"You didn't say anything wrong," she assured him quietly. "I just like to draw people. I don't consider myself a real artist."

Relief came instantly to his face. "Then you shall haff your two pencils, Miss Jones—no, a half-dozen pencils! My gift to you."

She was about to protest when he held up a hand. "Perhaps

one day when you consider yourself a *real* artist, you'll bring some of your work here for an old man's opinion."

~

Rachel barely felt the cobbled stones under her slippers on the way back to the train station. The thought of the pencils, wrapped in brown paper and tucked into her basket, kept a smile on her face.

He really wants to look at my sketches! she told herself again, giving wide berth to a couple of pigeons involved in a noisy tug-of-war over a potato peeling in the street. *And he wasn't just being nice, either!*

But another thought slowed her steps. *And then what?* For the most part, the paintings in Mr. Solomon's gallery were done in oils or watercolors, brilliant or muted tints that added realism and brought life to their subjects. Some, like the seascape he kept in a glass case, were the works of masters long gone. How could she even think of showing him pencil sketches on scraps of paper!

Another thought, even more dreadful, took the smile from her lips. *And what if he doesn't think I have talent?* She could picture him peering down at her work, his brow drawn as he tried to find gentle words to tell her that it was no good. That was a real possibility—Corrine had told her many times that her sketches were depressing. "Why do you draw such ugly people, when you could find so many nicer things to draw, like flowers or dresses?"

Rachel didn't know why she had this fascination with downtrodden people—chimney sweeps, rag and bone collectors, doorway orphans, and the like—but she certainly didn't find them ugly. Stories were etched in such faces, she thought

. . . tales of hunger and worry and despair, but sometimes of hope that hard times would get better.

She had even sketched Mr. Solomon's lined face after her first visit to his shop, capturing his warm, studious expression to the best of her memory. All of her drawings were done that way, for she had never had the nerve to actually *ask* someone to pose for her. Whenever she found a face that captured her attention, she committed it to memory until she could get it on paper.

Sometimes finding the time to sketch took a while, for Corrine and Gerald enjoyed being waited upon. Rachel's days began at six o'clock in the morning and ended only when the last dishes were washed and put away in the kitchen. She climbed up to her room many a late night too weary to think of anything but throwing herself on her mattress and sinking into oblivion.

~

When Rachel returned from the market, Gerald and Corrine summoned her to the sitting room.

"I'm hiring a hansom to take you to Mr. Burke's house," Gerald said. "We don't want him to think Corrine would send a servant on such a long walk, or can only afford to send you on an omnibus. So you are to appear grateful for her thoughtfulness should the subject come up."

Rachel stood before her employers with her hands clasped behind her back. "Yes, sir." She remembered all too well the five-mile walks to Corrine's favorite bakery when they had lived in Northampton, after Gerald had lost their horse and carriage in a game of faro. But she kept her face expressionless.

"Of course," he continued, "we don't expect that you'll

actually be invited to *speak* with the gentleman directly. But household servants are notorious gossips, and word usually gets around to their masters. So you must keep up appearances no matter who is around you."

Corrine, seated on the gold-damask settee, agreed. "Your livelihood depends on this, too, Rachel, so take our instructions to heart." She turned to Gerald. "I don't think we should send her in a hansom, though. No respectable lady would be seen in one without an escort."

He gave Corrine a smile that, to Rachel, appeared just a shade condescending. "That prejudice is only toward members of the gentry class, my sweet, not servants."

Turning his attention back to Rachel, he leaned forward in his chair. "Now, what are you to do when you give your mistress's message to the housekeeper?"

"I'm to say that Mrs. Hammond requests that I wait for a reply, if at all possible."

"Good," said Gerald. "I'm expecting you to come back with an answer, so don't fail us."

The weight of their scrutiny added to Rachel's discomfort by the minute, and she longed for the solitude of her room. Still, she had to make sure she clearly understood the instructions, for Gerald had struck her before when she had failed to obey him to the letter. Now more than ever, she didn't want his hands on her. "What should I do if Mr. Burke isn't there?" she asked.

"He'll be there. The man never leaves his home, so I hear." He shot a triumphant grin in Corrine's direction. *"Never!* Even though he's quite generous with charities, he sends his donations by messenger or post—never in person."

Nervously, Rachel twined her fingers behind her back. "Then why are we asking him for tea?"

Corrine gave a great sigh, as if instructing such a simpleton had become a wearisome task. "I'm not supposed to *know* that he never makes visits. We're counting on his being a gentleman. When he reads the urgency in my letter, he'll simply have to invite me to visit *him*. That is, if you've performed your duty correctly."

"Yes'm."

"Now," she continued, "is your uniform starched and pressed?"

Rachel nodded. While lavish with purchases for themselves—when they had money—Corrine and Gerald expected Rachel to provide her own clothes on the six shillings they begrudgingly doled out to her each week. The uniform, a crisp black poplin with a ruffled white organdy apron, was the only contribution they had ever made to her wardrobe. It was only a tool to be used when appearances mattered, however—and not to be worn while scrubbing floors or laying fires.

"You know . . ." Gerald squinted his pale eyes, studying Rachel with an intensity that made her want to bolt from the room. "Perhaps she shouldn't knot her hair up in her cap when she goes there. Don't you think her hair would look prettier tied with a ribbon at the back of her neck?"

Corrine's mouth fell open. *"What?"*

"Just a simple ribbon—she's still young enough to wear it that way. Her hair is really too lovely to hide away under a cap. And you could lend her a bit of your rouge as well."

"And for what purpose?" Corrine asked through her teeth, glowering at both Gerald and the maid who stood before her.

Gerald's tone became placating. "Just think for a minute,

Corrine. We want to entice this man with your beauty, right?" Hastily he added, "And there's no woman in England as beautiful as you. But it wouldn't be proper for *you* to go over there and meet him without sending a message first. I can't find any place in town that he visits, so we can't arrange for you to 'accidentally' bump into him, like we did with the others."

Corrine's eyes narrowed with suspicion. "But why could it possibly matter what a *servant*—"

"Just hear me out," he cut in, holding up a hand. "This Burke fellow is a strange duck. He moved to London after leaving the army seven years ago, yet none of his neighbors can recall ever actually seeing him."

"Then why did you go and *choose* someone like that?"

"Because if he can afford to give as much as he supposedly does to the charities around here, then the man has got to have more wealth than we can imagine. The fact that he's not married works in our favor, too. You can move much faster if you're not looking out for a wife.

"Getting back to Rachel," he continued. "How will Mr. Burke know by just reading your message how lovely *you* are? After all, he'll just have your words on a piece of paper to look at. For all he knows, you could be a toothless hag."

"Gerald!" The veins in Corrine's neck protruded.

Still standing there on the rug between them, Rachel wondered if they would even notice if she slipped out of the room. She took a tentative step backwards.

"Stay put, Rachel," Gerald ordered. Softening his voice again, he turned back to Corrine. "What I mean is . . . if our Mr. Burke gets a peek at Rachel when she delivers the message, at least it'll get his attention—and he'll be more inclined to answer. It's probably been a long time since he's been treated to the sight of a pretty woman."

"And if he doesn't see her?" asked Corrine, her voice laden with ice. "Most men don't stand at the door waiting for messages."

"Then the servants will get a look at her, and I'll wager they'll let him know how fair a hand it was that delivered the letter."

I just can't do this anymore, Rachel decided. *I'll go to the workhouse. I'll pack my bag and slip out the back door.* But even as she resolved to do so, an article in last week's *East London Chronicle* came back to her. She had heard Gerald snickering about it to Corrine over dinner, how some poor wretch had gotten part of his earlobe bitten off by a rat in one of those places on the East End.

Shuddering at the memory, she focused her eyes on the chintz-draped windows across the room and forced herself to block out the argument that was going on in front of her. She made a mental picture of kind Mr. Solomon, then of a stooped beggar woman she'd given a halfpenny to near the farmers' market today. *I'll draw her face tonight, if I can get to bed early enough.*

Suddenly she realized that Gerald was speaking to her.

"Did you hear me?" he asked, looking at her expectantly.

"Uh . . . I'm sorry, sir."

"I said, go change your clothes. Then come down here and let Corrine tie a ribbon in your hair."

"Yes, sir." Before leaving the room, Rachel looked at Corrine from the corner of her eye. The alabaster face had gone crimson with fury.

2

EAST London—bordered by the wooded glades of
Hackney to the north, the Tower walls to the west,
and, to the east and south, the rivers Lea and Thames—
was an area teeming with humanity and as different from the
rest of stately London as night from day.

Here vast numbers of immigrants—Irish and Jews,
Huguenots and Flemings—poured in each week in search of
a new start in life. While a few stately homes still graced parts
of Whitechapel Road and the surrounding area, most of East
London had been taken over by slums, chaotic aggregations of
cheaply built and badly maintained tenements that leaned
toward unpaved and sewerless streets.

Rachel's hired hansom cab, with the driver perched high
on his seat in back, weaved its way through the streets of the
parish of Stepney, turning off Commercial Road and heading
north past the textile factories. The air, now a little less chilly
with the afternoon sun, was permeated with the smells of
boiled cabbages, rotting fish heads, and, worse, the faint odor
of sulfate of ammonia from the chemical works several blocks
away.

Yet Rachel barely noticed the smells and sights surrounding
her, for every dull clop of the great horse's hooves against the

wooden-planked streets brought her nearer Mr. Adam Burke's house. *I'm about to help them ruin another man's life,* she thought, her eyes locked vacantly upon the footboard of the two-wheeled carriage. *I'm just as bad as the Mister and Missus. They cheat and steal, and I'm an accomplice . . . because I'll lose my job if I don't obey.* She reached into her drawstring bag for a hand-kerchief and blew her nose.

Too soon the cab was moving down Bow Road, a wide, tree-shaded avenue lined with magnificent houses behind neat hedges and crested wrought-iron gates. It pulled into the carriage drive of a large ivy-covered Italianate villa of stucco and mellow Cotswold stone. The fine lawn out front was studded with stately elms and beeches and a couple silver maples. A statue of Orpheus, its arms raised as if pointing to the boughs over its head, stood under the elm trees by the short front drive.

She saw no signs of life. Though the flower beds were obviously well kept, no yardmen or gardeners bustled about. That, she hoped, was a good omen. *If Mr. Burke is the hermit that Mr. Moore says he is, perhaps even his servants aren't allowed to talk with visitors. Maybe they won't even let me deliver Mrs. Hammond's note!* She reached into her apron pocket to touch the crisp linen-paper envelope, hating the very texture of it against her fingers.

"Miss?" The driver, a lanky, weathered man with slumped shoulders, was at the side of the carriage, holding his hand toward her.

Rachel looked down with a start. She had been so lost in thought that she hadn't heard him come around from the back of the carriage. "I beg your pardon," she said, taking his hand and rising to her feet.

As he helped her to the ground, the driver said, "I'll be waitin' right 'ere for you."

"Thank you," she told him sincerely. After all, she didn't blame him for the part he was unwittingly playing in this evil drama. Turning her face in the direction of Mr. Burke's house, she steadied her nerves and began her walk down a brick footpath leading around the side of the house.

At the back, the path stopped at the head of an iron-railed staircase. As in most English houses, the kitchen was below ground. Holding the rail, Rachel descended the stone steps and knocked at a heavy wooden door.

"Yes?"

The red-haired maid who answered the shaded kitchen door was a few years younger than Rachel and had a friendly smile. Instead of making Rachel feel better, the smile had the opposite effect; she had harbored a fleeting hope as she knocked on the door that she would be turned away.

The tumult of emotions she had felt since last night suddenly caused a lump at the base of her throat. "My name is Rachel Jones," she managed to say with a rasp. Before she could mention the purpose of her errand, a fit of coughing seized her. "Excuse . . . me," was all she could get out of her mouth between coughs.

The girl in the doorway reached out and took her by the elbow, beckoning for her to come inside. "It's that ammonia factory," she said, wrinkling her freckled nose. "Sometimes we get a whiff of it all the way over here. It ain't healthy, that's for sure."

Stepping through the doorway, Rachel found herself in a lofty kitchen that smelled of cinnamon and stewed apples. Baskets and copper pots swung from beams overhead, and side-by-side china cabinets displayed neat arrays of plates and crystal. Against the far wall, an open range squatted next to a bricked oven. A large, ruddy-faced woman with the same flaming red hair as the girl's looked up from a pie crust she was rolling at the table.

"You just sit right here, and I'll get you some water." The girl motioned to a stool near the table. Before Rachel could say that her throat was better, the girl was headed for a pump over a large metal basin.

"Sit, child," said the woman at the table, obviously the cook. "May as well rest your feet while you can."

Rachel obeyed, reaching for the mug of water when the young maid brought it over to her.

"I'm Lucy," said the girl, who couldn't have been more than fifteen. She watched with curious blue eyes as Rachel drained the pewter mug. "This is my mother, Bernice."

Rachel handed the cup back to Lucy. "Thank you," she said, giving a grateful nod to Bernice, too. "You've been very kind."

"Oh, we don't get many visitors," said Bernice. "Just delivery men and post carriers, that's all. Lucy gets excited when she sees someone closer to her own age than the rest of us old folks 'round here." Carefully lifting the pie crust, the woman draped it into a tin pie pan and began running a knife around the outside. "Now, what is it we can do for you?"

Rachel's heart sank. For a few minutes, she had been just a young lady visiting new friends, enjoying their company. Now she was drawn back into her deception.

"I have a message for Mr. Burke from Mrs. Hammond, my missus," she recited as was instructed by Gerald, not quite able to look the two servants in the eye. "It's of the utmost importance that he receive it today."

"Today?" Bernice glanced at her daughter. "Mr. Adam don't have a butler, and Mrs. Fowler ain't here. She's the housekeeper, and she handles all the messages."

Lucy nodded, her face grim. "She left yesterday—gone to Thruxton in Hereford for a couple o' months at least. Her sister's funeral and all that."

"We can give it to Mr. Adam after supper if you want," offered Bernice. "Have you got it with you?"

Reaching into her apron pocket, Rachel brought out the envelope with Corrine's spidery handwriting on the outside and wondered if her face showed the heaviness that was in her heart. "My missus would like me to return with an answer if at all possible. Is there any way that you could give him the message now?"

"I'm sure he's in his study," offered Lucy. She looked at her mother for approval. "I can take it over to him if it's that important."

"Well, I suppose it's all right," Bernice answered after a moment's hesitation. With a shrug she added, "If Mr. Adam's too busy, he'll just tell you so." After her daughter took the envelope from Rachel's hand, Bernice wiped her flour-whitened hands with her apron. "I'll fix us up a spot o' tea while we wait, you and me."

Rachel watched the girl's back as she headed for the door leading to the staircase and the rest of the house. *Why is everybody in this world so trusting?* she wondered. Just as Lucy's hand was reaching out for the doorknob, Rachel made an impulsive decision. She just couldn't do this anymore—she *wouldn't.* "Wait, please."

25

"Yes?" Lucy turned around, her eyebrows raised.

"Uh . . . perhaps Mr. Burke is too busy," Rachel faltered. "I really should bring it some other time." She would tear it up and throw it away . . . tell the Mister and Missus that they wouldn't even answer the door!

Lucy exchanged looks with her mother, who had stopped in the middle of the floor with a teakettle in her hand. "But you just said your missus . . ."

Rachel jumped up from the stool, growing bolder with her increasing determination not to hurt the people in this household. "I'm sorry," she said, walking toward the girl with her hand held out. "You've been very kind, and I can't explain this, but I have to go."

Just then Lucy jumped as the door she was standing near was pushed open from the other side. A man entered the kitchen, holding one of his palms clasped in the other. "Bernice, I've nipped my hand with the letter opener like an idiot! Can you tie something around it?"

Rachel froze where she stood. The man walking to the basin while Bernice and Lucy fluttered around him had the most badly scarred face she'd ever seen! The skin on the right side of his face and neck was brown and shriveled, veined with a mass of whitened lines, and as stiff-looking as shoe leather.

Aware that she was staring, she lowered her eyes, just as the man noticed her presence.

"This here's Rachel," Lucy told the man as her mother wrapped a strip of clean white dish towel around his hand. "She brought this message for you." Then as if suddenly remembering what had happened just seconds ago, she drew the envelope back a little and turned a helpless look in Rachel's direction.

Before Rachel could move, the man, who she now realized was Mr. Burke, had taken the envelope with his good hand. Giving her a nod, he slipped it into the breast pocket of his waistcoat.

"Ouch!" he exclaimed suddenly when the cook pulled the bandage tightly into a knot. "Have a heart, Bernice!"

"Sorry, Mr. Adam!" While the cook retied the man's bandage, Rachel discreetly ventured another look at him. Tall and broad-shouldered, he had the mannerisms and stance of a man in his early thirties, as far as she could tell. She darted her eyes back down at the floor when he turned his face toward her again.

"Do you need for me to look at this now?"

The back of her neck broke into a cold sweat. *Tell him you made a mistake . . . that you'd like to have it back.* But a picture of herself facing Gerald and Corrine came into her thoughts, and her courage vanished.

Besides, what reason can I give him? That I've changed my mind and no longer want to help my employers extort money from people? What if he sends for the police? She thought about Squire Nowells. She had had a hand in that too, delivering messages back and forth between him and Corrine, and standing watch outside various doors during their clandestine meetings. There was no doubt in her mind that Corrine and Gerald would implicate her if they were apprehended.

Before she could make up her mind, Adam Burke motioned with his bandaged hand to the kitchen door. "Well, come along then. I'll read this in my study."

Numbly, Rachel walked through the door the man held for

her, then followed him up a staircase to a wide, oak-paneled hallway. An open door was near the end of the hallway—Mr. Burke's study.

"Please have a seat, and I'll take care of this," he said, moving a thick book from the armchair in front of a cluttered mahogany desk. Then seating himself behind his desk, he brought the envelope from his pocket and broke the seal.

Rachel's face grew warm as she watched the man pull out Corrine's letter—unwittingly holding poison in his hands. She knew the contents well. She had heard Gerald dictating the words to Corrine as she wrote them.

Dear Mr. Burke,

I am a young widow just recently moved to London to escape the memories of my sainted husband, who was lost at sea two years ago. Our considerable estate in Bridgewater in Somerset is up for sale, and I expect to have such business cleared up shortly.

Meanwhile, it distresses me to see so many people in need in this city, particularly in the East Side. I am anxious to make plans to sponsor two or three charities, so that when the funds from the sale of my properties arrive, I can immediately put them to good use.

I have recently heard of your generous philanthropy and wonder if you could advise me about the organizations which serve the destitute of East London.

Time weighs heavily on my hands, Mr. Burke. The thought of being able to give of myself to others again is the only thing that keeps me from giving in to despair.

Would you please join me for tea one day this week at your convenience?

Sincerely yours,
Corrine Hammond

When he had finished reading, Mr. Burke looked across the desk at Rachel with his brow furrowed, as if deep in thought and not aware that he was staring. Then, blinking, he came out of his reverie. He turned up the left corner of his mouth, giving her a crooked and rather shy smile.

His eyes, Rachel realized with surprise, were quite nice—brown and thickly lashed and, like his eyebrows, untouched by the scars. His dark brown hair was combed with a side part and showed faint traces of auburn in the lamplight. *He must have been a handsome man at one time,* she thought.

"Your mistress seems quite desperate," he said kindly. "She sounds like a good person."

"Yes, sir," she said, swallowing. "A good person." The ticking of the clock on the wall behind her seemed to mock her, accusing her with every beat, *Li-ar, li-ar, li-ar!*

Mr. Burke tapped his pen on the top of his desk for a couple of seconds and glanced at the note again. Then suddenly he reached into a shallow wooden box on his left and brought out an ivory sheet of paper. After he'd scribbled several lines with his pen, he raised his head again.

"Please give this reply to Mrs. Hammond," he said, folding the paper and stuffing it into an envelope. When he held it out to her, Rachel rose to her feet and took it.

"Thank you, sir," she managed to say.

Already opening up a leather-bound account book, he

looked up at her and smiled again. "East India Dock Road is a far piece. Do you need someone to take you home?"

"Mrs. Hammond has hired a cab for me," Rachel told him.

"Good idea," he said. "Very considerate."

~

Rachel had no sooner stepped into the sitting room when Gerald and Corrine were at her side. "Did he answer my letter?" Corrine asked eagerly.

Rachel pulled the envelope out of her pocket and handed it over.

In a flash, Corrine's long fingernails were tearing the flap from the envelope. With Gerald looking over her shoulder, she read aloud:

> Mrs. Hammond,
>
> Please accept my condolences on the tragedy that befell your husband.
>
> Your question regarding local charities is most welcome, as there are so many souls out there who need the benevolence of those able to help. As soon as possible I shall ask my solicitor, Mr. George Cromer, to call upon you with information about the organizations that I sponsor.
>
> It is with regret that I must decline your kind invitation for tea, but I seldom make calls. However, I must commend you on your generosity, especially during what surely must be a trying time.
>
> Sincerely,
> Adam Burke

Spitting out an oath, Corrine crumpled the paper into a ball and threw it on the floor. "He'll have his *solicitor* bring me a list! Now what are we supposed to do?"

Gerald was frowning as he picked up Mr. Burke's letter and straightened it out against the front of his vest. "Did you get to see him?"

"Yes, sir—in the kitchen. Then he took me to his study and wrote down his answer."

With that, Gerald's eyebrows lifted. "Marvelous! But he said nothing to you about inviting Corrine to visit?"

"Not to me. He cut his hand," she offered, hoping that would suffice to end their questions.

But Corrine spoke up again. "Didn't he say *anything* about my letter?"

Rachel searched her memory for something, anything, that would satisfy her. "He said, 'Your mistress seems quite desperate' and that you must be a good person."

Folding her arms, Corrine said, "Well, that's *something.*" She turned to Gerald, who was now on his way to the settee. "It appears he wasn't so taken by Rachel's beauty as you thought he'd be." Her tone became faintly gloating. "Perhaps our Mr. Burke is blind as well as a hermit."

Gerald turned and stared at her through narrowed eyelids. "What are you implying, dear—that my ideas are foolish?"

"No," she answered immediately, almost meekly. After a pause, she added, "Do you think I should just call on him without an invitation?"

"No, not yet." Now seated, he sighed and sank back into the cushions. "We can't afford to waste time, but I don't want to spoil everything by getting *too* hasty. We've got to make plans."

Corrine let out a sigh, too, then walked past Rachel to join Gerald on the settee. "Go cook supper." She threw the command back over her shoulder.

~

Grateful to be away from Gerald and Corrine, Rachel fetched the potatoes from the larder and brought them over to the table. As she picked up the first potato and began to trim the peelings with a knife, she realized she hadn't told them about Mr. Burke's scarred face.

She couldn't understand why, but the thought brought some relief to her guilty conscience . . . as if by not mentioning his appearance, she was giving the man a small measure of protection. By the time the potatoes were ready to be boiled in a pot with sausages, she had figured out why. If Corrine found out about his scars, she would assume he was desperate for a pretty woman's company. And Rachel knew how bold her mistress could be.

She wondered about the scars. His face, though it had been a shock at first, had not repulsed her. Perhaps it was the kindness coming from his eyes that softened his harsher features. Scars and all, she thought Mr. Burke's face far more pleasant to look upon than Corrine's or Gerald's. While they both had handsome features, the effect was diminished by a predatory look about the eyes.

~

"The way I look at it, we have two options," Gerald was saying, his right hand caressing the back of Corrine's neck as she sat beside him. "One, we can wait for this Mr. Cromer to call, and you can turn the charm on him."

"But we're not interested in the solicitor. . . ."

"I know, but surely he'd mention to his client how beautiful and charming this wealthy widow is. Then afterwards you could send Adam Burke another letter, expressing your thanks and again asking him for tea."

"But don't you think he'll turn it down again?"

"We can most likely count on that," said Gerald. "But surely a man with that much wealth has been taught some social graces. Simple manners would *compel* him to return the invitation."

"Then that's what we should do," said Corrine.

Gerald nodded. "The only problem is . . . how do we know *when* Mr. Cromer will call? He might not think that it's urgent, particularly since your letter says that you have to wait for the estate to be sold before you can make any donations."

"You *told* me to put that in there."

"I know—and it served its purpose. I just don't like waiting when money is involved."

You mean when gambling debts are involved, thought Corrine. It was hard to keep her temper in check whenever Gerald brought up the subject of their desperate financial straits. *We've earned thousands of pounds these last few years, but it disappears as quickly as it comes!*

Yet she forced herself to hold her tongue, fearing a repeat of the episode last night when he had almost walked out. She glanced sideways at him as he sat there deep in thought with his eyes half-closed. She wondered, not for the first time, why she was so dependent on him. While she found him handsome in a callous sort of way, men much more handsome than Gerald had expressed interest in her.

Perhaps it was because he didn't fawn and stutter around

her, as most men did. He would leave her in a minute if she pushed him too far, and it intrigued her that someone would have that kind of power over her.

~

"Our only other option," Gerald began after a while, "is to send another letter saying that you'd rather get the information from him personally."

"Wouldn't he think that odd?" asked Corrine.

"Oh, I'm sure he would, at first." Removing his hand from the back of Corrine's neck, he steepled his fingers together against his chin and thought the situation over for a few seconds. "But what if you wrote that you appreciate his efforts and mean no offense—but that you don't trust solicitors?"

The tempo of his words picked up as he grew more excited. "You could tell him that . . . your father's trusted attorney managed to embezzle money from his holdings for years, so that when he died, your mother was left virtually penniless."

She couldn't help but snicker. "My father's holdings? My papa lived his whole life virtually penniless. I don't know if I could tell this 'dishonest solicitor' story with a straight face."

"You've told more outrageous stories than this one without batting an eye. Why would that be a problem?"

The smirk was still on Corrine's face, but she shook her head. "It wouldn't be a problem. I can tell this fellow anything you want me to tell him—and make him believe it."

Gerald laughed. "Of that I have no doubt. It's settled, then?"

"You mean . . . option number two?"

"I think so." He took her hand and gave it a squeeze. "Yes, that would be best."

Corrine turned her face toward him again and, closing her eyes, offered her lips for a kiss.

He responded by slipping his left arm around Corrine's shoulders and pulling her closer. As he pressed his lips upon hers, he strained his ears for the sounds Rachel was making as she set the table in the dining room. *I wonder if she's ever kissed a man?* He didn't think so, for when would she have had a chance?

"I'll have Rachel fetch my writing paper after supper," Corrine said when he released her. "Right now, I want to go upstairs and change."

There was a clatter of silverware from the dining room. Gerald gave Corrine a smile. "Yes, you do that."

~

With great relief Rachel closed the door to her garret room after supper had been served and the kitchen cleaned. Gerald's bold stares as she had tried to set the table had unnerved her, and she had almost dropped a plate from her shaking hands.

She lit the lantern on the night table next to her bed. *That must be why Corrine looked so angry at me last night,* she thought, almost feeling sorry for her mistress. *She must know what he's doing.*

Rachel had no illusions about Gerald being in love with her. For years she had watched married men succumb to Corrine's charms, and she had concluded that there were certain types of men who could not be faithful to just one woman. How any woman could settle for a man like that was a mystery to her. *If I ever fall in love with a man,* she thought, *it'll be because he's faithful and kind, and for no other reasons.* But

35

falling in love was hardly a possibility as long as she lived with Gerald and Corrine.

Crossing over to a small bureau near her washstand, Rachel pulled open the top drawer and took out a round, wooden cheese box. She lifted the lid. Inside were scraps of paper in all sizes and textures, and every blank space on most of them was filled with faces she had sketched.

She had no desk, but she preferred to draw by lying on her stomach across her mattress anyway. The lid of the box served as an adequate surface, and she smoothed out the brown paper with which Mr. Solomon had wrapped her pencils.

Closing her eyes for a few minutes, Rachel tried to picture Mr. Burke's eyes. It was too bad that she couldn't afford watercolors or oils or the lessons that would be necessary to learn to use them. It would have been much better to capture the expression in those rich brown eyes with colored paints—a kind expression . . . and lonely, she suddenly realized.

Pencils sketches on scraps of paper. Still, it was better than nothing. She didn't know what she would do if she couldn't come up here and draw.

Tentatively, Rachel began sketching Adam Burke's brow with short, feathery strokes. *What about his scars?* she wondered. *Should I leave them out? After all, he obviously hadn't been born with them.*

She had just about made up her mind to eliminate the scars when the pencil suddenly seemed to take on a life of its own. Carefully, using a piece of cotton for shading, she added a shadow to the right side of his face. His scars, after all, were part of him as well. She wondered if Mr. Burke had ever wished he could leave the real scars out—or erase them, just as she could on the paper if she wished.

She was putting the finishing touches on the sketch when the bells at the clock tower near the wharf began tolling midnight. Rachel held the paper closer to the lantern. The resemblance was remarkable, scars and all. There were times, rare ones, that the work of her hands filled her with a trembling sense of awe.

Weary to the bone, she placed Adam Burke's portrait onto the top of the stack of drawings in the cheese box. The face seemed to be watching her with a thoughtful expression. Just before closing the lid, she looked tenderly at the likeness she had created and whispered, "Be careful, sir."

3

BERNICE looked surprised to see Rachel at the kitchen door again the next morning. "Well, hullo, young miss," she greeted, opening the door a little wider.

"I've got another message from my missus," Rachel hastily explained.

The cook said nothing for a few seconds, and Rachel wondered if it was because of the bizarre way she'd acted yesterday or because of her appearance. Gerald, encouraged by the fact that she had met Mr. Burke and even spent some time alone with him, had ordered her to use Corrine's curling rod, a tortuous device that had to be heated in a pot of boiling water. Instead of being tied with a ribbon, Rachel's honey-brown hair now cascaded down her back in a mass of ringlets.

And the touch of Corrine's rouge on each cheek was a little heavier today. *No doubt she thinks I look like a doxy,* Rachel thought, shifting uneasily from one foot to the other. She wished she had followed her first impulse of destroying the message and telling Gerald and Corrine she had delivered it. Only the fear of what they would do if they ever found out had kept her from it.

"Now, are you *sure* you want us to give him your message this time?" Bernice asked as she stood in the doorway.

Rachel ducked her head in embarrassment as she took the envelope from her apron pocket. "Yes'm."

Bernice smiled and reached for the envelope. "I can't give it to Mr. Adam right away," she said, not unkindly. "He's havin' a meeting with his minister."

"He goes to *church?*" The words slipped out of Rachel's mouth before she could stop them. "I mean . . . I thought he never went anywhere."

Bernice gave her a strange look, then chuckled. "You thought right! Look, missy, I've got better things to do than stand in doorways. Why don't you come in and have some shortbread, and we'll talk. Lucy'll be glad to see you."

~

"You see, Mr. Adam ain't been to a church anywhere since he moved into this house," Bernice explained as she poured steaming hot tea into three stoneware mugs. "But he's a good Christian man, he is."

Her daughter smiled in agreement from across the kitchen table. "A good man."

"He has church right here," said Bernice.

"You mean there's a *church* in the house?" Rachel asked with wonder in her voice. Mr. Burke's house was big, but the churches she had seen were mammoth structures with imposing steeples and bell towers.

Covering her mouth with a hand, Lucy stifled a giggle. "We have meetings here every Sunday in the drawing room or the conservatory, dependin' on the season."

Rachel didn't understand. "But this is a house, not a church."

Bernice reached out a chubby hand to pat Rachel's on the

tabletop beside her. "The Lord's Book says that where two or three are gathered together, he'll be in the middle of them. Even with Mrs. Fowler away, there's seven of us servants. Mr. Adam and the good Reverend Morgan and his family are always present, too, so I reckon we qualify."

Rachel wanted to ask why Mr. Burke didn't just go to a regular church like most people, but she held her tongue, aware that she had pried too much already. Besides, she was sure that it had something to do with the scars on his face.

Her instructions had again been to wait for a reply from Mr. Burke if possible, but she couldn't bear the thought of having to lie to him a second time. Delivering the letter was bad enough. She was about to thank them for the tea and short-bread when Lucy asked innocently, "Where do you go to church, Rachel?"

Rachel knew that good people went to church, so it shamed her to tell them that she didn't go at all. There had been a chapel service every week at Freeman's—an hour of standing at attention in a classroom while Mr. Baker, the head-master of the orphanage school, droned Scripture in a barely audible voice. Since she had been "adopted" by Gerald and Corrine, however, she had not been exposed even to a mini-mal amount of religious training. But as embarrassed as she was, she was determined not to hide this. At least she could be honest about *something*.

"I don't go anywhere," she answered quietly.

The girl's eyes grew large. "Why not?"

"Lucy!" cut in her mother. "That ain't polite to ask."

"I don't mind," said Rachel. She gave the girl a smile across the table. "I guess I'd be afraid to go into one of those big buildings by myself. Anyway, I have to work Sundays."

Her face sympathetic, Bernice said, "Why don't you come here, then . . . to our Sunday meetings? You could ask your missus for a little time off, and I'm sure Mr. Adam wouldn't mind."

Lucy's face lit up. "That would be so nice! And you could have lunch with us afterwards. We all have lunch together on Sundays—Mr. Adam and all of us."

The very thought of such kindness overwhelmed Rachel. Unexpectedly, her eyes began to burn with unshed tears.

"I couldn't do that," she answered, pushing her chair out from the table and standing. Impulsively she bent down and gave the cook's shoulders a quick hug. "But I thank you for asking."

Bidding them farewell, she was out the door and on her way to the carriage, no longer caring that Gerald and Corrine would be furious that she hadn't waited around for a reply.

~

"Weren't you afraid this dastardly book would shake your faith in the Almighty?" Robert Morgan studied the leather-bound volume of Charles Darwin's *Origin of the Species*. The book had stirred controversy all over London since its publication in 1859, just four years before.

Adam Burke gave him a crooked grin, locking his hands behind his head as he leaned back in his favorite armchair. They had just finished a cutthroat game of backgammon and were enjoying each other's company in the library. "No, I'm not," he answered. "After all, I have *you*, my preacher friend, to see that my faith remains healthy."

"That reminds me; Reverend Harrison called me in for another talk yesterday."

42

Adam's eyes became wary. "And . . . ?"

"The same subject. He isn't quite sure that it's proper for us to be holding services here, when it's only your pride keeping you from attending the chapel at St. Andrew's."

"Only my pride?" Adam studied his friend thoughtfully. "And what did you tell him?"

Robert leaned forward, his stocky body rigid in the wooden chair. "Are you sure you want to know?"

"Tell me."

He sighed. "I asked him if he thought it was wrong for our ministers to visit the prisons. After all, John Wesley himself preached at Newgate many times."

"Why did you ask him that?"

"Think about it."

Adam blinked. "Are you saying that I'm a prisoner?"

"Aren't you?"

"Certainly not," he replied tersely. *"They* can't leave. I stay home of my own volition."

Robert shook his head slowly. "I don't think you can leave either." When Adam didn't reply, Robert looked at him with eyes full of compassion. They had become fast friends almost twelve years ago while attending Oxford University. After graduation, however, they had gone their separate ways—Adam to the British army, and Robert to serving God in the ministry.

Seven years ago, Adam had received with great joy the news that his friend was moving to London. He remembered the shock, however, when he had come to call on him for the first time. The Crimean War had left its mark on Adam's face and, much worse, had scarred his heart.

"I'm sorry if I hurt you, my brother," Robert said softly,

rising from his chair. He walked over to where his friend was seated and laid a hand on his shoulder for just a second. "I'll show myself out."

"See you Sunday?" Adam mumbled, still looking straight ahead.

"Of course."

"Robert?"

The minister paused, framed by the door to the hallway. "Yes?"

"Pray for me."

Robert looked back over his shoulder and nodded. "I always do, my friend."

~

When he heard the last, faint ringing of the minister's footsteps against the quarry tiles of the hallway, Adam got up and crossed the room to a small mahogany secretary against the wall. From the bottom drawer he brought out a black velvet pouch trimmed with gold cording. Holding it against his chest, he returned to his chair and sat down. With his pulse racing, he untied the cords that held the pouch closed and reached inside for the tintype of a young woman.

As he had done so many times in the past, Adam covered the scarred right side of his face with his hand as he brought the portrait up close. The young woman's eyes were focused at something just a shade to the left. She was exceedingly beautiful, with delicate features and flaxen hair.

He sniffed and was immediately disgusted with himself for the tears in his eyes. Still he drank in the image of the face he'd once loved until he could stand it no longer. Resting his head against the back of the chair, he closed his eyes. His imagination took over, dredging up memories that were at the same time sweet and bitter.

"Kathleen . . ." The name escaped his lips as a groan. "Why did you break your promise?"

She had been so distressed when his artillery regiment had received orders in the fall of 1854 to transport to Crimea and reinforce the troops already there. *But she was proud of me, too,* he thought. He had been able to see that through her tears.

Though he had not been a vain man even then, he was glad that Kathleen enjoyed being seen with him. Clad in the uniform of his regiment—dark breeches and a pale blue tunic faced with yellow and heavily braided in silver—he often escorted her down the cobbled streets of Gloucester, enjoying the pressure of her white-gloved hand resting in the crook of his arm.

After he had received his orders, there had been no time to plan the elaborate wedding of which she had dreamed. She had tearfully promised him that she would never love another man and would marry him when he returned.

Thirteen months later he was lying on a pallet on the dirt floor of a field-hospital tent, his face ravaged by exploding shrapnel during the siege of Sevastopol. Fortunately, he had thrown his left arm over his eyes just as the Russian shell hit the ground in front of him, saving his eyesight while doing minimal damage to the arm sheathed in the sleeve of his winter greatcoat.

Kathleen had received word of his injuries—and to Adam's great joy, she didn't act repulsed when he finally came home. Even as they walked through town in the light of day, she took his arm as in old times. After a short while, though, he began to sense a coldness in her feelings toward him.

Whenever he brought up the subject of wedding plans, she would answer woodenly, and the smile on her lips did not match the look of overwhelming resignation he sometimes caught in her eyes.

It's just your imagination, he had reminded himself frequently. After all, he had worried for weeks about her reaction to his disfigurement. More than once, back in the hospital tent, he had awakened in the middle of the night with his heart beating furiously from a nightmare in which Kathleen recoiled in horror at the sight of him. He was just being too sensitive, looking for monsters that weren't there.

Then, five weeks after his return, Adam found out by accident that his instincts had been correct. He had ridden on horseback over to her family's country manor house to visit her and found his younger brother Edward's favorite roan gelding tethered to the carriage rail out front.

Recent occurrences began assaulting his mind, such as the day before when Kathleen had accidentally called him Edward during their walk. She became flustered, and he had teased her about becoming forgetful.

Looking back, he realized that his brother had seemed uncomfortable in his presence since his return, never quite looking directly into his eyes. Adam had attributed his brother's actions to his facial injuries and figured that Edward would grow used to his appearance in time. Then they would again enjoy the camaraderie they had shared while growing up.

But with all the pieces falling into place, he wasn't so sure anymore. With a heavy heart he had slowly dismounted and tethered his horse. Anger began to quicken his steps, and by the time he reached the front door and brushed past the startled butler, his blood was pulsing in his ears.

He stopped just outside the closed library door, suddenly feeling foolish. Surely there was a logical explanation . . . after all, Kathleen and Edward both loved him. Just as he was about to knock on the door and confess his folly, their muffled voices reached his ears.

Despising himself for stooping so low as to eavesdrop, Adam put his left ear against the door. Kathleen was weeping, he realized. He could hear the voice of his brother, comforting her.

"We can tell him together, just like we planned."

"But that was before we found out about his face. How can I turn my back on him now with him looking the way he does?"

"That's not your fault," Edward was gently reasoning. "We fell in love months before he got hurt. Adam's a grown man . . . old enough to know that these things happen."

"But what about everybody else? You know how jealous all of my friends were when he asked me to marry him. Now everyone tells me what a 'good soul' I am, being so loyal . . . when I know, deep down, they're glad it's me that's stuck with him and not them."

"Adam's wealth still makes him attractive to women. I know at least a dozen who would jump at the chance to marry him." Exasperation crept into his brother's voice. "Anyway, who's more important—me or your silly friends? I can't believe you're even still considering this marriage!"

Kathleen and Edward. The only woman he had ever loved and *his brother!* Why hadn't he seen it earlier? When he had first stepped off the train at Gloucester Station and into their arms, why wasn't he aware that he had just become an intruder into their lives?

She was planning to go through with the marriage because she felt sorry for him. Pity had been the only cement that bound Kathleen to her promise—pity and the fear of being called heartless by her friends!

It took every ounce of willpower Adam possessed not to throw the door open and kill his brother. As it was, he scarcely remembered the five-mile ride back home. When he got there he wandered from room to room, ignoring the uneasy quietness of the servants, and searching—for what, he did not know.

He wished then that he hadn't surrendered his commission in the army. He belonged among men who were accustomed to looking at wounds and were, for the most part, unencumbered with such deceitful emotions as pity.

Oakleigh Park, the sizable Jacobean mansion and fifteen hundred surrounding acres, was legally his since the deaths of both his parents almost seven years before. His older sister had married and moved away when he was just a child, and he had no obligation to support anyone in the family. He could have turned Edward out into the streets . . . and for just part of the afternoon, he consoled himself by toying with the idea. When his brother returned, Adam refused to see him and instructed the servants that he would not see Kathleen either if she came to call.

Mercy and reason won out. It only took a week for him to realize that this was no kind of life. He decided to leave, and he arranged with a solicitor for the servants to be kept on— except for Bernice and her family, who agreed to go with him. Edward could even remain in the house with an adequate trust each month.

Adequate but not extravagant. He would not punish his

brother, but neither would he finance the kind of life he knew Kathleen was expecting. She was an only child, unashamedly pampered by her parents and used to the finer things of life. *Her dowry will be considerable,* he told himself bitterly. *She can provide the silk gowns and trips to Paris!*

The next consideration had been where to go. At first it seemed that the best way to remain anonymous would be to move somewhere even deeper into the countryside. Perhaps he would buy a crumbling medieval castle, moat and all, on the top of a cliff somewhere. Then it dawned upon him that, while he intensely wanted to get away from people's covert glances and sometimes even bold stares, he did not want to live in perpetual isolation.

That was when he decided upon London. In such a busy, bustling city, neighbors would be more apt to mind their own business. He would have access to his newspapers and journals, and he could even take his carriage out for rides at night if he wished. He chose the less prestigious East End for two reasons: He wished to have nothing more to do with the elite of society; and his old friend from Cambridge, Robert Morgan, was living there.

Still, it was several weeks before he could make himself send word to his friend of his new residence. Robert had a natural empathy for people, and Adam did not want his pity. His fears were put to rest upon their reunion, for the minister had simply enveloped him in a bear hug and exclaimed, "I never thought I'd see the day when *I'd* be more handsome than Adam Burke!"

Robert had been just what he needed. And his old friend's patient but persistent reasoning over the next couple of years brought him to the saving knowledge of Jesus Christ.

When Adam finally realized that God's Son understood how it felt to be betrayed, lonely, and physically scarred, it awakened a hunger inside to know more about this Savior.

For months after that he had spent hours in his study each day, poring over the pages of the Bible Robert had given him. He read with amazement the prophecies in the Old Testament book of Isaiah that described with uncanny accuracy the coming birth of Christ in Bethlehem and his sufferings on the cross. In the New Testament Gospels, he studied the accounts of Jesus' ministry on earth, the miracles he performed, and his rising from the tomb three days after his death.

At last Adam acknowledged the longing in his soul that couldn't be satisfied by Kathleen, Edward, or anyone else. He fell to his knees and asked Christ to forgive his sins and save his soul.

But Adam had balked stubbornly at attending any sort of public worship gathering. The very thought of imposing his disfigurement upon others, even fellow believers, made his blood go cold. He could just picture mothers whispering to their children to stop staring and well-intentioned men pretending not to notice his scars when shaking his hand. Worst of all would be the looks of sympathy sent in his direction— sympathy shaded with just a subtle amount of relief that it was he and not the onlooker who bore the ugly scars.

After weeks of trying to get Adam to change his mind, Robert came up with the idea of having worship services right here at the house. The servants would be the only other members of the congregation besides his wife Penelope and, later, his daughter, Margaret. He could come to Adam's every Sunday after he had preached at St. Andrew's, his own tiny chapel on Oxcart Road.

"This is just temporary," Robert had warned. "Sooner or later, you're going to have to get used to having folks look at you. If they have pity in their eyes, so be it! Look what our Lord and Savior had to go through—and it wasn't pity he saw most of the time, but hatred!"

The "temporary" arrangement had lasted four years now. So far Adam had been successful in getting Robert to continue. What he would do if Robert made good on his threat to stop conducting the private services, he did not know. One day, perhaps, he would have to stop living like a hermit, but he was determined to put that day off for as long as possible.

In the meantime, after much prayer, Adam had forgiven his brother and Kathleen . . . even though he knew he would always keep the portrait of Kathleen in his desk and the memory of her in his heart.

~

"What do you mean, he didn't send a reply!" Corrine exclaimed when Rachel walked into the sitting room empty-handed. "Didn't you ask if you could wait for one?"

Rachel met her mistress's glare with as blank a face as possible. "He was meeting with his minister."

"His minister?" Gerald folded the newspaper he'd been reading and set it on the floor next to his parlor chair. "But I was told he doesn't go anywhere, not even to church . . . even though he supports the Methodist charities here in town."

"That's *good* news, then!" Corrine settled into the settee, a rapacious gleam in her eyes. "If he doesn't answer my letter with an invitation to call, then I'll just arrange to make his acquaintance at church. After all, how many Methodist chapels can there be in East London?"

Gerald turned his attention back to Rachel, who stood just inside the arched doorway leading to the hall. "Did you happen to hear the name of this minister's church?"

"No, sir, I didn't," she replied truthfully. *Not likely that their little meetings have a name,* she told herself. The thought of Corrine wasting time on a wild-goose chase, visiting chapel after chapel, gave her such satisfaction that she had to struggle to keep a smile from her lips.

As it was, Gerald must have noticed something in her expression, for his icy blue eyes were studying her.

"Come sit here with us," he ordered softly, giving her a thin-lipped smile.

Crossing the room with feet that had suddenly turned to lead, Rachel chose a wing-back chair as far away from her employers as possible.

"Over here."

When Rachel had perched uneasily on the edge of the foot-stool nearest to his chair, Gerald spoke again, his voice still gentle.

"Why do I have the feeling that you're hiding something from us, our dear little Rachel?"

Much to her chagrin, she realized that her hands were beginning to tremble. She clutched them together in her lap and hoped he hadn't seen them. "I've told you nothing but the truth, sir."

"Then why am I having some doubts?" The tone of his voice became quietly menacing. "You wouldn't lie to your benefactors, would you?"

You're not my benefactors! her mind screamed, though she managed to keep her face expressionless. *You only took me from the orphanage so you wouldn't have to pay somebody decent wages to do your dirty work!*

"Rachel?"

"I wouldn't lie to you, sir."

Gerald drummed long, slender fingers on his crossed knee, obviously enjoying himself. "How long has it been," he began, his eyes sparkling, "since you had a switch put to you? Three years? Four?"

Rachel shot up from her stool. "You will *never* switch me again!" she cried, indignation rising in her chest. "I'll kill you first!"

A fleeting expression of shock crossed his face, then he grinned broadly. "My goodness, our little Rachel has a temper!" With a mirthful glance at Corrine, he asked, "Do tell me, how would you go about it? Killing me, I mean."

Standing there trembling with rage and wondering if she had ever hated anyone so much in her life, Rachel nonetheless forced herself to keep from further voicing her dark thoughts. She knew she could never actually take anyone's life, even one so cruel as Gerald, but she had imagined many times the satisfaction she would get from lacing his tea with poison. "If you ever beat me again, I'll leave," she finally stated, her jaw set.

"Oh dear . . . and where would you go?" Gerald said, feigning concern. "I don't remember giving you any references, and the streets are glutted with unemployed servants these days."

He began to toy with her as a cat plays with a mouse before devouring it. "Would you like to read today's newspaper, Rachel? There's an interesting article about an unfortunate young lady about your age at one of the workhouses. It seems that a group of fellows who weren't quite gentlemen—"

"Why don't you leave her alone, Gerald?" Corrine, who'd been quietly sitting there for the past few minutes, finally spoke up. She yawned. "This conversation is becoming a dreadful bore."

"What?" He turned incredulous eyes to her. "She's obviously holding something back from us, and you—"

"No, she's not." Flashing Rachel a look of scorn, Corrine said, "She's too dull witted to plot against us . . . and I'm starving. Let her go fix lunch."

Moments later, Rachel's hands were still shaking as she dropped some chopped carrots into the pot of mutton stew on the stove. But her soul blazed with a new intensity, brought on by the victory she had won over Gerald and Corrine in the sitting room. The fact that it had been a small victory at best couldn't put a damper on her spirits.

She hadn't told them everything!

~

Corrine was waiting in the kitchen when Rachel returned from the market the next morning. "What took you so long!" she demanded.

"I . . . I didn't think I was taking a long time," stammered Rachel.

Corrine shook a piece of paper. "This was just delivered. Gerald hasn't seen it yet, but when he wakes up, he's going to be furious!"

Setting her basket on the table, Rachel took the letter that was thrust at her.

Dear Mrs. Hammond,

I am distressed to read of your past troubles with your father's solicitor. While I can assure you with all candor that Mr. Cromer is a decent, honest man, I can certainly understand your reluctance.

Enclosed is a list of the charities I have been privileged to sponsor. While most are maintained by Methodists, there is also a Catholic soup kitchen that tries to meet the needs of the unemployed in the Irish section. If you desire to visit any of these worthy establishments, please send word and I shall contact the proprietors to make appointments for you.

If I may be of further service to you, please do not hesitate to send word.

Sincerely,
Adam Burke

P.S. My cook has invited the young maid who delivers your messages to our Sunday services here in my home. Please tell her she is most welcome to come. We meet at eleven and share the noon meal afterward.

Corrine snatched the letter out of Rachel's hands when she had barely finished reading the postscript. "I'm going upstairs to show him this right now!" she hissed. "You lied to us after all, you stupid girl!"

Ashen faced, Rachel put a hand on Corrine's arm. *"Please* don't tell him," she begged. "You didn't ask me about the meetings at his house."

"You *knew* we would want to have that information!" Shaking Rachel's hand from her arm, Corrine was about to wheel around and head for the stairs with the evidence of

Rachel's duplicity when she suddenly remembered Gerald's threat to use a switch on the girl. She paused—not from compassion but because of the disturbing realization that he would get a sick enjoyment from inflicting such a punishment.

"I don't know what I'm going to do about this," she said, lowering her voice but still glaring at the stricken face in front of her. "He needs to know about that invitation."

"You could just show Mr. Moore the list of charities Mr. Burke sent *with* the letter!"

"But he'll know that a man like Adam Burke wouldn't send a list without some sort of note. Gerald has to know about the Sunday meetings so he can help me figure out a way to get invited. I've got to find a way to meet this man!"

"What if you . . ."

"Hush!" Corrine ordered. She was silent for a moment, pursing her lips. "Perhaps there's a solution to both problems," she finally conceded.

Before Rachel could say anything, Corrine motioned toward the stairs. "Go change into your good clothes right now. I'll write another letter, thanking Mr. Burke for the advice about the charities and for inviting you to his 'church,' or whatever he calls it."

She spoke more to herself than to Rachel. "I'll tell him how I long to find a place to worship as well. . . . Might I impose upon his generosity by coming along with my maid this Sunday? I'm just going to have to be bold, because he certainly doesn't take hints very well."

"But what about Mr. Moore?"

"I'll tell him you and I were invited to Mr. Burke's meetings when you delivered the note I'm about to write."

"Oh, thank you!" Rachel cried. Impulsively, she threw her

arms around Corrine—then, as if realizing what she had done, immediately took a step backward. "I'm sorry, ma'am."

When the shock had worn off, Corrine frowned, putting both hands on her hips. "You just make sure you get back here with an invitation for *both* of us, and I'll burn this letter in the fireplace!"

~

Thirty minutes later, after Rachel had left on her new errand, Corrine listened for any signs of life upstairs. Hearing none, she slipped down into the kitchen. As she helped herself to a seed cake, she recalled the look on Rachel's face when the girl realized Gerald wouldn't find out about her deliberate omission of information. Corrine had never seen anybody look so grateful.

Strange. For those few seconds, Corrine had felt something that was completely new to her. She couldn't identify it, but it was a strange, unsettling feeling.

4

SUNDAY morning Rachel got up even earlier than usual, for she had to lay fires, cook and serve breakfast, clean up the kitchen, and then help Corrine with her gown and hair. By the time she was able to fly up the stairs to get dressed, Corrine—grouchy from having to get up so early— was downstairs fuming about the possibility of being late.

The fleeting bond she had felt with her mistress just a few days before had vanished with a fury, for Corrine had become more demanding and insulting than ever. Rachel couldn't imagine what she had done to deserve such scorn. Was it because she had caused Corrine to keep a secret from Gerald? Or maybe because she, a servant, had dared to touch her?

After hanging her work dress on a hook on the wall, Rachel picked up the yellow-sprigged muslin. The joy of having a new dress was tainted with the knowledge that it was just more ammunition for the pursuit of Mr. Burke. "It wouldn't be proper to send her to church, or whatever it is, dressed in a maid's uniform," Gerald had told Corrine over dinner two days ago. "And we can't have her showing up dressed like a beggar woman. The man obviously has a soft spot for servants. He might get the idea that you mistreat her."

With her hands behind her back, Rachel fumbled with the

tiny horn buttons. It seemed to take forever, but she had no intention of asking for Corrine's help, not with Gerald hovering about. When she finally finished with the buttons, she coiled her long hair into a chignon at the nape of her neck and fastened it with a comb. She grabbed her drawstring bag from the foot of her bed and left the room.

Gerald stood at the second-floor landing, looking up at her. "It's time for you two to leave," he announced, giving her an appraising stare with eyes that were still puffy from hours spent the previous night in a smoke-filled gin house. "Why did you put up your hair?"

His presence there startled her. Was he about to climb the stairs? She resolved to keep her door locked *any* time she was in her room.

"Rachel. Your hair?"

"You didn't tell me not to fasten it up," she said with as much defiance as she dared. *Besides, Miss Corrine's the bait,* she added to herself.

He looked as if he was about to say something, then glanced at the stairs below him and sighed. "You best get on your way."

"Yes." She waited until he turned to leave, determined that he wouldn't be behind her on the staircase. It was bad enough she had to face his lecherous scrutiny every day—she didn't want the feel of his eyes moving down her back today.

~

What in the world possessed me to invite visitors here? Adam upbraided himself as he held his left cheek taut for Hershall's razor. He watched absently in the mirror as the sharp instrument glided skillfully over the soapy lather that covered half of his face.

It wasn't so bad that the young maid who had delivered those letters from her mistress was coming—after all, she had already seen his face. But manners had forced him to invite this Mrs. Hammond, too. He could kick himself now for allowing Bernice to bring about this change in his comfortable, safe routine.

Though he resented this turn of events, he knew deep down that it was not the fault of the two women, who were probably on the way to his home at that very moment. How could he fault anyone for wanting to worship?

He sighed as Hershall wiped the traces of soap from his face with a warm towel. He was a gentleman, and he would do everything in his power to make his guests feel welcome. But deep down, he would be praying that by next week they would find a church of their own.

~

"We really should hire a footman," Corrine fussed as she and Rachel stood on Adam Burke's terrace, awaiting the answer to Rachel's knock on the front door. Corrine looked exquisite in an azure and gold striped gown, her glossy dark hair cascading in ringlets from behind a matching silk bonnet. Around her neck hung a costly strand of pearls—a gift from one of her previous suitors. "If Gerald wouldn't go through money like it was water, I wouldn't have to travel around in rented carriages with only a maid to accompany me."

Rachel winced inwardly at the scornful accent her mistress put on the word *maid*. She had been looked down upon for so many years that she sometimes wondered if there would come a day when she would actually believe herself worthy only of contempt. She had seen such people before, even some who were younger than she, whose expressions showed a resigned acceptance of being beaten down by life. Would she be like that one day? Grateful for any crumb of kindness, even when it came from a hand that dealt with her harshly? She straightened her shoulders, trying to look as dignified as a mere servant could. *I hope I die before I ever get that hopeless!*

She was wondering if she had rapped loudly enough on the brass knocker when the door in front of them swung open. A middle-aged woman with striking blue eyes let them in and took their capes, then led them down a wide hall.

Adam Burke's drawing room, to the left of a long central hall, was twenty-five feet square and elegantly furnished. Above the rich cherry-wood wainscot, the walls were painted pale green with a handsome white cornice. A tiered chandelier of delicate brass hung from a carved ceiling medallion, and on the floor lay a rug of green, Prussian blue, and umber floral patterns. Three rows of shield-back chairs had obviously been arranged for the occasion.

Adam Burke came through the door before they could be offered seats. Clad in a black worsted frock coat and silk cravat, he appeared startled upon first sight of Corrine. An instant later, however, he had recovered enough to introduce himself to her.

"Oh, dear," Corrine remarked sweetly as she held out a gloved hand. "You seem surprised to see me, Mr. Burke. You *were* expecting me, weren't you?" She didn't seem taken aback at his disfigurement, but Rachel knew that Corrine was an expert at appearing any way she wished to appear.

"Of course I was," he replied, bowing slightly over her

hand. "I just didn't expect . . . such a beautiful lady to be gracing my home."

To Rachel's surprise he turned and spoke to her. "Bernice and Lucy will be here shortly," he said with a crooked smile. "They'll be glad to see that you came. Would you ladies like to sit down?"

Without having to even think about it, Rachel knew that Corrine would want her as far away from her and Adam Burke as possible, so she walked over to the back row and took a chair. Corrine, of course, found a place on the middle of the front row, and Adam sat in the chair to her right. Rachel wondered if he had chosen that seat deliberately, so that Corrine wouldn't have to look at his scars.

"I'm so grateful to you for extending this invitation to me as well," she could hear Corrine purr softly to Adam, her eyes fixed unwaveringly on his face. "And may I say that I admire your concern for your servants' spiritual well-being?"

Letting out a soft sigh, Rachel found herself wishing Lucy and Bernice were here. Corrine's worries about being late had been for naught, for even the minister hadn't yet arrived.

"They're more than just servants," Adam was saying as Rachel tried unsuccessfully to drown out their conversation with her thoughts. "They're my brothers and sisters in Christ as well. I can't imagine not including them during our worship services."

"What a refreshingly unique way to look at it." Corrine smiled.

To Rachel's quiet dismay, Adam was smiling back. "I believe you'll find Reverend Morgan a true expositor of the Word."

"Oh, you don't know how good it is to hear that!" She was

gushing now, her eyes lit up with rapture. "Such an answer to prayer!"

"Where did you attend church in Bridgewater?" he asked.

Corrine hesitated for a second. Inflecting just the right note of pathos in her voice, she murmured, "I'm afraid to confess I became bitter after the death of my dear husband. But when my maid came home with the news of your small gathering, I realized how much I had been longing to worship again."

From the back row, Rachel sickened to hear such lies. And the way Corrine was gazing at him—as if he were the most handsome man on earth! Her mistress would show her true feelings, Rachel knew, once she got home to Gerald. Many times in the past she had heard them laughing at Corrine's description of Squire Nowell's portliness or some other man's bowed legs or bad teeth.

What was worse by far was the way the man was looking back, his head tilted slightly towards her, as if he couldn't get enough of her words. *Are all men blind and deaf?* Rachel wondered.

She was so absorbed in her thoughts that she didn't hear Bernice and Lucy until they slid into seats on her row. "I was prayin' you wouldn't change your mind," said Lucy from beside her. The girl looked freshly scrubbed and pretty in a blue cotton dress, her red hair pulled in a topknot and covered with a cap of velvet and ribbons.

Next to her daughter, Bernice leaned forward, wearing a black dress and bonnet. "After all, you got a history of doin' such," she whispered. The good-natured grin on the woman's face showed that she was teasing, and strangely enough, Rachel didn't mind. Never before had she experienced the lightheartedness that comes from enjoying a private joke with friends, and she found it much to her liking. She smiled back just as Bernice was beginning to look worried that she'd offended.

Other servants began to filter into the room. Two middle-aged women she supposed to be housemaids took seats in front of them on the second row. They turned and smiled at Rachel as Lucy introduced them.

"Glad to have you with us," said Marie, the woman with the striking blue eyes who had answered the door earlier. The other woman, Dora, was thinner, but with eyes almost as blue.

"They're sisters," Lucy informed her. The two maids were joined shortly by an older woman with sharp features who nonetheless gave Rachel a shy smile before seating herself.

"That's Irene," whispered the girl beside her. "She's the upstairs maid. I'll introduce you to her later . . . she's a bit bashful."

Rachel wondered what they must think of Corrine, who was still regaling Mr. Burke with her melodious voice. *She must have practiced all morning,* she thought. Usually her mistress used a deeper, more sultry tone with her victims, but she'd obviously figured that Mr. Burke would require special treatment.

A huge man with iron gray hair and a thick mustache came into the room next. Dressed in a brown muslin shirt and corded trousers, he looked to be several years older than Mr. Burke. His weathered face lit up at the sight of Bernice and Lucy, and he came over and settled into the vacant chair next to Bernice.

"Papa's the gardener," Lucy whispered, rolling her eyes after her father reached over and gave her a light cuff on the chin. "They've been married for eighteen years, and he's still daft about Mummy."

Rachel leaned forward just a bit so she could watch the couple from the corner of her eye. The man had Bernice's hand clasped in his great paw.

She hadn't even thought to wonder if the cook had a husband! Growing up in the orphanage and then living with Gerald and Corrine, she had had limited exposure to *real* families. She didn't know who she envied more—Bernice, for having a loving husband, or Lucy, for having a mother and father.

A bell sounded from the front of the house. "That would be Reverend Morgan," Lucy told her. The low hum of conversations ceased as the group waited expectantly. Minutes later another manservant ushered in a short, balding man—though Rachel suspected he was younger than his lack of hair suggested. With him were a young woman, her pleasant round face topped with brown hair under a lace cap, and a curly haired girl of about three years of age.

"Good morning to you all," boomed the minister as he led his wife and child to chairs in the front row. "I hope we haven't kept you waiting too long."

"Worth the wait, sir!" declared Bernice's husband to the laughter of the others.

"Papa always says that," Lucy whispered to Rachel.

From her seat on the back row, Rachel watched as Mr. Burke introduced Corrine to Robert Morgan and his wife, whose name was Penelope. The little girl ignored the introductions and turned in her chair to stare with shining dark eyes at the people seated behind her. When she got to Jack

Taylor, the gardener crossed his eyes and made a face at her, causing her to break into an appreciative grin.

Why, the little one's got dimples just like mine! Rachel mused. She hoped the child would look her direction, too, but just then her mother turned her around to face the front.

Reverend Morgan noticed Rachel, however, as he came to stand in front of the group. He gave her a quick smile, then asked that everyone rise for prayer and hymns.

"Dear heavenly Father," he began, "we thank thee for allowing us to worship together, and we humbly ask thy pardon for our sins. Give us the desire to do thy will in every task that we undertake, and an appreciation of the blessings thou hast bestowed upon us. In Jesus' name, amen."

When all heads were raised again, Irene, the housemaid with the sharp features, slipped out of her chair and walked over to a mahogany piano in the corner of the room. She took a seat on the bench behind the instrument and, with a nod from Reverend Morgan, began to play beautifully, her features softening as she played.

"Come, thou fount of every blessing, tune my heart to sing thy grace. . . ."

Rachel stood silent as the people around her sang the hymn. If Lucy and Bernice were aware that she wasn't singing, they pretended not to notice. She wondered how Corrine was handling what had to be an even more awkward position—after all, she had told Mr. Burke that she used to attend church. Leaning slightly to the right so she could see past the housemaid in front of her, she noticed that Corrine had her head bowed slightly, as if still praying. Of course! She would probably tell Mr. Burke that she was so caught up with emotion that she had to thank God again for allowing her to be here.

It would most likely work, too, for Mr. Burke glanced over at her occasionally as he sang. She had seen that same look on other men's faces: a mixture of concern and admiration.

When the hymn was finished, everyone sat back down and the minister cleared his throat and began to speak. His voice was gentle but rose when he spoke of how a group of deeply religious men called the Pharisees were prideful about their good works. Caught up in the words of the sermon, Rachel forgot to watch Corrine as she heard about one of these Pharisees named Nicodemus and the visit he made to Jesus one night.

"Nicodemus had everything!" Reverend Morgan thundered. "A respected position in his church, high morals, and vast knowledge of the Holy Scriptures! But our Lord and Savior Jesus Christ told such a good man . . . you must be born again!"

Born again? Rachel wondered at such an impossibility. *Besides, being born once was bad enough!* Then she realized that the minister wasn't referring to a literal returning to the womb. But what else could it mean? After trying to figure it out for a few minutes, she gave up and let her mind drift, becoming absorbed in watching the back of Adam Burke's head. From behind, it was impossible to tell that his face was scarred. *How did it happen? Had he ever wished he had never been born, as she had sometimes wished?*

When Robert Morgan was finished speaking, he bowed his head again and closed his eyes, as did the rest of the tiny congregation. Rachel lowered her head, too. For five minutes no one made a sound, not even the little girl on the front row. Then a quiet amen came from the minister, and people began to raise their heads.

Mr. Burke stood, clasped the preacher's hand, and turned to face the others. "Let's all move to the dining room. I'm hungry!"

Rachel knew they had been invited to lunch, but it seemed so unnatural for servants and their employers to be dining together. Why, in the six years she had lived with Corrine and Gerald, she had never shared a meal with them. As she followed Lucy and her parents into the hall, she touched Bernice on the shoulder. "Would you like some help in the kitchen?"

"No thank you, child." The cook turned to give Rachel a smile. "We laid it out ahead of time."

"Mr. Adam don't want us to have a lot of work on Sundays," explained Lucy. "It's just some cold meats, cheese, and the like."

"By the way, I'd like you to meet my husband," said Bernice, nodding toward the man beside her. "Jack, this here's Rachel . . ."

"Jones, sir," Rachel supplied, wondering if she was supposed to offer to shake hands. She had read in *Mrs. Bertram's Rules of Social Etiquette for English Ladies*—one of the few books that Corrine possessed and was willing to lend her—that the woman was supposed to offer her hand first. But the book didn't mention if that custom applied when servants were introduced to each other as well.

The man solved her dilemma by scooping up her hand with his huge rough one. "Jack Taylor here, missy."

"I'm pleased to meet you, Mr. Taylor."

"Call me Jack," he said, putting an arm around Lucy's shoulder. "Now let's go get some o' that lunch my two lovely ladies have prepared."

Just across the hall from the drawing room was a spacious

dining room. The cream-colored walls were stuccoed, and one end was dominated by a black marble fireplace with a large open grate. A sideboard, groaning with silver and jasperware, sat against the north wall.

Reverend Morgan, Mr. Burke, and the manservant—a short man named Hershall—were standing behind their chairs at an oval dining table when Rachel walked into the room with the Taylors. The other women were already seated, and to Rachel's amusement, Corrine was three chairs down from Mr. Burke . . . and didn't look happy about it. What must have been even more disconcerting to her mistress was the fact that sisters Marie and Dora sat between them, and Irene, the older maid who had played the piano, was on her other side.

Reverend Morgan pulled out a chair for Rachel right beside his little girl. Mr. Burke held the next chair for Lucy, and Jack Taylor seated his wife before taking his seat.

Once everyone was at the table, Mr. Burke said grace, and everyone began to pass platters of cold meats, cheeses, breads, and fruits around the table. The conversation was hearty and full of laughter, with the servants speaking as freely as anyone else. Rachel imagined that this must be the same kind of comfortable intimacy that large families shared.

The minister's little girl, whom Rachel had overheard addressed as Margaret, was a delight. A copper pot had been placed upside down in her chair, and in her pink-flowered dress, she sat perched upon it like a queen. Her mother, on the other side, had served the child's plate with small portions of food. But Margaret was more impressed with the cheese and sliced beef sandwich that Rachel had put together for herself, and she asked for a bite.

"Margaret!" scolded Mrs. Morgan.

"It's all right, ma'am," Rachel told her. "I haven't taken a bite yet. Would you mind if I give her a little bit?"

"Not if you don't mind sharing it."

"Not at all." Rachel picked up her knife and cut her sandwich in half, then cut one of the halves again and trimmed the heavy brown crusts. When she set it over on the little girl's plate, Margaret surprised her with a lisping attempt at "Thank you."

"You're welcome," answered Rachel. The familylike atmosphere around the table had eased some of her shyness, and she added, "And might I say that you have lovely manners for one so young."

"Aside from begging for food at the table," said Penelope Morgan, giving Rachel a wink. "Do you have little brothers or sisters?"

"No, ma'am."

"Oh? You seem to have such a way with children—I'm surprised."

"At the orphanage . . . ," Rachel began, then immediately wished she hadn't. She had to complete her sentence, however, because everyone seemed to be listening. "The older children helped out with the younger ones." She busied herself with her food and waited for someone to say something, anything, that would take the attention away from herself.

Instead, Reverend Morgan looked at her with sympathetic interest. "An orphanage? How old were you when you lost your parents?"

"I believe I was two, sir," she answered quietly.

"Do you remember them at all?" This time Mr. Burke was speaking, and Rachel didn't even need to look up to know that Corrine's gray eyes would be filled with barely disguised irritation at the attention her maid was getting.

"No, sir." She would be going home with Corrine later, so she had to make amends while she had the opportunity. "Mrs. Hammond here generously provided employment for me when I was thirteen."

Corrine jumped in quickly, as if she had been just waiting for the conversation to turn her way. "It was really quite impulsive of me," she confessed, her lips turned up in a self-effacing smile. "I had no *need* for another servant. But when I visited the charity home and saw that Rachel was about to be set out on her own, my heart went out to her."

She sent Rachel a manufactured look of warmth from across the table and sighed. "Isn't it wonderful how, when you set out to do a good thing for someone else, it turns into a blessing for yourself? When I decided to leave Bridgewater after my husband died, I knew I couldn't manage without her—she's been a hard worker and a cheerful companion. In fact, sometimes I feel that she's more like a *sister* than my maid."

At the far end of the table, Jack Taylor was wiping his eyes with his napkin. "That's right good to hear, ma'am. Ain't it somethin' how the good Lord works things out that way!"

Even though he was just a servant, Corrine batted her eyes at him. "It never ceases to amaze me!"

From beside her, Irene looked at Corrine as if she were an angel from heaven. "I wish somebody like you would have hired me when I was a young one," she said with a trembling, quiet voice. "Not everybody's as good to their servants as you or Mr. Adam here."

"I'm so sorry," Corrine sighed, tightening her lips and giving her pretty head a shake. She reached over to pat the

72

woman's bony hand with her small white one. "Unfortunately, some members of the upper class need lessons on treating others decently."

Adam Burke leaned forward. "What were you doing at the orphanage, Mrs. Hammond?"

"Why, charity work, Mr. Burke! I believe I mentioned in our correspondence how much I like to be involved with helping those less fortunate."

There were nods of approval from half the people at the table, and the other half looked appreciative . . . except for Bernice. Rachel noticed with surprise that the woman had an appraising look on her face as she listened to Corrine's words.

"You know," began Adam, "that might be the answer to your dilemma."

Corrine lifted her eyebrows. "Excuse me?"

"I sponsor an orphanage in the Spitalfields parish. Someone with your compassion for children could do some great things there."

"You flatter me," she murmured, lowering her eyes. With a sigh, she raised them again. "Unfortunately, my financial situation is static until my estate in Bridgewater is sold."

Adam drew his eyebrows together as if in deep thought. "Your letter . . . ," he finally said. "You don't mind if I mention your letter, do you?"

"Of course not." Except for little Margaret, the other guests and servants had stopped eating and were listening with obvious interest.

"You wrote in your letter that time was weighing heavily on your hands." He gave her a lopsided smile. "You could spend some of that time with the children at the orphanage."

"With the children?" Corrine absentmindedly put a hand

73

up to her pearls, and Rachel could detect a slight tremor at the corner of her mouth. "You mean . . . visit them?"

"Oh, more than just visits," said Adam, still smiling. "Think about how much good you could do by mothering the little ones a bit. I know for a fact that the nurses haven't the time to sit and rock the babies or to hold the others in their arms."

"What a grand idea!" exclaimed Robert. "And it wouldn't cost you a penny. Think of all the children who go to bed every night without a mother's touch. What joy it would bring you to add love to those little lives!"

"Now there's a heartwarming thought, Mrs. Hammond." At the far end of the table, Bernice had finally decided to speak. "And you certainly have the experience."

"Experience?" The corners of Corrine's mouth were turned up, but her eyes were anything but smiling as she turned her face toward the cook. "But I have no children, dear."

"Yes, ma'am," said Bernice, smiling back benignly. "But you mentioned that you met Rachel when you was doin' some charity work at an orphanage . . . didn't you?"

"Oh, that!" Corrine waved a hand and gave a little laugh. "How silly of me. I had it in mind that Mr. Burke was speaking of *babies,* when my experience has been exclusively with *older* children."

"There are all ages at the Methodist home," said Penelope Morgan, wiping her daughter's mouth with her napkin. "In fact, I spend some time there once a week. . . . Would you like to go with me this Tuesday?"

"This Tuesday? I believe I have—"

"Or we can go another day if you prefer."

Corrine's shoulders fell slightly, but she lifted her chin and said, "Tuesday's fine."

~

The fine, misting rain that had begun when Corrine and
Rachel left Mr. Burke's house turned into a thundering tor-
rent shortly afterwards. Rachel sat as still as possible in the
hired carriage, lest Corrine take notice of her and decide to
vent the wrath that was surely building up in her mind. Right
now the woman sat with her bag clenched in her lap and a
definite frown on her face. That made things even more ominous, for Corrine was too wrinkle conscious to let herself
frown for very long.

Unfortunately, a vegetable cart on Sidney Street had overturned just moments before, and the carriage had to come to a
dead stop. Drivers of omnibuses, landaus, coaches, and drays
yelled curses at the hapless merchant, who, with the aid of a
few sympathetic passersby, was trying to right his cart and
retrieve at least a portion of his sodden wares.

"Can't you go around them?" Corrine called at the driver
through an opening in the back of the canvas. She had to
shout twice to be heard above the rain pummeling the hood.

"Sorry, ma'am!" called the man, bundled in oilskins. "Not
till they move that wagon!"

Corrine apparently decided she could use the time more
productively, and she turned venomous eyes upon Rachel.
"You weren't going to mention what a freak Mr. Burke is,
were you? Were you hoping when I met him I'd appear
shocked and ruin my chances with him?"

"No ma'am. He's not a freak, and besides, you never asked
me about his looks."

"And I suppose you're happy about the mess you've gotten
me into!"

"Me?" Her mouth fell open. "How did I—"

"You just *had* to tell that charming little story about my taking you out of the orphanage, didn't you!"

A dull ache started pounding Rachel's temples. "You wanted Mr. Burke to see you as kind, charitable—"

Corrine's nostrils flared. "But I certainly did not want to get trapped into visiting such a dreadful place. You knew all along that would happen, didn't you?"

"How could I know that would happen?" For years Rachel had borne the blame for everything that went wrong in Corrine's life. Now she squared her jaw and forced herself to stare back. "Why would I even *want* to do that, ma'am?" she asked in an even tone, hoping to appeal to any sense of reason that her mistress might possess.

"So that you can stay home with Gerald while I traipse over to the slums with the minister's moonfaced wife!" Corrine sneered, folding her arms across her chest. "You've wanted to get me out of your way for months now, and don't think I don't know it!"

"Stay home with Mr. Moore!" Rachel could hardly get the loathsome words out of her mouth. "That's not true!"

"I've seen the way he's been looking at you! And what kind of looks are you giving him when my back is turned?"

"Giving him?" A cold nausea gripped the pit of her stomach at the very idea of flirting with Gerald. "I . . . I'm not . . ."

Corrine was eyeing her sharply and seemed to take Rachel's reaction as proof that her accusations were true. "Well, from now on, you're not to be alone in the house with him. And that means you'll come with me to that orphanage, too!"

"Yes, ma'am." The relief made Rachel go limp against the back of the seat.

"And don't let me catch you making those doe eyes at him again, or so help me, I'll kick you out with no references!"

~

Hours after his guests left, Adam Burke was reading in his library when Bernice appeared in the doorway. "Sir? May I have a word with you?"

"Come in, Bernice," he said, lifting his feet from the footstool.

"Oh, don't go gettin' uncomfortable for me," she scolded lightly. "Next thing, you'll be bowin' like I'm the queen of England."

He smiled and propped his feet back on the stool. "Queen Bernice—I like the sound of that. Will you have a seat?"

She nodded and eased into the armchair across from him. Before she could speak, Adam asked, "Are you in pain, Bernice?"

She waved away his concern. "Bit o' rheumatism, sir. The damp weather and all."

"Are you taking anything for it?"

"It ain't so bad that I have to do that. But I didn't come to talk about *me,* sir. . . . Do you mind?"

"All right," said Adam, closing his copy of *Foxe's Book of Martyrs.* "What's on your mind?"

The woman hesitated as if searching for the right words. "When I came to work for your family," she finally began, "I was just a girl of fifteen. You was about five years old. Do you remember them days?"

"Of course. You were the . . ."

"Scullery maid," she finished for him. "But I was determined not to spend the rest of my life scrubbing pots and pans, so I watched Dorsey, the cook, every chance I got. And I asked questions. When she got too old to work and went back to live with her family, I was given a chance at her job."

"I remember you used to let me slip into the kitchen and have sweets once in a while," said Adam.

"Well, I should have been canned for that!" Bernice exclaimed heartily. "Now that I've got me own child, I know it ain't right to let them go behind their parents' backs."

He smiled. "You were young. I don't think you spoiled me too much . . . do you?"

"Heavens, no! You turned out to be the best o' the bunch." Her ruddy face grew even more flushed. "I'm sorry, sir."

Adam knew why she was so embarrassed. His older sister Judith had married in haste, and then years later the rift had happened with his brother over Kathleen.

"Please don't apologize," he said. "There aren't any skeletons in my family closet that you don't know about. Now, what is on your mind?"

"May I speak freely?"

"Of course."

Bernice shifted in her chair. "It's that fancy woman."

Lifting an eyebrow, Adam asked, "Do you mean Mrs. Hammond?"

"Yes . . . her."

Adam leaned his head back against his hands, an amused grin on his face. "What about Mrs. Hammond? Are you wanting to invite her for tea?"

She was obviously offended. "Now, don't be makin' sport of me, sir. You know I wouldn't be in here if I didn't care what happens to you."

"Of course you wouldn't," he told her. He moved his feet from the footstool again and sat up straight. "I'm sorry."

"It's all right," she sniffed. "But I've got to warn you about her."

So I was right, Adam mused. He had sensed a coldness coming from Bernice toward the woman during lunch when they had spoken about the orphanage. "You don't like her, do you?"

Bernice's lips tightened for a second before answering. "I try not to judge people, Mr. Adam. Most people have *some* good in them, and it just ain't Christian to be lookin' for faults."

Adam smiled again. "I know that. You've always been a kind person."

Embarrassed, she looked down at her roughened hands. "Oh, well, I try to be. But this Mrs. Hammond . . ." She paused, then rushed ahead. "I don't see any good in her at all, and I think she's after your money!"

"My *money?*" Bernice looked so worried that Adam couldn't resist teasing her. Putting a hand to his chest, he feigned surprise. "You mean she's not chasing me for my looks?"

"Mister Adam!" The cook pulled herself out of her chair. "I can see that you ain't interested in hearing what—"

He was on his feet in an instant, walking over to put his hands on her shoulders. "I'm sorry again, Bernice. Here you are, trying to help me, and all I can do is make jokes."

"Well, certain things don't need to be laughed at."

"You're right again. Now, please sit down."

She complied but fixed him with a wary expression. "Are you ready to listen?" When he nodded, she continued. "I overheard her talkin' with you before the meeting. The things she says just don't ring true."

"You mean about longing to worship again and all that?"

"That's just what I mean—and that bit at the table about visitin' orphans and the like!" Bernice snorted. "You can tell she ain't got a charitable thought in her head. Why, it's plain to see even her maid is afraid of her."

"Rachel, you mean."

"Yes. The first time that girl came over here with one of Mrs. Hammond's messages, she looked like a scared rabbit. Then she went and changed her mind and almost took the letter back from Lucy. Would have happened, too, if you hadn't walked in the kitchen."

Adam nodded. "Come to think of it, I remember she looked a little worried. Why is that, do you think?"

"I think the girl knows what her missus is doin' and feels bad about it. You probably ain't the first rich man this Mrs. Hammond's tried to get her claws into."

"That's a good possibility."

Bernice looked up with a start. "You mean, you *know* what she's doing?"

"It only took a little while to figure it out." He gave her a knowing wink. "Five to ten minutes, and I knew all about her."

"But how? Even my Jack's thinkin' she's a saint from heaven."

A sad, uneven smile came to Adam's lips. "I started questioning her motives right away when she started flirting with me. I'm not exactly the kind of man that women throw themselves at."

"Mr. Adam, I wish you wouldn't say that," implored Bernice, her expression pained. "There's someone out there for you."

He shrugged. "Perhaps. But getting back to Mrs. Hammond, I noticed myself what you said about her words not ringing true."

"Are you disappointed?" Her tone became sympathetic. "After all, she's a beautiful woman, to be sure."

Adam shook his head. "I didn't find her beautiful."

"You didn't?"

"Well, perhaps at first. But not after I discovered the greed in her eyes."

"And all that talk about gettin' her to visit the foundling home?" The cook grinned delightfully. "You was just pullin' her along?"

He grinned back at her. "I was. But come to think of it, it might do her some good, don't you think?"

Bernice looked doubtful. "If she don't end up poisonin' the poor little orphans."

"Do you think I should tell her not to come to the meetings again?"

She pursed her lips thoughtfully, then shook her head. "I know how the Lord can change even the most rotten heart. Just look at my Jack. When he first came to work for your family, I thought he was the worst rakeshame I ever saw."

"He's a good, decent man now."

"And the girl . . . Rachel," she continued. "If you tell Mrs. Hammond not to come back, she's the type that would keep the girl away from here, just for spite. I have a feelin' that me and Lucy are the only friends she's got."

"Then it's decided," Adam declared. "We'll continue the invitation indefinitely."

Bernice nodded. "And we'll pray for that woman's soul!"

81

5

A T ten o'clock Tuesday morning, Penelope Morgan was at the front door to fetch Corrine for the visit to the orphanage. "Good morning, ma'am," Rachel said as she held the door open. As was standard procedure when her mistress was expecting a caller, she had already transferred Gerald's cloak and hat from the rack at the door to the pantry off the kitchen. "You didn't bring your little girl?"

The minister's wife, dressed in a simply cut but attractive blue muslin gown, stepped into the hallway. "My husband stays home to prepare his sermons on the days I make charity visits. Between him and our housekeeper, they manage to keep her out of trouble."

"I can't imagine such a sweet girl causing much trouble."

"Thank you. She's a sweet girl, all right, but I've never yet seen a three year old who didn't require a watchful eye."

Rachel led the woman into the sitting room and offered her a place on the settee. "Mrs. Hammond asked if you'd mind waiting here," she told her. She knew that Corrine, still upstairs fussing with her hair, would be in no hurry to come down. *"Just offer her some tea and cakes, and keep her entertained until I get ready,"* she had instructed. *"I don't want to spend a minute more than I have to at that dreadful place!"*

"That color you're wearing really shows off your eyes," Mrs. Morgan remarked after declining Rachel's offer of refreshments. "Is that a new dress?"

"Yes, ma'am." She absently brushed the folds of Nile green broadcloth gathered at her waist and starched new apron— more stage props for the drama that Corrine was acting out. Still, when she considered the alternative of staying home, Rachel didn't mind so much playing her part as the pampered servant today. Gerald was upstairs asleep, and she was determined never to be alone with him. She had avoided him as much as possible since Sunday and had taken to locking her attic-room door even on the rare occasions she went up there in the daytime.

She was disappointed that Margaret wasn't here. In her apron pocket was a sketch of the little girl. She had portrayed the tot seated on a cooking pot in a chair, smiling as she held a bit of sandwich in her fingers. Rachel had wanted to see her face when she handed her the picture.

Her hand inside her pocket, she touched the linen paper she had trimmed from an envelope Corrine had thrown away. *Should I give it to her mother now,* she wondered, *or wait till Sunday?*

Penelope Morgan was beginning to look a little anxious, occasionally glancing at the stairs. She smiled, though, at Rachel. "Won't you sit down, too?"

"Oh—yes, ma'am." Rachel sat in the nearest chair and folded her hands in her lap, wondering what she could possibly talk about that would interest someone as near perfect as a minister's wife must be. They had nothing in common. After all, Rachel had been such a belligerent child during most of her childhood—out of necessity, for the meek children in the orphanage were tormented incessantly by the others.

And even now, though she'd been cowed by Corrine and Gerald into outward submission, she rebelled inwardly. Had Mrs. Morgan, kind and gentle, ever hated anyone the way she hated Gerald Moore? The very idea seemed absurd. What would the good lady think if she knew the servant sitting before her often entertained thoughts of her employer choking to death from a poisonous batch of tea?

"Did you enjoy the service Sunday?" Mrs. Morgan asked at length.

Rachel didn't want to lie—she had lived with so many lies that she had grown to hate them. And she *had* enjoyed the singing and seeing Lucy and Bernice and sitting next to Margaret at lunch. But between worrying about Corrine's deception of Mr. Burke and her confusion about the "born again" part of the sermon, she had left the big house with the beginnings of a headache. Corrine's tongue-lashing in the carriage had added considerably to the tension so that Rachel's head had been pounding by the time they got home.

"Your husband is a true expositor of the Word," she said solemnly, remembering what Mr. Burke had said to Corrine. After all, Mr. Burke didn't seem the type who would lie, so Reverend Morgan was most likely an outstanding expositor . . . whatever that meant.

The woman had a little smile of amusement on her round face. "Thank you, dear." She glanced back at the stairs again. "Perhaps your mistress would like some help dressing?"

"Oh, no, ma'am. She told me to stay down here and keep you entertained."

"Then tell me about yourself," Mrs. Morgan said, crossing her arms and settling back against the cushions.

"About myself?"

"Yes. What do you do in your spare time—do you like needlepoint?"

Rachel shook her head. Hesitating briefly, she offered, "I like to read, whenever I can get a book. But mostly I like to draw."

"You do? Well, what do you draw?"

"People." She took a deep breath, brought the paper out of her pocket, and handed the portrait to Mrs. Morgan. "I drew this last night."

The woman's eyes grew wide as she studied her daughter's image in the sketch. "Why, this is very good!" she cried with delight, putting a hand up to her cheek. "Look how you've even shown her dimples!"

"I haven't had as much practice drawing bodies, so I think I made the arms a little too short," Rachel said. "Would you like to have it?"

"Would I like to—why, I'd *love* to have it!" The woman looked up at her. "My dear, I think it's perfect, and I have a little silver frame that's just begging for this. But I insist on paying you for it."

"Oh, no, ma'am. It's a gift."

"Are you sure? Because I can tell you worked hard on it."

"I'm sure, ma'am."

"Well, I thank you!" Mrs. Morgan smiled down at the portrait of her daughter. "I can't wait to show Mr. Morgan . . . and I'd love to see some of the other things that you've sketched."

"You would?" Rachel brightened, then her shoulders fell.

Margaret's portrait was on about the nicest cut of paper she
had ever used. She couldn't show a fine lady like Mrs. Morgan
a cheese box full of scraps and bits. She was just going to have
to buy a sketchbook.

She had been saving for a new pair of shoes to replace the
leather work slippers that were wearing out. The pair of laced
boots she was wearing now had been bought as part of her
fancy maid's uniform and were to be used only when Corrine
wanted to impress someone. There always seemed to be something she needed, and she had considered drawing paper a lux-
ury. But she hadn't had to pay for the pencils, and some good
vellum paper would be so nice. Maybe the shoes could wait a
bit longer.

"They're not very fancy," she finally said, in answer to Mrs.
Morgan's interest in seeing more of her work.

"Oh, but that doesn't matter," said the minister's wife. "I'd
really like to see what you've got. Quality is much more
important than 'fancy,' don't you think?"

Rachel's heartbeat quickened. Besides Mr. Solomon, no
one had ever expressed an interest in seeing her sketches. But
the pleasure on Mrs. Morgan's face when she saw the portrait
of her daughter gave Rachel new courage. "They're upstairs in
my room," she said, rising from her chair. "But I can fetch
them quickly, if you don't mind. . . ."

"I'm sure they'll be worth the wait," Penelope assured her
with a smile.

Two minutes later, Rachel was back with her cheese box.
She placed it on the settee beside Penelope and took a seat at
the other end. Only after she opened the box did she remember Adam Burke's portrait at the top of the stack. Her cheeks
burning, she reached for some papers at the bottom of the box

and piled them on top of the others. "This was a boy who cleaned our chimney once. . . ." She almost said *in York,* but then remembered that Corrine claimed to be from Bridgewater. Abruptly she stopped and shuffled the drawings, hoping that Mr. Burke's portrait would stay hidden.

Rachel couldn't understand why it disturbed her so much, the thought of having this kind woman spot that particular portrait. Was it because Mrs. Morgan was Mr. Burke's friend and might think she had some romantic interest in the man? Or was it because she didn't want him to find out and think the same thing?

"These are incredible!" Mrs. Morgan was saying, taking out several of the papers and spreading them in her lap. "What talent you have, my dear girl."

"Thank you," Rachel told her, pleased in spite of her uncomfortable predicament. While Mrs. Morgan was studying the sketches in her lap, Rachel caught sight of Mr. Burke's face, half-hidden by the other papers. Quietly she reached in the box and, pretending to sort through the sketches, hid the portrait in the palm of her hand. Then she slid it under the box, hoping to slip it back inside when they were finished.

She was just breathing easier when the rustling of skirts and horsehair crinoline sounded from the staircase. Corrine floated down the steps in an apricot-colored poplin gown, a smile fixed on her face as she held the banister and shook her head helplessly at the minister's wife. "My dear Mrs. Morgan."

The minister's wife looked up from the sketches with what Rachel believed to be reluctance. "Good morning, Mrs. Hammond."

Corrine was at the bottom now and came toward Penelope

Morgan with her arms outstretched, the scent of Vivre le Jour trailing after her. "I'm so sorry to keep you waiting," she breathed, bending to kiss her on the cheek. Without batting an eye she added, "I feel so foolish! Just a moment ago, the hem of the gown I started out with got caught on one of my dressing-table latches and ripped, so I had to change into another one. I'm almost feeble without Rachel to help me get dressed."

"You should have called for her," Mrs. Morgan said. "In fact, we both could have helped you."

"Oh, heaven forbid! I couldn't have you left down here all by yourself—and I don't ask my guests to do servants' work. I hope you haven't been too bored."

Mrs. Morgan glanced down at the sketches in her lap. "Not bored at all. Rachel's work is fascinating." She turned to the girl and smiled. "I wish I had more time to look at these, but we're expected at the orphanage. May I see them again sometime soon?"

"Yes, ma'am," Rachel answered, returning her smile and hoping she hadn't angered Corrine by bringing out the box of sketches. *After all, she did order me to entertain her,* she rationalized. *If only Corrine weren't so touchy about anyone getting attention besides herself!*

"Well then, we should be going," said the minister's wife, gathering her purse from the arm of the settee before standing.

"Do you mind if Rachel comes with us?" asked Corrine. "It would be such a good experience for her."

Mrs. Morgan cast a doubtful glance at Corrine's wide crinolined skirt, but said, "I believe we can squeeze together in the coach."

Corrine turned to Rachel, who was now gathering up her

collection of sketches to dash them upstairs. "Just pick them up later," she ordered, kindly because of Mrs. Morgan's presence. "We mustn't keep the children waiting any longer."

~

The brick, two-story Methodist Charity Home for Orphans sat on the north side of Blossom Street. Rachel looked around at the crumbling tenements and recognized the general hopelessness etched into the faces of the ragged people in the doorways.

Spitalfields, abutting the city wall, had once been a prosperous middle-class parish with most of the residents involved some way in the silk trade. The introduction of the power loom in the late eighteenth century and its widespread use by the early nineteenth century brought about massive unemployment and starvation wages. It would be safe to guess that, while the majority of the one hundred and sixty children who resided in the home were true orphans, a good number had been left on the doorstep by desperate parents.

Corrine, Penelope Morgan, and Rachel were ushered into the building by a gray-haired man who walked with the aid of a cane—Mr. Garland, the administrator of the home. "Mrs. Morgan," he said with delight as he took her hand, "I was beginning to worry that you weren't going to be able to come today."

Mrs. Morgan leaned forward to put a kiss on his lined cheek. "Well, we're here now. And don't you worry—we'll just stay a little longer to make up for the time."

Rachel noticed the crestfallen look that swept across Corrine's face. Nonetheless, her mistress recovered with typi-

cal speed and held out a gloved hand while Penelope introduced her to Mr. Garland.

Servants were almost never included in the civilities that
members of the middle and upper classes practiced with each
other, so Rachel was surprised when Mrs. Morgan gave her
name to Mr. Garland as well. Etiquette book or no, she decided
to extend her hand to the man, who warmly took it in his own.

"There's a nursery for the tiniest infants on this floor, as well
as the kitchen and serving hall," Mrs. Morgan told them after
Mr. Garland took his leave. She began leading them toward a
wide staircase. "An office and room for washing clothes, too.
Upstairs are two classrooms and beds for the rest of the children."

Rachel took careful note of their surroundings. The building itself was old—it had once housed a textile factory—but
the inside looked clean and well maintained.

"Do they stay inside all the time?" asked Rachel as they
made their way up the stairs. She hoped not, because her only
fond memory of the orphanage in Liverpool was of the huge
yard shaded with oak trees that were perfect for climbing.

"Goodness, no. While the courtyard isn't as big as one
would prefer, the children are brought out in groups to play.
There's also a park nearby where they're taken on Saturdays—
the children that are old enough."

"What are we supposed to do here?" asked Corrine, drag-
ging herself up the wooden staircase as if headed for her own
execution.

Mrs. Morgan reached the landing and stepped aside. "The
school-aged children are having their lessons."

As she spoke, Rachel could hear the familiar sound of tre-
bled voices reciting something in unison . . . the continents?

"We'll be with the younger ones," the minister's wife said.

~

"Babies?" Corrine cleared her throat. *Not babies. Please, no. . . .*

Penelope smiled. "Not the very littlest—they're downstairs." She started walking again, leading them down a long, paneled hallway. Corrine could hear muted sounds behind heavy wooden doors from both sides.

Penelope paused in front of the last door. "Mr. Garland believes that children not only need their physical needs looked after, but their spiritual needs as well. But how can you teach them about *God's* love if they haven't experienced the most basic human love, that of a mother to her child? The nurses here have all they can do just keeping them clean and fed. The children need more love and affection."

Corrine faltered. "I . . . I don't think I can do this." She shook her head. "As I said before, I only have experience with older children."

"Well, let's see," said Penelope, folding her arms in front of her. "Perhaps you could help the oldest ones study their Scripture or arithmetic drills. Most likely the teachers could use another hand."

Corrine glanced back over her shoulder at one of the classroom doors from which was coming a muffled recitation: *"By faith Abraham, when he was called to go . . ."* She couldn't do that either.

"On the other hand, the young ones probably need us the most," she declared quickly, motioning for Penelope to open the door.

The door opened into an enormous room lightened by six windows on the opposite wall. Indentations in the planked

floor indicated where giant looms had once sat, and against
two walls were rows of little iron cots. The third wall was
taken up with a dozen metal cribs, lined front to back like cars
on a train.

Some sixty or so chattering little ones from the ages of one
to four years played in the middle of the floor, tended by two
tired-looking women. Several of the children had looked up
when Penelope opened the door and were now watching the
callers with a mixture of expectancy and curiosity.

The two nurses raised hopeful eyebrows at Corrine and
Rachel, then glanced at each other. One, a tall, dark-haired
woman, set down the toddler whose diaper she had just
changed and walked over to them. "Grand to see you, Mrs.
Morgan!" she said in a thick Irish brogue.

The woman still had the wet diaper bunched up in her left
hand as she offered her right one to Penelope. The minister's
wife shook the hand that was offered without hesitation.
Cringing inwardly, Corrine put both gloved hands behind her
back and pretended to stare at the windows against the far
wall.

"Good day, Mrs. O'Reilly. This is Mrs. Hammond and
Rachel," Penelope told the woman while patting the tops of
little heads that had begun to cluster around her. "They're
going to start coming with me every week."

Corrine whipped her head around. *Every week!* She had to
say something, make some excuse—and quickly—before she
found herself stuck here every Tuesday for the rest of her life.
"Not *every* week, I'm afraid," she corrected. "I mean, we'll *try,*
but sometimes I have other appointments."

"Well, we're appreciative of any time you can spare," Mrs.
O'Reilly said. She pointed to the barely visible form of a little

child lying under one of the cribs. "That one just arrived yesterday, and she's a pitiful thing. Maybe one of you could sit and just hold her for a little while."

"Mrs. Hammond—would you like to?" Penelope asked. "There's a rocking chair over there in the corner."

Corrine was about to tell her that she didn't want to wrinkle her dress, but the minister's wife was already leading Rachel to a group of older children. Letting out a sigh, she gathered her skirt and walked over to the crib. She bent at the waist to try to get a look at the child, who had scooted further out of her reach.

"Come out," she ordered sternly, drumming her fingers impatiently against the metal railing of the crib as she waited.

When no movement came from underneath, Corrine's voice rose a little louder. "I'm to sit and hold you now, so come out from under there."

Mrs. O'Reilly appeared at her side. "You'll have to coax her a bit, dearie," she whispered. "Her mum left her out on our doorstep yesterday, and the baby's grievin' for her. Perhaps if you let her see you holding out your arms for her?"

"Well, I certainly can't crawl down there and get her with this dress on, can I?" Corrine snapped. Turning back to the crib, she tried to soften her voice this time when she called to the child, but to no avail. Finally she straightened and folded her arms. "Isn't there something else I can do around here?"

"I tell you what," said the Irish woman. "Why don't you go sit down, and I'll bring her over."

Corrine clenched her teeth and nodded, then moved with resignation to the rocking chair in a corner. With her crinoline billowing about her, she could only perch on the edge of the seat, which served to irritate her even more. Seconds later

Mrs. O'Reilly followed with the crying and struggling little girl in her arms, a thin waif who appeared to be less than three years old. "Here you go, ma'am," she said, lowering her into Corrine's arms.

"Tell her to stop crying," Corrine said loudly over the wails. Any hopes she'd had of keeping her dress unspotted were crushed when she realized the child's eyes and nose were wet.

"Maybe a lullaby would do it," coaxed Mrs. O'Reilly before walking away. "I've got to finish diaperin' now—yer doin' fine."

Wrinkling her nose in disgust, Corrine reached into the purse she had hung on the chair arm and pulled out a linen handkerchief. "There, there now," she said stiffly as she wiped the little face. The child only cried louder, taking in deep, shuddering breaths between sobs.

"Oh, why don't you just shut up!" Corrine hissed through her teeth, then immediately glanced up to see if anyone had heard her. Relieved that no one had noticed, she tried to make her voice kinder. "We mustn't cry now, child," she cooed, wondering how anyone so little could make so much noise.

The crying continued. Surely someone else could deal with this brat! She tried to catch Rachel's eye, but the maid was seated on the floor with her back to her. Two or three children were piled in her lap and others on the floor at her side as she told a story. Penelope was in a chair across the room, rocking a baby. Mrs. O'Reilly and the other nurse bustled about, too busy to look over at her. The only thing that kept Corrine from setting the little girl on the floor and leaving was that she knew word would get back to Adam Burke and spoil any chance she would have with the man.

"All right now," she soothed woodenly, drawing the child closer. The child stopped struggling but held her little body stiff as she continued to cry.

Then Corrine remembered Mrs. O'Reilly's advice about the lullaby. She began humming a tune while gingerly rocking the chair—and sure enough, after a while the child stopped crying and relaxed against her, staring up at her face with half-closed eyes. Encouraged by the change, Corrine wiped the little nose again and started singing in a low voice bits and snatches of a song she had learned sometime in childhood.

> . . . *and so he asked the mighty ship at sea,*
> *"Were you once a little boat like me?"* . . .

When the child's eyelashes finally touched her pale cheeks, Corrine supposed she was asleep. Just then the child opened her eyes for an instant, raised her arm, and touched Corrine's face with her little hand. A faint sigh escaped her lips, and she closed her eyes, her arm falling back to her side.

A hollow feeling rose up in Corrine's chest, the feeling that often came in the stillness of night before the brandy she took to soothe her nerves could put her to sleep. *My little girl was almost this age when I . . .*

She shook her head abruptly, trying to push the thought aside. But a picture of Jenny kept coming to her mind. So small and delicate the child had been, with huge gray eyes that regarded her mother with a mixture of fear and longing. She would be ten years old now. Did Jenny remember her at all? Or had she, over time, come to think that her Aunt Mary was her mother?

No! Corrine clenched her teeth until her jaw began to ache. *I won't think of such things!*

But she couldn't take her eyes off the child who lay sleeping in her arms.

~

In the dining room Gerald finished the bread and marmalade that Rachel had left out for him, then drained the last of his tea. Corrine hadn't known what time they'd be back, but he assumed that he still had a couple of hours alone.

He was on his way through the sitting room to finish the rest of his newspaper in his favorite chair when he noticed the round wooden box. Setting the folded newspaper on the tea table, he moved over to the settee.

Rachel had obviously left her drawings out, something she'd never done before. He lifted the lid and set it aside. One at a time he picked up the scraps of paper and studied the faces she'd drawn. *She even seems to capture their personalities!* he thought with wonder.

A great emptiness suddenly came to his chest. Here was someone, a servant, who used the talent she had been given— by whom, he wasn't sure. The fact that she hadn't the proper drawing equipment didn't hinder her from trying to perfect her craft.

He had had talent, too . . . once. A star student at Oxford University, his idols had been Keats, Wordsworth, and Coleridge. Verse seemed to flow effortlessly from his pen like wine from a cask, and he imagined that one day every library in Great Britain would contain volumes of his works.

Then trouble had come, during summer holiday at his family's manor in Holdenby. Just as he had been ready to start his third year at the university, the girl from the village, the wheelwright's daughter, had brought him the dreadful news. Gerald's father had been generous with money and had given him the funds to quiet the girl's family. But the girl, a simple-minded fool who had taken his declarations of undying love to heart, had insisted on marriage.

The thought of becoming chained throughout life to such a creature haunted his dreams for days. He woke up one morning with the idea that he would go mad if the problem were not resolved. Pretending to have renewed affection for the silly lass, he had asked her to meet him at a certain spot in the forest where their earlier assignations had been. He had only wanted to reason with her, without her father and brothers around. But she had made him angry with her babbling on about how happy they would be as a family . . . so angry that he had lost all sense of reason.

He stormed back to the pen beside the grain house for his father's hunting dogs. The hounds had done their job; he hadn't even needed to dirty his own hands with the girl. Her death had been an accident—a terrible, unforeseen accident. And no one, not even the law, could hold Gerald Moore accountable.

A great deal of money had pacified the girl's father somewhat, but the bitter result of Gerald's rage had been estrangement from his own family and expulsion from the university. Eventually he found a replacement for his first love, poetry. While decks of cards and bottles of gin did not give him the same satisfaction as penning words in perfect meter, they demanded nothing from his soul. Yet he wondered, in his low hours, how different his life might have been. *If only . . .*

He frowned suddenly, despising himself for wallowing in self-pity. Sentiment was for fools, and he was no one's fool.

Turning hardened eyes back to Rachel's sketches, he realized it was a shame he couldn't profit from her talent. He had seen artists, with their pencils and sketch pads at Hyde Park, doing hurried portraits for sixpence or even less. But that wasn't the kind of money he was interested in; and he certainly didn't want her discovering that she could earn a living another way.

A piece of paper caught his eye, peeking out from beneath the wooden box. He reached for it and brought it close. *Adam Burke,* he realized by the scars. Corrine had described him as hardly looking human, but Rachel's rendering of the man showed handsome dark eyes and a studied intelligence.

Why did she draw him? She had never, to Gerald's knowledge, sketched himself or even Corrine. And come to think of it, Rachel had seemed more reluctant than ever to play her part this time. Was it because she had some feelings for the man?

He looked at the sketch again. Impossible. Most of her pictures were of freaks and beggars . . . this was just another one of the freaks.

But if Rachel *did* have some feelings for the man, wouldn't that double their chance of success? The fact that she was just a servant wasn't a hindrance. Though marriages between the classes seldom occurred and were frowned upon, many a squire's son—himself included—had learned to find his way down the servants' staircase in the dark. She was growing more beautiful every day. What man could resist having *two* lovely women from which to choose?

Gerald smiled. He liked those odds—and he didn't mind sharing, not where money was concerned.

He tossed the scrap of paper back in the box and began to close the lid when a sudden thought erased the smile from his face. If this Mr. Burke took an interest in her, what would prevent him from luring her away from them? She was nineteen years old now and not so easy to control as she once was. It would be useless to forbid her to leave if she had somewhere else to go.

And then what? Gerald had always taken for granted that Rachel's forced involvement in all of their schemes would keep her silent about them. He had played upon the guilt she obviously felt, telling her that if he and Corrine were ever arrested, they would make sure the authorities knew about her as well.

Still, she was no longer the naive little girl they had taken from the orphanage. What if one day she realized that, as a young servant obeying orders, she would most likely not be held liable for anything they did?

We can't risk that, he told himself. *She's got to stay dependent on us.* As hopeful as he had just been about using Rachel to gain access to Mr. Burke's money, he just couldn't do it. He would have to tell Corrine to make sure that she was the one who got Burke's attention, not Rachel.

~

"Is your mistress all right?" Mrs. Morgan whispered in Rachel's ear. In the coach, they were squeezed together in one seat so that Corrine could have the one facing them. Ever since the coachman had helped her into the carriage, Corrine had sat there with her head turned, staring through the window at nothing in particular.

"I don't know, ma'am," Rachel whispered back, reasonably sure that Corrine couldn't hear her over the noise of the hooves and wheels against the cobbled stones.

"Do you think that the child's situation made her sad?"

Rachel glanced at her mistress and shrugged her shoulders. *More likely she had a fight with Mr. Gerald last night.* She knew that Corrine had left her husband and baby several years ago, but Rachel had never seen her express any sorrow for having done so, or any sympathy for her own abandoned flesh and blood. Why would she feel any more for a child who was a stranger to her?

Still, she thought she had seen Corrine's eyes glistening when Mrs. O'Reilly finally took the sleeping baby from her arms.

6

MY dear Miss Jones!" Mr. Solomon's face was wreathed in smiles Thursday morning as he made his way to the front of the shop. "I had so hoped you would come today!"

Rachel shifted her heavy market basket over to her left arm. "You had?"

"I want to show you something," he said with a wink. Taking the basket, he led her to his worktable at the back corner. "It was brought in yesterday to be cleaned and reframed."

On the table lay a canvas portrait of a middle-aged man clad in the type of hunting coat worn in the late eighteenth century. Browns, grays, and flesh tones were the primary colors, with a splash of deep scarlet for the jacket.

"Do you know who painted this?" he asked.

Rachel drew closer to study the signature scrawled in the left corner. "Reynolds?" Impressed, she looked up at Mr. Solomon. "Sir Joshua Reynolds . . . I've heard of him but I've never seen any of his work."

"You still haff not, my dear—not in this place, at least. Although I did manage to acquire and sell one of his paintings just last year."

"Then who is it?"

"His younger sister, Frances. She never achieved the fame that her titled brother did, but she was quite good for an amateur artist."

"A woman?" Rachel shook her head incredulously.

Mr. Solomon smiled again. "And surely you haff heard of Rosa Bonheur of France?" When she nodded, he said, "So you see, it is possible to be a woman *and* a great artist."

"Yes, it is," she murmured. "But how did they do it?"

"Talent first," said the man. "But talent alone will seldom suffice. Mademoiselle Bonheur was trained by her father, and I assume Miss Reynolds's brother was generous with practical advice."

Rachel leaned over the portrait again and studied the texture of the paint on the canvas. "He almost looks as if he could speak to us, doesn't he?"

"And what would he say?" laughed Mr. Solomon. " 'Please help me . . . I haff been trapped in this portrait for eighty years'?"

Smiling, Rachel retrieved her basket from him. "I have to go home now," she said. "Thank you for showing this to me."

"Of course." He walked with her toward the front of the shop. At the door, he said quietly, "You know, I would still like to see some of your sketches."

"But why?" She shook her head. "They aren't anything you could sell."

"Let us just say I am curious. You haff an eye for quality work. Usually God awards such a love for beauty with the talent to create more beauty."

"And what will you say if you don't like my work?" asked Rachel.

The old man gave her a beatific smile. "I will tell you to

draw for your own enjoyment and not to waste your time trying to sell it."

Rachel wasn't taken aback by his answer. Somehow, the
fact that he would be honest and not try to spare her feelings
made it easier to consider asking his opinion. But still, what
would it change? She couldn't afford the lessons necessary to
advance her skills, not to mention paints and canvases.

"One day," she told him, impulsively putting a hand on his
shoulder. "By the way, I'd like to buy a sketchbook."

~

"You can't be serious!" Corrine sat at her dressing table,
blending rouge into her cheekbones with her fingertips. "Why
would a man like Adam Burke even look Rachel's way?"

Gerald took a chair from the corner and set it next to her.
"I'm not saying that he would. It's just a possibility that we
need to look out for now that she's more . . . mature."

"But she's just a maid. She scrubs *floors* for a living!"

"I know. And that's why I'm not overly concerned." He
picked up a hairbrush and began pulling it through her hair.
"But we still don't know a whole lot about this Burke's character. Even though he's a praying saint, some men are attracted
to lower-class women. Didn't you say he was chummy with
his own maids?"

Corrine leaned her head back and closed her eyes. "But not
in that sort of way. Besides, he could hardly keep his eyes off
me this past Sunday."

"And who can blame him?" Gerald said with a low chuckle.
"I'm sure you're right. It's just that when I found the man's
portrait Tuesday, I started wondering if there was something
we needed to watch out for."

"If Rachel drew his picture, it's because she draws everyone she sees. She knows better than to get infatuated with someone I'm involved with." Opening her eyes again, she looked at him in the mirror. "By the way, what were you doing in her room?"

The brush stopped in midair. "I wasn't in her room, if you must know. She left her sketches in the parlor. By the way, I believe this house is leased under my name. Isn't it?"

"Well, yes, but I just don't want . . ."

"The girl needs to be watched so we'll know she's not plotting anything against us. I can't help it if you're uncomfortable with that."

Corrine sighed, studying in her reflection the fine lines around her eyes that seemed to have appeared overnight. "I'm just worried that you're taking too great an interest in her lately."

Smiling, Gerald resumed brushing her hair. "If that's all you're worried about, you needn't. I'm only interested in one woman, and she's right here in front of me."

She closed her eyes again, trying to convince herself that she had only imagined the feelings of coldness coming from him lately. Then she remembered the way he had been looking at Rachel. She wasn't making it up.

"So, are you still going to bring her with you when you drop in on Mr. Burke today?" Gerald asked after a while in a casual voice.

Turning to take the brush from his hand, Corrine nodded. "I think that's best." *For more reasons than one,* she added silently.

~

Two hours later, Dora was showing Corrine and Rachel through Adam Burke's front door. She led them to chairs in the front parlor, then told them she would see if Mr. Burke was able to receive guests.

Presently he stepped into the room, wearing a black waistcoat over a white shirt and gray worsted trousers. "Why, Mrs. Hammond," he said cordially.

"Please call me Corrine," she implored, holding out a hand. "And I do hope you'll forgive my rudeness—popping over unannounced like this."

Adam walked over to take her extended hand, then nodded at Rachel before taking a seat in a chair facing Corrine. "There is nothing to forgive. It's not every day that I get a visit from two lovely women."

Corrine gave him her best imitation of a modest smile, then said, "You see, we were just out shopping, and we came across a lovely gingham apron." With a gloved hand she indicated the package that Rachel held in her lap. "Well, Rachel here said right away, 'That would look so nice on Mr. Burke's cook!' Bernice is her name, right?"

"Bernice. And so you bought it," observed Adam, folding his arms across his chest.

"Didn't I mention before how impulsive I am?" she said with a tittering laugh. Nervously she brushed the wrinkles from her blue sateen skirt. "Anyway, we were about to start for home when Rachel said, 'I don't think I can wait until Sunday to see Bernice's face when we give this to her!'"

Taking a moment to send an affectionate look in her maid's direction, she continued, "We didn't have anything else pressing, so we talked it over and decided to drop in. Are you sure you're not terribly angry?"

Talked it over? Rachel thought bitterly. *When did we do that?* Suddenly aware that Mr. Burke was looking her way, she made sure her expression was sufficiently bland to please Corrine.

"Of course I'm not angry," Adam was saying. "And it was so kind of you to think of Bernice. I'll send for her right away."

"Oh, don't do that," said Corrine. "I'm sure she's busy. Besides, since it was Rachel's idea, I thought it would be nice if she took it to her."

Adam shrugged his shoulders. "Certainly, if that's what she would like to do." To Rachel he asked, "Can you find your way to the kitchen? I can have someone lead you there."

"I can find it, sir." With the package in her arms she got to her feet, relieved to be leaving the room.

~

When Rachel was gone, Adam turned back to Corrine. "How was your visit to the children's home?"

"Oh, wonderful!" she exclaimed, smiling broadly. "It was such a joy to bring some happiness to those little lives. I can't thank you enough for suggesting it!"

"Well, it was good of you to go with Mrs. Morgan. Mr. Garland has convinced a few other women to give the children some time, but Penelope's the most faithful. I really admire her for that."

"And so do I," Corrine agreed. "There just aren't enough faithful people in the world today, and they stand out like jewels when you find them."

"Does that mean you'll be going with her every week?"

Covering her discomfort with a smile, she replied, "Of course. Those children need us. And I must confess I was charmed by them—they're so beautiful!"

"Yes, I imagine they are."

"You mean you've never seen the children you're helping support?"

"No, I haven't," he answered just a bit tersely.

"Oh dear, have I offended you?" Corrine panicked, mentally kicking herself for speaking without thinking. She rushed to explain. "I only meant . . ."

"No offense taken, Mrs. Hammond." He smiled a little, as if to put her at ease. "I believe I mentioned in one of my letters that I seldom make calls."

"Yes, you did, come to think of it." Corrine realized then that her faux pas could turn into a golden opportunity. Softening her voice, she said, "Mr. Burke . . . do you mind if I call you Adam?"

"Of course not."

"Then I must insist that you call me Corrine." She sat up straight and fixed her huge gray eyes on his face. "Adam, is the reason you don't make calls because of your scars?"

"I just don't like being stared at." His tone softened. "And I wouldn't want to frighten the children at the orphanage."

Careful to put as much warmth as possible in her tone, she said, "You're still an attractive man, Adam. Don't you realize that?"

~

Stunned by Corrine's blatant flattery, Adam could only look away. Her words, however insincere, caused a sense of longing to grip his heart. *Why can't it be true?* he wondered darkly. *There's more to me than just my face. Isn't there a woman somewhere who would be willing to look beyond it and see that I still have some worth?*

Here seated opposite him was such a woman, one who professed a willingness to ignore his disfigurement—but the only worth she cared about was in pounds sterling.

Corrine obviously mistook his silence for embarrassment, for she began speaking again. "Forgive my boldness, but if there's one thing I've learned in life, it's to speak the truth when it needs to be pointed out. When I first met you this past Sunday, the first thing that came to my attention was how nice your eyes are. Brown eyes are so attractive on a man."

"Well, thank you," he said. Suddenly tired, he wished this woman's maid would come back so she'd leave.

She apparently wasn't finished, however. "I've got something to confess, Mr. Burke," she said, lowering her eyes. "Adam. I'm not being quite honest with you."

An eyebrow lifted. Was she about to turn around and admit that the words she'd just spoken had been pure flattery? Did she have a conscience after all? If she did, it certainly worked fast! He propped an ankle up over his knee and watched her face. "You weren't?"

"No," she murmured, looking deeply ashamed. After a deliberate pause she said, "You see, Rachel and I *could* have waited until Sunday to bring the apron to Bernice."

So this confession's to be as phony as her compliments, he thought as he waited for her to continue.

"We've just been so lonely ever since we moved to London," she was saying. "And you and your servants are the only people we know . . . besides the Morgans now, of course."

Even though he felt she was lying again, he would not let himself be anything but a gentleman. "Aren't there women's societies you could join?"

Corrine sighed deeply. "Please don't think me a snob, but I find most women . . . well, shallow. All they care about is fussing over themselves and gossiping about each other."

Adam struggled to keep from smiling. "Do they?"

She nodded. "You have no idea!"

"And what made you turn out different?"

"I take that as a compliment," she said with a little smile. "You see, I grew up an only child, and my father treated me as his equal." She was looking over Adam's shoulder now, with a dreamy cast to her face. "At the dinner table, when the ladies would retire to the drawing room so that the men could light cigars and speak of hunting and window taxes and India and such, I was allowed to stay. I grew up appreciating the way men look at the world."

"And so you prefer the company of men."

Corrine put a hand up to her cheek and looked directly into his eyes. "That sounds so . . . so wanton. But actually, I do. So when Rachel and I couldn't bear the loneliness this morning, I immediately thought of you. I did so enjoy your company last Sunday."

~

"I should leave now," Rachel was saying to Bernice and Lucy at the kitchen table, over the rattle of cups and saucers.

"Oh, do you have to?" cried Lucy. "Why, you haven't even finished your tea."

Rachel had to laugh. "That's because you poured another cup before I was done with the first one."

"We would enjoy havin' you stay a little longer," Bernice told her, her sweet face marked with concern, "and I do so appreciate the pretty apron. But we don't want you gettin' into any trouble with your missus now."

Nodding, Rachel remembered Corrine's earlier instructions to take as long as possible in the kitchen. *My missus would prefer I stay in here all day,* she thought. She regarded the friendly faces of the cook and her daughter. *And I'd like that, too . . . very much. But I just can't do that to Mr. Burke.*

"Well, maybe five more minutes," she said as Lucy clapped her hands with delight. "But please don't pour me any more tea!"

~

Gerald was waiting for Corrine's report when she returned. "And how was your visit with Adam Burke?"

"A kiss first," Corrine replied, opening her arms.

Gerald took her in an embrace and pressed his lips to hers. Then he walked with her into the sitting room and said, "I hope that wasn't your *first* kiss of the afternoon."

"Don't be so impatient—he's not as forward as most men. Besides, I've only been alone with him once so far."

"And I get the feeling the idea doesn't appeal to you, does it?"

Corrine shuddered. "Kissing Adam Burke? It doesn't, but I always manage to do my part."

Putting his arm around her waist, Gerald led her over to the settee and took a place next to her. "You do, indeed. By the way, where is Rachel?"

"I sent her downstairs to cook supper."

"How did she act around Mr. Burke?"

Corrine shrugged her shoulders. "The same way she acts most of the time. Like a deaf-mute."

"Good," he said. "And did she leave the two of you alone?"

"Just as we planned. It was a stroke of genius, suggesting I get that apron for the cook."

Gerald kissed her again. "I have my moments."

~

"I don't believe anyone can prepare poached turbot like Bernice can," Robert Morgan said as he held his plate out for seconds. He and Penelope were in Adam Burke's dining room for their customary Friday evening meal with their friend. Across from each other, they sat adjacent to Adam at the end of the table.

Adam nodded in agreement. "She says her secret is plenty of lemon juice and just a touch of basil."

"Well, so much for your ability to keep *secrets,*" quipped Penelope. "I'll have to try it next time we have fish."

Pretending to be frightened, Adam winced and looked over his shoulder. "Just don't tell Bernice, and I won't be murdered in my sleep."

Robert let out a laugh. "As if you would! That woman spoils you to death—I'll bet she'd roast a donkey for you if she thought you had a craving for it."

"And when did the good parson start gambling?" inquired Adam with an eyebrow cocked.

"All right, I know when to hold my tongue. Just wanted to let you know, if you ever decide you've had enough of the good life and want to let her go, we'll treat her with the respect she deserves."

"I'll keep that in mind. Now will you pass that platter, or do you intend to have the rest for yourself?"

After supper they went to the library, where Adam and
Penelope settled into leather chairs while Robert browsed
through the books on the shelves. "For a man who never goes
anywhere, your collection of books gets bigger every week,"
he said, thumbing through a volume of *The Mill on the Floss* by
George Eliot.

"Borrow it if you like," said Adam. "I have an arrangement
with Lackington's in Finsbury Square. They send me a crate of
the latest books to inspect every fortnight or so. I just send
back what I'm not interested in buying."

Penelope brought out her crocheted purse. "Oh, Adam, I
have something to show you." She reached over to hand him
a linen handkerchief wrapped around something hard and flat.

Leaning forward to take the object in his hand, he opened
the handkerchief and brought out the silver frame. A slow,
crooked smile spread across his face. "Why, it's Margaret!
When did you have this done?"

Penelope smiled. "We didn't *have* it done—someone
sketched it from memory. Would you care to guess who?"

He studied the portrait again and shook his head. "You'll
have to tell me."

Exchanging amused glances with her husband, who had
now taken the chair on her other side, she said, "Rachel."

"Rachel. Rachel who?"

"Mrs. Hammond's Rachel. She gave this to me before we
left for the children's home. Did you know she was an artist?"

"No, I didn't!" He brought the portrait closer. "She's really
quite good, isn't she?"

"Quite good, indeed!" exclaimed Penelope. "I must tell you I was surprised."

"Did she show you anything else?"

"I asked her to, but she seemed bashful about it. When I finally convinced her that I truly wanted to look at her sketches, she eagerly raced to get them. Regrettably, Mrs. Hammond was ready to leave before I was able to see many."

"Ah, the lovely Mrs. Hammond," Robert said. He winked at Adam. "I believe she's set her cap for you, my friend."

Adam took one last look at the portrait, then handed it back to Penelope. "I believe you're right."

The minister looked surprised. "Well, it's good to hear you acknowledge that. There was a time when you thought no woman would even want to look at you again."

Adam's hand went to his scarred cheek. "That was before I realized how attractive money can be."

"What do you mean?" asked Penelope. "She seemed nice to me."

"Everyone seems nice to you," Adam said, giving her an affectionate smile. "Why else would you have married old Robert here?"

Robert merely snorted at that remark. "Why do you think she's after your money?"

"Let's just say I have a strong hunch. Bernice thinks so, too, and I'd consider her about the best judge of character I know. Did I tell you she came over here yesterday?"

"You mean Mrs. Hammond?"

"Yes, with Rachel. Only she sent the girl to the kitchen as soon as propriety would allow—a gift for Bernice was the reason. Then when we were alone, she . . . well, flirted with me. I could tell she didn't mean it, though. She's a good actress, but not *that* good." In a wry tone, he added, "However, I do believe she'd make a perfect Lady Macbeth on stage."

"Perhaps you should suggest it," Robert joked, then sobered up at the sharp look from his wife. "And then, perhaps not."

Penelope shook her head. "I'm surprised, Adam . . . and disappointed. You certainly deserve better than someone like that."

"What are you going to do about her?" asked Robert.

"Nothing."

"Nothing?" Glancing again at her husband, Penelope said, "But if she's after your money . . ."

"Unless she comes here with a mask and a pistol, my money's perfectly safe," Adam told her. "And unless she makes a habit of popping in to see me too often, I'll let things just stay as they are. You don't mind allowing her to go along to the orphanage with you, do you?"

"Not at all. She actually was a great help last time." Penelope made a face. "Even if it was only to get your attention."

"So she's still welcome to our Sunday meetings then?" Robert asked.

Adam gave his friend a nod. "Would you have it any other way?"

"No, I wouldn't. I can't see turning anybody away from hearing the gospel, even if she's come for the wrong reasons."

Wiping the corner of her eye with the back of her hand, Penelope smiled at her husband. "You're such a good man." She then turned to Adam. "You, too."

Robert reached for his wife's hand and smiled back at her. "And not to mention the maid Rachel," he said softly. "She's not likely to be allowed to come if her mistress is turned away."

"Bernice mentioned that, too," said Adam. "Speaking of Rachel, may I see that portrait again?"

~

Groaning to herself, Corrine turned over in bed to lie on her stomach and press her forehead against the pillow, trying to ease the pain that gripped the top of her head. The throbbing was so intense that she had left the table before finishing her supper.

She wished Gerald had come upstairs with her. While he had looked sympathetic when she pushed her plate away and told him she was hurting, he simply ordered Rachel to help her up to her room and fetch her a pot of strong tea. *He didn't miss a bite,* she thought reproachfully. She'd waved away the tea when the girl returned, opting instead for a glass of brandy. Rachel had to steady the glass in her shaking hands and hold it up to her mouth.

The brandy wasn't helping, even though she had taken it a good twenty minutes ago. *Maybe I should have another glass.* Yet she was hurting too badly to even raise her head, let alone reach for the bottle on the bedside table.

It's my own fault—I've got to stop thinking about that child! She wished now, more than ever, that she had never been talked into going to that dreadful orphanage.

~

"Thank you, sir." Downstairs in the kitchen, Rachel reached for the tray of plates and silverware Gerald brought from the dining room. "But I really can clear the table myself."

"And have you climbing up and down those stairs with your arms full? I just wish I could help you more often, but . . ." With a jerk of the head he indicated that Corrine was the reason. Something inside warned Rachel not to turn her back on him. She waited until he had gone upstairs for another trip to the dining room before turning to put the plates in the washbasin. After she washed them and set them in the rack to dry with the glasses, she put the copper roast-beef pan down in the water and began to scrub it, keeping her ears alert to any sounds on the kitchen stairs. They were stone and easy to slip up or down without making noise, so she turned to check them every few seconds with her eyes as well.

She had just glanced at the stairs and then became absorbed in scouring the crust from the pan with a cloth. She was about to turn her head to look again when she felt a presence close behind her.

"You know, your hair is like spun gold," came an oily whisper in her ear. A hand touched her shoulder.

Rachel froze, a wave of nausea churning in her stomach.

Gerald stepped closer and ran his hand down her back. "I wonder if you realize how beautiful you are."

With tears in her eyes, Rachel groped in the dishwater for the carving knife she knew was still there. She grasped the handle in her hand and suddenly wheeled around, sloshing water on both of them. "Don't ever do that again!" she cried as she held the knife pointed at the middle of his linen shirt.

He eased a few steps backward, a half-smile on his face. "Well now, she's got a temper!" Smoothly he added, "Don't you think you're overreacting? I only meant—"

"I know what you meant," she said through her teeth as she

took a step towards him. "You meant to try to have your way with me!"

He took another step back, bumped into the worktable and began edging sideways. "Oh, come on. Can't you take a compliment?"

"Not from the likes of you, I can't! And if you want to send me to the workhouse, go ahead. I'd rather have to watch out for the rats than for you!"

Gerald glanced at the stairs, then put a finger to his lips. "Not so loud!" he ordered.

"Leave this kitchen if you want me to be quiet!" Her teeth had begun to chatter and her hand trembled, but she managed to keep a firm grip on the knife.

It was not firm enough. In an instant he lunged at her. With one arm he circled her body, pinning her arms to the side, and with his other hand he pried open her fingers so that the knife clattered to the floor.

"Don't you dare hold a knife to me again," he snarled. His breath reeked of gin. "If you do, I promise they'll be fishing your body out of the Thames the next day."

She couldn't answer but stood there trembling in his grasp.

His arms tightened around her. "Do you understand me, Rachel?"

"Y-yes."

"Good." He let go of her and stepped back. "Not a word of this to Corrine, or you'll be sorry." Turning in the direction of the stairs, he smiled back at her and added, "She wouldn't believe you anyway."

Her knees began to weaken, and she propped herself against the edge of the table. *I'd be ashamed to tell a soul!*

~

Hours later, up in the attic, Rachel got up from her rumpled bed and went over to the dormer window. She peered outside. The night was cloudless, with stars crusting the sky like sprinkled sugar. Beneath the sky she could see only the dark silhouettes of houses. Not even one window was lit up.

Everyone in London is asleep but me, she thought, suddenly feeling lonelier than ever. Closing her eyes, she pressed her forehead against the glass. *Please help me, God,* she prayed silently, not even sure if he was listening. *Surely there's somewhere safe I can go.*

7

I'M sorry, but we have no positions available," said the
woman standing at the door of the third domestic agency
Rachel visited that Saturday morning.

"Already?" Rachel's shoulders fell. "But I just bought this
newspaper two hours ago. Your advertisement says . . . "

The woman in charge, quite possibly a former servant herself, gave a weary sigh and looked past her to another young
woman coming up the path. "And you're the fifteenth person
who's applied," she said kindly. "Number sixteen's coming up
behind you."

"Isn't there *some* work I can do?" she pressed. "I don't need
a big salary."

"I'm truly sorry."

"Yes, ma'am. Thank you for your time."

"Take a little advice, dear," said the woman at the door
with a sad smile. "You're a pretty one and polite, too; but you
won't get a position without a letter of reference. Why don't
you get your former employers to write one for you?"

"Yes, I'll have to do that," said Rachel, backing up the
steps. Murmuring her thanks again, she turned and nodded at
number sixteen as she passed. She was young, too, and had an

anxious expression on her face . . . the same look Rachel knew had been on her own face all morning.

~

When she got back home, Corrine had gotten up and was waiting at the kitchen worktable.

"Where have you been?" she demanded as soon as Rachel walked in the back door. "I had to make my own hot chocolate, and there aren't any pastries left."

The fear that had been a part of her life as long as she could remember seized Rachel, but she fought against it. After the episode with Gerald last night, she was determined to get out of this household as soon as possible, and if it took incurring her employers' wrath, then so be it.

"I'm sorry, ma'am, about the chocolate," she said. "And there were three pastries in the jar last night."

Corrine glanced at the kitchen stairs. "Well, I get hungry when my head aches," she said defensively. Frowning, she stepped closer. "Where were you?"

Don't back down! Rachel told herself. "I had some errands to take care of." She squared her shoulders and met Corrine's gaze without flinching. "Now, would you like me to go to the bakery for you?"

"First I want to know where you've been." She pointed to the newspaper tucked under the maid's arm. "You've been looking for another job, haven't you!"

"I had some errands to take care of," Rachel repeated softly, amazed at her own boldness. Turning her back to the angry woman, she reached up for her market basket. "What kind of pastries would you like, ma'am?"

~

Corrine folded her arms and studied the girl's back. It was obvious that Rachel no longer believed her threat to tell any new employers that she was a thief, else why would she be looking for another position?

I ought to kick her out right now, she told herself. *Let her try to get a job without references!* But then what? What if she decided to go to the police? Or what if she actually did find a position somewhere else?

Then Corrine would have the problem of explaining to Adam Burke why Rachel was no longer with her at the Sunday meetings. She could always make up some reason, but what if Rachel kept up her friendship with that cook and her daughter and told them the truth? In fact, what would keep the girl from telling them *everything?*

Adam was far too softhearted about his servants. He would believe them. Then she would have no chance at all with him.

There wasn't time to find another prey. Their money situation was only two or three months away from desperate—that is, if Gerald had only moderate losses at the card tables. She couldn't understand why Gerald failed to see that he was throwing their money away with his gambling. For every quid he pocketed, he lost five the next night.

Just this past Sunday, when she was dressing to go to Adam Burke's, she had noticed Gerald staring at the strand of pearls around her neck with a calculating expression. When she got back and he was not in her room, she hid them in the toe of a seldom-worn pair of slippers in the far recesses of her wardrobe. They were the prettiest thing she had ever owned and her most valuable possession. She was determined they wouldn't be used for gambling debts . . . or any other of Gerald's debts, for that matter.

There was another reason she wanted to hang onto the pearls, one she didn't like to think about. If Gerald ever left her, he would probably take every penny they owned. She had to have some assurance of an income, at least for a while, and selling the pearls would give her that.

Corrine studied the maid in front of her, standing there with her market basket on her arm. *Rachel's changing,* she thought, *and she'll leave if we don't treat her differently.* Part of her would welcome such an occurrence. Rachel was turning into a beautiful young woman, and Gerald had obviously noticed. But until they moved on to another town, they couldn't risk her turning on them.

"I'd like some pastries," she finally said. "But I can wait if you're too tired."

Rachel blinked. "Ma'am?"

"You look tired." Corrine wasn't used to saying words of consideration, and she had to stop for a second and clear her throat. "Perhaps you should sit and rest a while first."

Dumbfounded for a few seconds, Rachel said, "I'm . . . I'm not tired. And I can get some eggs while I'm out, too."

"That would be nice." Corrine started for the stairs, then turned back to face her. "And, Rachel . . ."

"Yes, ma'am?"

"Why don't you leave your newspaper here?"

~

Corrine poured Gerald a cup of tea at the dining-room table. It was early afternoon, and he had just gotten out of bed. He opened the newspaper. "Where did Rachel disappear to?"

124

"Market," Corrine answered, turning her back to him so that she could add a second spoonful of sugar to her own cup of tea.

"Didn't she go yesterday?"

"She forgot the eggs then."

Gerald shrugged his shoulders and turned his attention back to the newspaper. He looked up again, however, when Corrine pulled out the chair across from him.

"I won twelve pounds last night," he announced.

"Really? How much did you lose the night before?"

His face darkened. "That doesn't matter. I'm on a winning streak now—I can tell."

She ignored this rationalization. She had heard it all before. "I want to talk with you about something."

"Yes?"

"It's Rachel. Have you noticed anything different about her?"

"Different?" Gerald searched Corrine's eyes suspiciously. "How so?"

"She went looking for another position this morning."

"Another position!" he snorted. "I don't even have to ask if she found one."

"She didn't, but—"

"And she won't," Gerald interrupted. "Not if *I* have anything to do with it."

Corrine was tempted to ask why he felt so strongly about keeping Rachel. She was pretty sure that his reasons were not the same as hers. But she was in no mood for an argument, so she got up to refill their cups, then sat down again.

"We can't keep her with us forever," she said. "One day she's going to find another place, with or without references."

Turning the newspaper to another page, Gerald ignored her for the time it took to read another article, then without looking up, muttered, "Hundreds of unemployed servants looking for jobs these days. It's good that she's finding out just how hard it is to find one."

"There's something different about her," Corrine persisted. "It's almost as if she's grown up overnight. I'm telling you, she's not as frightened of us as she used to be."

"And how is her newfound courage going to change the domestic employment situation in London?" asked Gerald sarcastically.

She shook her head. "I don't know. She seems determined enough to find a way."

~

Gerald thought back to their confrontation in the kitchen and the expression on Rachel's face when she held the knife at him. She would have used it on him if he hadn't backed off. Perhaps Corrine was right. "What do you suggest?" he asked.

"I think we should start treating her better—a whole lot better. That means giving her a bigger salary, too."

"But we can't afford—"

"Her salary's a pittance. We spend more on lamp oil than we do on her. What we can't afford is to lose her right now."

He didn't have to be convinced of that. "Then we'll just have to do it."

"Also, we need to let her know right away that we've had a change of heart about the way we've treated her. So she'll stop looking for another position."

"Do you mean something like . . . a *religious* conversion, my dear?"

Corrine shook her head. "She'd never believe that. And are you prepared to convince her by giving up the cards and gin—and letting Adam Burke off the hook? Not to mention . . ."

"I see your point." Tugging at the ends of his mustache, he leaned back in his chair and weighed their options.

"We could just come out and admit that this job-hunting incident made us realize how much we don't want to lose her."

"Good idea." Gerald nodded slowly. "But I believe *I* should be the one to speak with her."

"Alone?" Corrine's eyes filled with suspicion. "Why?"

"I know what you're thinking." He reached across the table to take her hand. "And you're wrong. I just feel that I'm the one who's treated her the worst, so the apology should come from me."

"But why not both—"

"Because we don't want to make too much of this. If Rachel thinks we've become desperate to keep her, then she'll start demanding more than we're prepared to give her. I won't have a tyrant for a servant."

Corrine frowned. "I just can't see her acting that way."

Gerald couldn't see it either, but he didn't want Corrine around when he apologized to the girl. The incident in the kitchen last night was minor in his own mind, but he was sure it was the reason she went out job hunting this morning. And he didn't want her blurting out anything that Corrine shouldn't hear.

"I grew up in a house with servants," he reminded her. "Trust me, you don't ever want them to feel they're not expendable."

"If you insist," said Corrine.

Gerald watched her as she got up to refill their teacups and smiled at her back. *She thinks I don't know she's slipping more sugar into hers,* he thought. She was becoming so predictable. For all her beauty and refined ways, Corrine Hammond was still just a country bumpkin.

~

Rachel was cleaning up after Saturday's supper when Gerald came down the kitchen stairs.

"Now, don't start getting edgy," he told her as she stood poised to sprint. "I'm going out in a few minutes, but I wanted to have a word with you."

She glanced at the carving knife she had kept next to the sink all day, and she watched in silence as he pulled out a chair at the worktable. He was dressed in a dark broadcloth suit and had a diamond stickpin in his silk cravat, his usual attire when frequenting the gaming rooms.

"Would you have a seat for a minute?" he asked, motioning to the chair across the table from him. When she didn't move, he said, "I promise to be a gentleman."

Wiping her hands on her apron, Rachel glanced at the knife again, then walked over to the chair and sat down.

"Do you know why I'm here?" he asked.

She shook her head, refusing to look at his face.

"I want to apologize for last night. I don't know if you realized it, but I had taken in quite a bit of gin during the evening, and I wasn't myself. Still, there's no excuse for what I did."

Rachel couldn't believe what she was hearing. *First Corrine, and now him!* When she had recovered from her surprise, she steeled herself and said quietly, "It wasn't just last night."

Gerald's eyebrows lifted. "Excuse me?"

"You've been . . . making me uncomfortable for a while," she told him, still staring at her hands folded on the table.

He started to protest, then thought better of it. "Yes, you're right." He lifted his hands helplessly. "I really can't say anything in my own defense either. You've turned into such a beauty that I began to forget my manners."

Rachel frowned and looked up at him. "You're doing it again."

Appearing to be genuinely surprised, he put a hand up to his chest. "Am I? You mean the compliment?"

She nodded. "I don't like your saying things like that."

"Then I'll quit." Gerald put a finger up to his lips. "Never again, and that's a promise."

Rachel couldn't believe it. He had certainly never apologized to her before, for anything. Was it because she went looking for another job? Whatever his reasons, she realized she might never get an opportunity again to tell him what was on her mind. She sat up straight in her chair. He was going to hear all of it, even if she ended up sleeping at the workhouse that night!

"It's not just the things you say," she went on. "I don't like you . . . looking at me the way you do."

His expression turned pained. "I've really been a cad, haven't I?"

"Yes, sir." Her voice was a whisper now, but she still made herself look straight into his eyes.

"Then I must make amends," he said, brushing a bit of lint from his sleeve. "If I promise to leave you alone, will you stop all that nonsen— I mean, will you stop looking for another job?"

Suddenly it dawned upon her why he was doing this. It

wasn't just to keep her from finding another position. He was afraid she would tell Corrine!

"By the way," Gerald continued as if reading her mind, "I confessed everything to Corrine this morning while you were out getting eggs."

Rachel's expression turned wary. "You did?"

"I did." He shrugged his shoulders. "Go ahead and ask her if you don't believe me."

"What did she—"

"What did she say? After she shouted at me—which she had every right to do—we both realized that we've been treating you rather badly. Me, especially. That's when we decided to raise your salary. Double it, actually."

His thin lips stretched into a magnanimous smile as if he had just bestowed a great favor on her. Rachel had lived with the couple for too long to accept his words without some skepticism, but she couldn't figure out the sudden change of heart.

"Don't you have anything to say?" Gerald finally asked.

"Say?"

"Well, I would think you'd be happy to hear all of this."

She took in a deep breath. "I can never be happy here."

"Why?"

"Because of what you do—you and the Missus."

His expression hardened for a second, then he leaned forward and gave a labored sigh. "You mean, how we make money."

"You steal it."

"Not so," he insisted, shaking his head. "If people want to give Corrine money, then she's not foolish enough to turn it down."

"But she pretends to care for them."

"And you think she's the only woman who's ever chased a rich man? My dear child, people do that all the time."

She still couldn't believe he was allowing her to talk to him like this. Years of self-loathing over her part in their deeds brought a bitter taste to her mouth. "Most of the people she got money from were married. And look at Squire Nowells."

"That was unfortunate about Nowells," Gerald replied, shaking his head. "But Corrine didn't hold the gun to his head. And if a married man is unfaithful to his wife, I think he deserves to lose a little money."

"Deserves to have it stolen?"

The color began to rise in his cheek. "These haven't been innocents, Rachel. And they've been rich enough to absorb any loss of the funds they've given—I repeat, *given*—to Corrine."

"What about Mr. Burke?" asked Rachel.

Gerald studied his fingernails. "What about him?"

"He's not being unfaithful to anybody."

"I wouldn't worry about the good and kind Mr. Burke. The man obviously gets happiness from sharing his money, and Corrine is just going to make him a little happier."

"By tricking him."

"By being *kind* to him," Gerald insisted. "You're too young to understand such things, Rachel, but men enjoy having a beautiful woman pay attention to them. Adam Burke probably can't believe his luck right now."

"But she'll leave him one day . . . after she gets his money."

He held up a hand. "After he *gives* her *some* of his money."

"And how will that make him feel?" Rachel persisted. "He'll know he was being used."

"Not at all. Corrine will simply tell him that her husband

was found alive, rescued from some remote island, and that she has to go back home." Smiling, he added, "And Mr. Burke will be left with the realization that he's not unattractive to women. That should be worth a little expense along the way."

Suddenly Gerald took his watch from the fob pocket at the front of his vest and looked at it. "I'm late for an appointment," he said, picking up his silk hat from the table. He pushed out his chair and stood. "By the way, I forgot to mention that you're to get Sunday afternoons off, too, starting tomorrow. Corrine would still like you to go to those church meetings though, but we assume you won't mind that."

Rachel knew he was expecting her to thank him, but she couldn't bring herself to say the words.

"Well," he said, setting his hat on his head, "good evening." With that, he turned and headed for the steps.

She sat there for a moment after he left the kitchen, wondering at the things he had just told her. Did the men Corrine pretended to love really deserve what happened to them? Even if they did, did that make what she was doing right? Gerald had made her deceptions sound almost noble.

It wasn't right. And it wasn't right for her to be a part of it. Getting up from the table, Rachel gathered her skirts and sprinted up the kitchen steps.

~

Gerald turned when he heard footsteps behind him. He was in the back parlor, just about to leave the house. "What is it, Rachel?"

"I want to know why you won't give me a reference," she said, her eyes blazing.

Gerald leaned his walking cane against the door and studied

the face of the girl before him. *I could get lost in those green eyes,* he thought. Deep set and innocent, they almost looked out of place over lips that were full and sensuous. He thought of a line from Byron: *She walks in beauty, like the night.* While he was drawn like a magnet to her innocence, the desire to take it away from her dominated his thoughts more and more lately. *Let you go? Never!*

He put both hands in his pockets and frowned. "You're still wanting to leave us, Rachel? After I gave you my word we'd treat you better?"

Biting her lip, Rachel nodded. "You can hire somebody else. You told me yourself that there are plenty of servants looking for jobs."

Stall her, he told himself. If he could get her to stay with them a bit longer, he could always think up some way to talk her out of leaving. "I tell you what," he finally said. "If you'll forget about looking for another job until we get ready to leave London, I'll have Corrine write you up a grand letter of reference."

He turned to go, then had a second thought. "In fact," he added, "how about when we leave here we give you enough money to rent a room somewhere while you look for a job— say for three months?" Gerald arranged a warm smile on his face. "It's the least we can do, after all the years of service you've given us."

~

Perhaps he's right, Rachel rationalized to herself as Gerald waited for an answer. *Maybe Mr. Burke does enjoy the attention Corrine is giving him.* She had never thought about it, but it was possible that men needed to feel handsome, just as women wanted to be told they were beautiful. And if the man had enough money to be giving some away, he could probably well afford to pay for Corrine's bolsters to his ego.

"Do we have an agreement?" Gerald was asking.

Hesitating briefly, she said, "Are you sure you'll let me have a reference letter then?"

Gerald picked up his walking cane and tipped the brim of his hat with its ivory knob. "You have my word, Rachel."

~

Hours later, Gerald pushed his chair away from the card table at the Waterman's Arms Tavern, situated upon the Thames in Limehouse. "I believe I shall call it a night," he told the three other men in the smoke-filled saloon.

A thin man with bushy muttonchop whiskers slammed down his cards and let out an oath. "That's two nights in a row! Why don't you give me a chance to win some of my money back?"

Gerald grinned at him as he picked up the eight one-pound notes from the table. "You've picked my pockets enough in the past, Harold. Let's be gentlemen about this."

"Don't you want to try for more?" growled a heavyset man across from him.

"Tomorrow," said Gerald.

He made his way around the noisy patrons and giggling saloon maids until he came to the front door. When he stepped onto the cobbled stones of Narrow Street, he turned to the left. Gerald walked a block and a half, stopping in front of a narrow, wooden two-story building. The four sash windows at the lower level glowed with a soft amber light, while no light came from the ones at the second story.

Though the windows were dark, Gerald knew that people were up there. He had never been to this particular establishment, but he had frequented others like it. What drew him here tonight was the sight he had caught earlier of one of the girls who worked here. She had been with a patron in the Waterman's Arms for just a few minutes, and Harold, one of his card partners, had told him where she could be found.

It was pure luck that Gerald had won anything tonight, for he hadn't been able to keep his eyes off the girl. When she first walked past his table with a man's arm around her waist, he looked up with a start. Had *Rachel* followed him here? But when the girl turned her head, flipping her long honey-colored curls past her shoulder, he noticed that she had more angular features than the maid and lips that were not quite as full.

But she was young, perhaps even younger than Rachel's nineteen years, and the jaded expression cast in the faces of the older women in her profession had not yet hardened hers.

Gerald glanced back up at the windows, wondering which one was hers and how long he'd have to wait to see her.

For a while, at least, he would have relief from the torment of living under the same roof with a girl who bewitched him with her freshly scrubbed looks, not to mention her chastity. He could pretend, up there in the darkness of the second floor, that things were different, that it was Rachel's soft, young body under his control. *One day it will be,* he vowed to himself as he knocked on the door.

I am the good shepherd." Robert Morgan held open a leather-bound Bible and read from a book he called St. John. "The good shepherd giveth his life for the sheep."

Rachel stopped watching Corrine and Adam and paid attention to the minister's words. She remembered a painting she had seen in the lobby of the children's home, of a bearded man in old-fashioned garments holding a lamb in his arms. "The Good Shepherd" had been inscribed underneath. Was that man supposed to be Jesus?

She had heard about Jesus, of course, even before last Sunday's meeting. He was God's Son, and he died on a cross for people—and even rose from the dead three days later. She never understood why such a thing had been necessary, but she had in mind the kind of people for whom it had been done. Good people, like Queen Victoria and the late Prince Albert, the Morgans, and Bernice and her family. Mr. Burke. But not for someone like herself. Not for someone involved with deceptions so that she could keep her job, someone who had shockingly hateful thoughts toward her employers.

"My sheep hear my voice, and I know them, and they follow me: And I give unto them eternal life; and they shall never perish, neither shall any man pluck them out of my hand."

Rachel found the words beautiful, but they evoked a feeling of sadness deep down inside her. Why couldn't *she* be one of those sheep held safely in God's hand? The everyday misery of life wouldn't matter so much if she had eternal life to look forward to.

At that moment, Robert Morgan lowered his Bible and looked directly at her. "Jesus said that he came to seek and save those who are *lost,*" he said gently. "And that is why he allowed himself to be killed on the cross—as a sacrifice for the sins of everyday people. Those who rely on their own *goodness* to save their souls are, in a sense, telling Jesus that his sacrifice doesn't matter."

Oh, Lord, I'm not good, Rachel found herself thinking. *I wouldn't dare try to count on my goodness to save me. But what else is there? Lord, please help me to understand.*

~

In the dining room, Rachel watched Corrine grow increasingly agitated as Adam Burke's gardener took charge of the dinner conversation.

"You'll never catch me in one o' them underground carriages," Jack Taylor said as he spread butter on a chunk of brown bread. "It ain't natural, for sure."

From the head of the table, Adam Burke pointed his fork in the gardener's direction. "Didn't I hear you say the same thing about trains a few years ago when we were all set to move to London?"

"He did," said Bernice, her voice full of mirth. With a sidelong grin at her husband, she related how he had said it wasn't "natural" to be traveling across the country at thirty miles an hour.

The huge man actually blushed. "Yep, but that were different. And I'm man enough to admit I was wrong about that."

"Well, I'm with you, Mr. Taylor." Penelope Morgan gave up her attempt to coax Margaret to eat something besides grapes. "I'd be afraid the ground would cave in on me." She glanced down at the little girl seated on a copper pot in the chair beside her, happily spitting seeds into her little hand. "And I absolutely forbade Robert to take Margaret with him."

Stunning in a rose-colored taffeta gown, Corrine looked at the minister with affected awe. "You actually went down into that tunnel?"

Robert laughed. "It's not like a rabbit hole, Mrs. Hammond. You should go and see for yourself sometime—the air's just a bit heavy with sulfur, but not unbearably so. And it's lit up quite nicely."

"I've read in the newspaper that more routes are being planned," said Adam. "One day people will be able to go from one end of the city to the other in a matter of minutes."

Rachel noticed the glow in Adam Burke's eyes as he spoke of this latest marvel, the London Underground. *He looks like he's dying to go see it for himself. . . . Doesn't he go anywhere at all?*

She suddenly realized that he had turned his face in her direction and was in fact looking directly at her. Embarrassed at having been caught staring, she dropped her gaze to the place setting before her.

"Forgive me for changing the subject," he said to her. "But Mrs. Morgan showed me the portrait you drew of Margaret. You have an incredible talent for someone so young."

"Thank you, sir," Rachel murmured, still watching her plate and hoping the pleasure on her face wasn't obvious. *An incredible talent,* he said!

"We were wondering if you would mind bringing some of your drawings next week," asked Robert. "My wife tells me that you have others."

With all her heart she would have loved to show them her work. The satisfaction she had received when Mrs. Morgan had praised the portrait of her daughter had left her with a craving for more. She wanted the whole world to look at her sketches and confirm that she had talent, a gift, that brought a spark of light into the drudgery that was her life.

Still, she shook her head. If only she'd had time to work in her sketchbook. "Just bits and pieces," she said to the minister. "Nothing good enough to show everybody."

"She's just being modest," Corrine said quickly. "She's got quite a bit of talent."

Rachel's heart leaped with hope. But Corrine's praise only turned out to be an attempt to steer the conversation to herself. "I've *always* encouraged her to develop that talent. In fact, I'm thinking of having her do my portrait."

Lowering her voice to a solemn, breathy tone, she added, "My late husband often asked me to have one made. He would say, 'Corrine, your face should be immortalized on canvas, so that years from now our great-grandchildren will still be able to enjoy your—your beauty.' I put it off though, never seeming to find the time. Now it's too late." She wiped the corners of her eyes, and a silence lingered among the people in the dining room.

~

Watching Corrine Hammond's face, Adam finally recalled the words he had been searching his memory for during her narrative. It was a line from one of Sir Francis Bacon's essays: *It is the wisdom of crocodiles, that shed tears when they would devour.*

At length Corrine looked up again and put on a brave little smile. "Now, would you just look at what I've done—spoiled a lovely gathering with my sad memories!"

"Not at all, ma'am," came the quiet voice of Marie, one of the housemaids. "That was touching."

After a minute or two Bernice, at Rachel's right, cleared her throat. She had sat dry-eyed through Corrine's story, and she seemed to have been waiting for an appropriate amount of time to pass before bringing the subject back to Rachel's artistic skills. "You know, I'd like to have one o' them portraits made of Lucy."

Jack nodded in agreement while Lucy, seated between her father and mother, put a hand up to her reddening cheeks. "That's a grand idea!" he exclaimed. "How much would you charge to draw her picture?"

"I wouldn't charge anything," she told Lucy's parents. "I don't have colors, though. Does that matter?"

The cook reached over to squeeze her hand. "I saw little Margaret's picture. Anything you draw will be beautiful. And we'll talk more later about payin' you."

"Try if you will, Bernice," Penelope leaned forward and advised. "But she wouldn't take any payment from me."

"I don't charge my friends," Rachel said, giving the minister's wife a quick, shy smile.

Silently watching the interchange before him, Adam was both touched and amused by Rachel's reaction to being the focus of everyone's attention. *The girl's positively glowing from the praise of her talent!* he thought. *Yet she looks like she'd like to crawl under the table any minute.*

Before his injuries, when he was a brash, young officer out to conquer the world for England's sake, he would have been irritated by that kind of timidity. While he had never been one to lord his position and wealth over people of lower social stations, he had often mistaken their meekness for signs of weak character.

Now having experienced rejection by those closest to him, he understood the necessity to keep one's feelings sheltered against any possible hurt. *And she's definitely been hurt sometime in her life . . . perhaps back in the orphanage. Or perhaps Bernice is right about Corrine Hammond mistreating the girl.*

"Why don't you come over one day this week and have Lucy sit for you?" he found himself saying. "I must confess, I've never watched an artist at work—I'd be interested in seeing how you go about it."

Before Rachel could speak, Corrine responded, "That's a wonderful idea. We'll be here tomorrow afternoon."

"Sorry, ma'am," Bernice said, "but we do the baking for the week on Mondays. Takes up the whole day."

"And we have our children's home to visit on Tuesday," added Penelope.

If Corrine was disappointed at the delay, she didn't let it show. "Oh, well," she said brightly. "How about Wednesday?"

Bernice first glanced at Adam and then nodded. "If you don't mind sparing her for a few hours, ma'am. But you don't have to bother about getting out. Jack can fetch her with the market wagon or the carriage."

"Oh, I *adore* watching Rachel sketch," Corrine said with a smile that didn't reach her eyes. "And it'll be a fun outing for me, too." She turned back to Adam. "That is . . . if you don't mind my coming along with her."

Adam looked at her intently. She was lying—he knew it

instinctively. She had never watched the girl work; she had probably never shown any interest at all in Rachel's talent—until now, when it would suit her purposes.

"You don't mind, do you?" she repeated, fluttering her eyelashes at him.

"Of course not," he replied politely.

~

Rachel studied Mr. Burke as he busied himself with cutting the roast beef on his plate. She wondered if she had imagined the disappointment, moments before, that had briefly shadowed his scarred face. Never had she seen *any* man who didn't find Corrine irresistible. Could Adam Burke be the exception?

Come to think of it, she had noticed the same fleeting expression the day she and Corrine dropped over with the apron for Bernice. But why? After all, Gerald had said that any man would be delighted to be the center of a beautiful woman's attention. And surely a man like Mr. Burke, disfigured as he was and lonely as he seemed to be . . . wouldn't he prove Gerald to be right?

Was it just possible that he could see through her act? Maybe some men weren't as blind as she thought. Maybe this Mr. Burke was different from other men—and not just in appearance. She couldn't help but smile at the thought. Gerald Moore and Corrine Hammond might be in for a surprise!

She glanced at the people seated around her. In all the places she'd been with Corrine and Gerald, she had never heard of a household where servants were invited to break bread on Sundays at the table with an employer. *He's a decent man,* she told herself. And it was obvious that he cared deeply about the Jesus that Reverend Morgan spoke about. Why else would he have church services at his house?

A pang of some indefinable longing touched her heart. She found herself glancing covertly at Mr. Burke again. What would it be like to have someone as decent and kind as him care for her? She immediately rejected the thought. She was still just a servant, after all. They might be eating together at the same table, but for all the difference it made, they might as well be on different continents.

~

At the orphanage on Tuesday, Mrs. O'Reilly greeted Rachel, Corrine, and Penelope with a weary smile. "Mrs. Morgan, you and your friends are a balm to me soul."

Penelope and Rachel were already enveloped from the knees to the waists by the hugs of chattering little ones. Corrine stood a bit off to the side, searching the huge room with her eyes.

"Are you looking for the little girl?" asked Mrs. O'Reilly after Penelope and Rachel had led their young charges to the middle of the floor.

Corrine frowned, reluctant to admit it. The child had come to her thoughts several times during the week, in spite of her efforts to forget about the orphanage. It was bad enough that she had to *come* here every Tuesday—she resented having it pop up in her mind in the meantime. Still, she couldn't help wondering if the little girl would recognize her.

She had left her crinoline at home this time, too.

Mrs. O'Reilly took a step over to her and pointed to a little bundle in the furthermost corner of the room. The child lay on her side with her knees drawn up to her chest, watching the other children with a listless expression. "She's not wantin' to eat," said the Irish woman, shaking her head.

"Not anything?"

"She'll drink a little water now and then, but she won't touch her milk or porridge. We've had to force what we could down her, but it ain't enough."

Corrine looked over at the little body again and winced. "Force her?"

The Irish woman shrugged her work-rounded shoulders. "Sounds heartless, but she's got to have nourishment."

The child stirred, lifting her head from the wooden floor. She seemed to scan the room for a few seconds, then closed them again and laid her head back down.

"She's still lookin' for her mother," explained Mrs. O'Reilly. "Perhaps you could sit with her for a while, like you did the last time."

"All right." Ignoring the children who stood between her and the corner, Corrine swept around them, her steps moving faster as she neared the child.

The girl lifted her head again, watching Corrine with disinterested eyes. Instead of calling the child to come to her, this time Corrine simply bent down and took her up in her arms. She expected a struggle, but the child lay limply in her arms as if resigned to whatever should happen to her.

Alarmed, Corrine held the girl against her shoulder and sought out Mrs. O'Reilly, who was putting a baby into one of the cribs. "Why won't this child cry?" she demanded.

The woman tucked a blanket around the sleeping baby and turned to Corrine. "I don't know." She reached out a finger to touch one of the child's blond curls. "But I can tell you they don't last long when they get to this state."

Corrine was horrified. "Don't you care what happens to her?"

Mrs. O'Reilly gave a sigh, and the lines in her face seemed to deepen. "I don't want the child to die, ma'am. But if she does, by the very next mornin' we'll have another, just as pitiful, to take her place. If we grieved every time somethin' like this happened, we couldn't work here."

"It just sounds so cold."

"Cold? Meanin' no disrespect, I'll tell you what's cold—it's when folks have to spend twelve hours a day in the mills or factories just to keep a roof over their heads and a bit of food in their families' bellies. Sometimes there's no place for a little one like this to stay if she ain't got other family to help care for her. Then the mother and papa have to give her up, hopin' their child'll have a better chance here."

Corrine instinctively tightened her arms around the limp form. "I should think she would get hungry enough to want some food after a while."

Mrs. O'Reilly shook her head. "Most times they do, but sometimes the sadness gets in the way of the appetite. Don't forget—she don't understand that her mother might have left her for her own good. She just wants her mama back."

Corrine rested her chin over the top of the little blond head as she carried her over to a rocking chair and sat down. She moved slowly, listening to the squeak of the chair and patting the child's back as she thought about how sad the world could be at times . . . and not just for little children.

Why, I can't even remember the last time I was happy! When she and Gerald had started making money, she'd been insulated from any sorrow for a while. The excitement of high living had given her little time to reflect on the emptiness of her lifestyle. But then the sleepless nights started, and the thoughts that raced so furiously in her head made her worry for her own sanity.

She thought back to Robert Morgan's sermons. Though she had successfully blocked out most of the minister's words, one thing had found its way through. She was a sinner. She glanced down at the baby in her lap, whose fair head rested against her bosom. *The worst kind. The kind who abandons her own child.*

What was her daughter Jenny doing at this very moment? Was she happy? Did she ever wonder about her mother, the mother who had abandoned her?

Corrine shook her head abruptly. To avoid the painful questions, she forced her imagination to lead her elsewhere, to people she had laughed with, dresses she had worn, places she had been taken by wealthy admirers. It worked for a little while, but then the ugly thoughts about herself began to creep back in.

She looked down at the girl. "You're too young to die," she whispered into her little ear. "Why won't you let them feed you?"

Suddenly she had an idea, and the next time she caught Mrs. O'Reilly's eyes she beckoned for her.

"Yes'm?" the Irish woman said, wiping her hands on her apron.

"What is this child's name?" asked Corrine.

"There weren't no note with her or anything, so we've taken to callin' her Anna."

"Anna." Corrine ran her fingers through the girl's fine hair. "I was wondering if you've tried giving her a bottle."

"She's more than old enough to drink from a cup, ma'am."

"I have a feeling I could get her to take some milk. Don't you have bottles downstairs for the younger babies?"

"We do."

Corrine gave the older woman a smile. "Do you think you could get one for me . . . with some warm milk?"

Mrs. O'Reilly left the room, shaking her head and muttering to herself, but several minutes later she returned with a glass bottle of milk. Wordlessly she handed it over and went back to work.

Corrine turned the child's face up to look at her. "Now, you're going to drink some of this, Anna . . . for me." Making soothing little sounds, she coaxed the rubber nipple between the girl's teeth.

The child stared up at her with unblinking eyes, her lips not moving. Corrine began to rock the chair gently again and, for the first time in her life, found herself breathing a prayer. *Please make her drink the milk—I don't want her to die.*

After several minutes Anna seemed to come out of her lethargy long enough to take a tentative pull on the nipple in her mouth.

Corrine took in a quick breath. "That's a good girl. Take the milk," she urged.

The child's first hesitant drinks turned into thirsty gulps, and she drained the bottle in a matter of minutes. Corrine set the empty bottle down on the floor beside her, then hugged Anna to herself and marveled at the feeling of great warmth that had come over her.

Penelope had observed the child's plight and was making her way over. "You persuaded her to drink some milk?"

Corrine nodded. "She took the whole bottle. I believe I could get her to eat something else as well."

"I'll go down to the kitchen and ask for a bit of bread or fruit," offered the minister's wife. She smiled at Corrine. "What a blessing you've been to this child."

"I think *she's* the blessing," Corrine found herself answering.

"What's her name?"

"Jen—," Corrine started to reply, then realized her mistake. "Anna," she sighed. "Her name is Anna."

~

Corrine was reclining on the settee, halfway through a penny dreadful when Gerald came downstairs.

"Back so soon?" he said as he rubbed his hands down the front of his white linen shirt.

She closed the book and swung her feet to the floor, then turned her cheek up to accept his kiss. "I've been here for three hours. When did you get home?"

"Oh, sometime this morning," he said, taking a place beside her. "The game went longer than I planned, but don't worry, nobody saw me come in the house."

"You played cards *all night?*"

Gerald only smiled. "Where's Rachel? I'm dying for some tea."

"She should be back any second. I sent her to Adam Burke's with a message telling him to expect us at two in the afternoon tomorrow."

"Why? You already settled that Sunday, and you know he'll be home."

She smiled. "We never discussed an exact time, so I want to be sure he'll be prepared for us. I'd hate to get there and find

that he's shut up in a room with that minister or taking a nap
. . . or whatever it is the man finds to do."

"Smart thinking," Gerald said with an appreciative nod.
"It's a good thing that Rachel has given you an excuse to
spend an afternoon at Burke's house again. I believe the fellow
is as good as in the net." He then glanced at the book in her
lap. "How can you read such rubbish?"

"Rubbish? This is a good story—I can barely stand to put it
down."

Crossing his legs, he settled back and gave her a condescending smile. "Let me guess. The heroine is a poor baroness
whose fortune was stolen by an evil cousin."

"It was her uncle," she said defensively, yet she brushed the
book from her lap to the cushion beside her. Gerald could be
an unbearable snob sometimes. *Just because he was highborn, he
thinks he's better than me.*

Gerald yawned, covering his mouth with a neatly mani-
cured hand. "How was your mission of mercy today?"

"It was a good visit," Corrine found herself saying. She told
Gerald how she had managed to coax the child Anna into taking some milk and even a bit of bread.

"You can't imagine how . . . useful it made me feel. I
believe the child would have let herself starve to death if I
hadn't gotten her to drink from the bottle."

"I'm not surprised," said Gerald.

Then again, he can be terribly sweet at times, she thought. "You
aren't?"

He leered back at her. "You've had *men* eating out of your
hand for years now . . . why shouldn't children as well?"

Gerald had looked at her that way countless times before,
but today there was something about it that made her feel

dirty and cheap. As she did at the children's home, Corrine had to force herself again to put such thoughts out of her mind.

"Why do you do that?" Gerald suddenly asked.

"Do what?"

He frowned. "Jerk your head like that. I've seen you do it several times lately."

Corrine frowned. How could she explain to Gerald, who seemed to have no regrets for anything he ever did, the need to quiet the voices in her head, accusations that sometimes attacked her so violently she had to shake her head in an attempt to get rid of them? "I didn't realize I was doing it," she offered as a feeble explanation.

Taking up her hand, Gerald put her fingers to his lips. "We'll have to work on that before it becomes a habit. You don't want Mr. Burke thinking you've got a tic, do you?"

"Don't worry," she said, lifting her chin. "Adam Burke won't have any reason to criticize me."

Gerald kissed her hand again, but the eyes he turned to her were questioning. "Are you saying I'm too critical?"

"I am."

"Then I apologize, my love," he conceded. "I just want what's best for you."

She sighed. "Then you shouldn't point out every flaw that I have."

"Is that what I've been doing?"

"It would seem so." Corrine squeezed the hand that still held hers. "I need your encouragement, Gerald. Now more than ever."

"Why more now?"

Closing her eyes for a second, she admitted, "Because I've been feeling so . . . ugly lately."

His reply was to laugh, which irritated her. "Why is that so funny?" she asked.

He rolled his eyes. "Because you know very well that you're beautiful!"

"I'm not talking about my face. Inside. I feel ugly *inside* sometimes. Can you understand that?"

~

Gerald stifled another yawn and began to wonder when Rachel would get back. He hadn't had anything to eat since he woke up, and while he wasn't terribly hungry, he wished for a cup of hot tea. Corrine seemed determined to prattle on and on about whatever had brought about her sudden blue mood, and he couldn't change the subject without appearing disinterested. *I'll let her get whatever's bothering her out in the air now, then perhaps she'll shut up for a while.*

"I think I understand," he replied, letting go of her hand so that he could put an arm around her shoulders. "Having to become involved with religion the past two Sundays has affected you. What did that preacher say that's got you so melancholy?"

"Nothing, I suppose." Corrine shrugged. "But there are times I can't help but wonder about the people we've . . . hurt. Like Malcolm's widow."

"Mrs. Nowells? She's most likely happy that the old bore's not around anymore, don't you think?"

"Perhaps she loved him."

"And perhaps not. Now, what can we do to get you into better spirits?" He rubbed his mustache. "What if I took you to the theatre? Here we are living in London, and we haven't even been yet."

"I don't think so."

"You could wear a veil, just in case. . . ."

"I'm not in the mood," Corrine said listlessly.

Exasperated, Gerald fought the urge to leave the room. She would only get sullen and not speak to him afterwards if he did. He sometimes felt trapped. Although he was becoming increasingly bored with Corrine, he knew that keeping her happy allowed him the lifestyle he preferred without having to work. The idea of actual labor was much more abhorrent than the problem of boredom. One day he would put away the gin and cards and write poetry again, he told himself often. He would show his family—the world—of what greatness he was capable.

But until then, he was dependent upon the woman beside him. He tried another tactic to cheer her up. "Tell me again about this child you got so attached to."

Her expression immediately took on a happier cast. Seconds later, though, Gerald regretted his choice of subject.

~

"You want to do *what?*" Gerald stared at Corrine as if she had lost her mind.

"I'd just like to go over there and see about little Anna every day for a while . . . just until she starts eating regularly."

"*Every* day?"

"Only until she gets stronger. You don't object, do you?"

"I certainly do. I know you were pressured into going there once a week with that woman—and it's likely working in our favor. But this is overdoing it, don't you think?"

"I don't see how."

Taking his arm from around her shoulders, he turned to fix upon her an incredulous stare. "Have you forgotten *why* we came to London?"

Corrine shook her head. "Of course I haven't forgotten. But I have enough extra time. How can an hour or so at the orphanage interfere with that?"

"The idea is to get *all* the time you have committed to Adam Burke," he said through clenched teeth. "Not to go around wet-nursing a little bas—"

"Gerald!" Corrine couldn't believe he was being so hateful about this.

"Next thing you know they'll be giving you sad tales about other brats there. I might as well buy you an apron and cap, and you can move over there and be everyone's nurse." Gerald glared at her as he crossed his arms. "How could you think of doing such a ridiculous thing!"

"You don't understand. The child would have *starved* if I hadn't gotten her to take milk from that bottle." She put a hand on his sleeve. "Can you imagine how that made me feel?"

Gerald sighed and shook his head. "It's really quite ironic, don't you think?"

"Ironic?"

"I mean, what would the good people at that orphanage say if they knew?"

Eyebrows raised, Corrine regarded him with an icy stare. "If they knew what?" she said evenly.

His thin lips stretched into a smile. "If they knew what kind of mother you really are. How you left your own child—*Jenny* was her name, wasn't it?"

She moved her hand from his arm. "Why are you—"

"I wonder how many times your little daughter cried for you? And perhaps she refused to eat, just like your new little friend." He put a hand up to his mouth, feigning shock. "You don't think she starved to death, do you?"

"Gerald, how could you!" Tears sprang to Corrine's eyes. "I'm not going to sit here and—"

Quick as a heartbeat, Gerald reached out and clasped her chin with his hand. Roughly jerking her face around to just inches from his, he hissed, "I just don't want you to forget what kind of person you are. And what your purpose is."

"I haven't forgotten." She attempted to pry his hand from her chin, but he was stronger. With his other hand he grabbed her small hands and pulled them down to her lap.

"Let me go!" she cried, trying in vain to free herself. "Or I'll pack my things and leave!"

He merely held tighter, watching her struggles through half-closed lids. Slowly he moved his thumb around to her bottom lip and pressed it against her teeth. "And go where?" he growled.

"I don't know!" Every time Corrine tried to pull her hands away, he tightened his thumb against her lip. "Just stop hurting me!"

Gerald looked surprised and began bearing down harder with his thumb. "This *hurts,* you say?"

With tears coursing down her cheeks, she tried to nod but couldn't even move her head. Why was he being so hateful? She knew he could be cruel, but he had never been physically brutal to such a degree. And he professed to love her, yet there was an unmistakable satisfaction in his pale eyes.

Though her vision was blurred by tears, Corrine wondered

if she was seeing him clearly for the first time. "Please," she whimpered. *"Please* stop."

~

After the driver helped her into the tilbury, Rachel looked back to the front corner of Adam Burke's house. Mr. Burke was still standing there watching. She wondered if it would be proper for her to wave farewell to him. Just because they had shared a friendly conversation didn't mean they were social equals; but surely a simple wave wouldn't be overstepping the boundaries Corrine and Gerald had so diligently drilled into her head.

Why can't people just be people? she wondered. The driver flicked his leather reins and let out a whistle, and the wheels of the open gig began to turn with a creak of wood and metal. Deciding that what her employers couldn't see was none of their concern, she lifted her hand and waved. Just before Mr. Burke was out of her vision, Rachel saw him raise a hand in return.

Turning to steady herself in the slightly jouncing seat, she smoothed out the folds of her fancy maid's uniform, closed her eyes, and imagined that she was still standing at the top of the staircase leading down to his kitchen door. . . .

~

"Rachel?"

Just about to lower her foot to that first step, Rachel had started at the sound of Adam Burke's voice to her right. She had turned to find him almost out of sight behind a grape trellis in the kitchen garden.

"Mr. Burke?" she said, taking a step in his direction.

156

He came from behind the trellis and smiled at her. He was casually dressed in brown corded trousers and a white shirt with the sleeves rolled up to his elbows. "Isn't tomorrow when you were going to sketch Lucy?"

"Yes, sir." Putting her hand in her apron pocket, she said, "I'm here to—"

"Don't tell me. You're here to deliver a message."

"Yes, sir," she said again, chagrined that he would look so amused. It wasn't her fault that Corrine sent her over so often. "Would you like me to give it to Bernice?"

He shook his head. "I can take it now, unless you just want to visit Bernice and Lucy."

She would have enjoyed visiting the two very much, but instead she walked over to him and took the envelope from her pocket. "Thank you anyway. I'm sure they're busy, and I should get back soon."

Adam took the envelope from her. Not looking at Corrine's handwriting on the outside, he slipped it into the pocket of his trousers. "Do you have time to come see something?"

Surprised, Rachel could only nod. She followed him as he beckoned and turned toward the garden. They walked past trellised vines and blooming shrubs before coming to a young pear tree. First putting a finger up to his lips, Adam moved aside a clump of leaves and smiled back at her. "Have you ever seen robin nestlings?" he whispered with something close to reverence.

She stepped closer to the low tree branch, from where she could hear faint peeping sounds. The sight of the nest and five tiny, brownish pink baby birds made her gasp with wonder. Beaks wide open, the birds were clustered together as one wriggling and chirping mass among bits of blue-green eggshell.

"Do they have parents?" she whispered.

He stepped beside her and touched the very edge of the nest with a finger. "Yes, they are both out searching for food."

"I hope they won't be by themselves for too long."

"I saw one of them—the mother, I believe—fly away just before you came, so she'll probably be back any minute."

Rachel looked over her shoulder toward the sky. "Shouldn't we leave so she won't be frightened away?"

"That might be best," he answered, gently replacing the clump of leaves. "Wouldn't want the little ones to go hungry."

As they walked away from the pear tree and out of the garden, Rachel ventured, "I read once that birds eat nearly three times their weight every day."

"You don't say! No wonder the parents are so busy." They walked a few more steps, then he stopped, crossed his arms, and studied her. "So, you like to read, too, do you?"

"Whenever I have the chance."

"Which do you do more? Reading or sketching?"

Rachel knew that he was just being polite and that she really shouldn't take up any more of his time. But he was so easy to talk with, and he didn't leer at her the way Gerald did. Besides, it would be rude not to answer his questions. "I like them both, sir, very much. The last house we stayed at in York had shelves in the parlor with several books, and I read them all. One was about the habits of animals—that's how I learned about how much birds eat."

"You mean the house in Bridgewater, don't you?"

"Sir?"

"Isn't Mrs. Hammond's estate in Bridgewater?"

"Oh, of course," she lied, hating herself for doing so.

If Adam Burke noticed the discomfort in her eyes, he didn't show it. "You know, I have a considerable library inside with more books than I can possibly read. Would you like to borrow some?"

She brightened. "Do you think it would be all right?"

Laughing, he said, "I believe I can get permission from the head of the house." There was a sound of leaves rustling then, and he stopped. Shielding his eyes against the sun, he glanced back toward the tree, its top just visible over the white trellis. "I believe that was the father I just spotted."

Rachel turned to look. "I'm glad they're being taken care of." She reminded herself that her errand was over and that the carriage was waiting. She gave him a bashful smile. "Thank you for showing me the nest, Mr. Burke."

He gave her a slight bow. "And thank you for allowing me to show it to you. Wouldn't you like to pick out some books before you leave?"

She didn't want to seem ungrateful, but Corrine had told her not to stay too long. "May I tomorrow?"

"Of course," he answered. "In fact, how about if I collect a few of my favorites and have them ready for you? You could read what you like and swap them when you've finished."

"That would be wonderful!" she replied with as much enthusiasm as her shyness would allow. "Thank you again, sir."

His eyes crinkled at the corners as he returned her smile with a crooked one of his own. "It'll be my pleasure, Rachel."

~

Rachel stood in the dining room with the tray in her hands as she had for the last ten minutes. The steam wisping from the

159

spout of the teapot had dwindled down to a ghostly thread. If she didn't serve the tea soon, she would have to go back downstairs and brew another pot.

The voices in the sitting room had become lower, and Rachel hoped that it was a good sign. She had witnessed countless altercations between Gerald and Corrine, but her presence had never been voluntary . . . and she had certainly never *knowingly* walked in during one of their arguments.

Then she heard Gerald's voice rising again. She let out a sigh and, with a regretful glance at the teapot, turned to head back for the kitchen steps. How long had they been at it? Usually their fights ran down after a while. Perhaps they would be finished by the time she had made another pot.

She stopped abruptly, tilting her head at another sound. This time it was Corrine's voice, filled with distress. Did she just tell him to stop hurting her?

It was none of her business, Rachel tried to tell herself, yet she turned to set the tray on the table. Taking quick steps over to the open doorway that separated the dining and sitting rooms, she stood just out of the couple's sight and listened.

"I'm sick of having to cater to your every whim!" Gerald was saying with vehemence. "You were a low-class *nothing* until I taught you how to get what you want!"

Corrine's answering sob sent a chill up Rachel's spine. He was obviously hurting her in some way. She remembered the strength in Gerald's hands when he wrestled the knife from her hand in the kitchen.

What could she do? she wondered, then questioned why she cared to do anything. Her mistress had never expressed any sympathy for her own situation. Yet she couldn't get out of her mind the picture of Corrine at the children's home this morning, beaming while she fed the child in her arms some milk.

Rachel steeled herself and picked up her tray. She hoped the tea was still warm enough to serve. Pretending not to notice the scene before her, Rachel walked into the sitting room. "May I pour you some tea?"

At the sound of Rachel's voice, Gerald released Corrine's hands and lunged to his feet. "It's about time!" he snarled.

Rachel darted a glance at her mistress, who had a hand up to her mouth and was quietly weeping. "I'm sorry, sir," she told him as she set the tray on the tea table in front of the settee. "I'll just pour—"

"Never mind!" Ignoring Corrine, he stomped over to the coatrack and grabbed his hat and cloak. He had taken two steps toward the hall when he wheeled around to point a finger at both of them.

"You *will* concentrate your efforts on Mr. Burke!" he growled at Corrine. "And if you're considering leaving me, think again! I can fix it so that *no* man will ever want to look at you!"

His face dark with rage, he shot a furious look at Rachel. "And the same goes for you!"

9

RACHEL heard the windows in the front of the house rattle as Gerald slammed the door. Corrine flinched at the sound, and inexplicably, Rachel's heart again went out to the woman who had treated her with such indifference and scorn for so many years.

"He's gone, ma'am," she said gently, kneeling in front of her mistress. "Did he hurt you badly?"

Her eyes red and wet, Corrine moved her trembling hand from over her mouth and frowned at it. "My lip's not bleeding, I don't think."

"I'll get some water for it so it won't get swollen." Rachel took off for the kitchen, returning minutes later with a wet dish towel.

"Here now," she said, seating herself next to Corrine. "Hold this over your mouth for a while."

"It won't swell." Corrine touched the tender place on her bottom lip. "He's too smart to do anything to ruin my looks." Nonetheless, she took the wet cloth Rachel held out to her.

Rachel clasped her hands together in her lap and watched. Corrine alternately pressed the cloth to her lips and wiped her eyes with it. "Why do you stay with him, ma'am?"

163

Corrine shrugged her shoulders. "I love him." Her tone was flat, emotionless.

"But how can you?"

Corrine cut her eyes over to Rachel. "You're too young to understand. I deserve someone like Gerald." She let out a mirthless laugh, and Rachel wondered if she'd suddenly gone mad.

"I left my home to go with him," she continued bitterly, "because I thought I deserved better than what I had. Now I deserve just what I've got—a man who pretends to love me while he sends me to the beds of other men."

She evidently noticed the blush that came to Rachel's face. "You're embarrassed, aren't you?"

Rachel shook her head, but she felt her cheeks burning.

"You see how jaded I've become?" Corrine rubbed her eyes, sinking back into the cushions of the settee. "The things that decent people only whisper about have become so commonplace in my life that I mention them without blinking an eyelash."

"What are you going to do?"

Corrine handed the cloth back to Rachel. "Why, have a glass of brandy and go to bed."

"That's all?"

She shrugged again. "What else would you suggest?"

"I would—" Rachel stopped abruptly. She had always thought of Corrine as strong, but Rachel was dumbfounded by Corrine's apparent willingness to accept her situation. After all, she had enough money to go somewhere else, and she didn't have to wait for references.

"You'd leave." Corrine gave a bitter smile. "Is that what you were going to say?"

"Yes, ma'am. We could pack our things right now."

"We? You mean you'd go with me?"

"I certainly wouldn't stay here alone with Mr. Moore."

"And where would we go?"

"Why not the place you came from? I could work. . . ."

"Home?" interrupted Corrine. "My dear, I don't think I'd be welcome in Leawick. And besides, it's the first place Gerald would look."

"Just tell him you don't want to be with him anymore."

"Didn't you hear what he said before he left?" Corrine shuddered visibly. "His threat to fix it so no man would want to look at me. He wasn't joking."

"You mean he would . . ."

"I don't want to even imagine what he's capable of. Why do you think his family disowned him?"

Rachel knew, or thought she did. She had heard Corrine throw that up to him during one of their heated arguments. "The girl in his village?"

Corrine nodded. "Gerald didn't want to marry the girl, nor did he like the notion of a child who looked like him running about for everyone to snicker about. He ordered the girl to go with one of his servants to Shepton to see a woman who could . . . get rid of the inconvenience."

~

Corrine watched the rapid succession of emotions that moved over Rachel's face. The girl couldn't possibly understand.

But Corrine knew, and the memory made her shudder. She herself had been to the woman three times since she had started living with Gerald. Three times she had submitted to that frightful old crone with sour breath and rotting teeth. . . .

Rachel's voice brought her back to the present. "Do you mean he wanted the girl to give the baby away?"

"He didn't want the child born," Corrine answered flatly. "But the girl refused to go see the woman, insisting that Gerald should marry her. When she threatened to have the vicar disgrace him publicly, he took her off in the woods and 'eliminated the problem.'"

"He *killed* her?"

"Well, not directly. He set his hounds on her, then claimed they'd gone off their leash and acted on their own. It was only his father's money that soothed the tempers of the sheriff and the girl's family."

"And he wasn't arrested?"

"It was a large sum of money," Corrine said. "But he had to leave Holdenby because of the scandal. And because certain members of the girl's family were not that easily appeased."

Rachel stared at her without speaking for a minute. Finally, she said, "You *knew* about this?"

Corrine shook her head. "Not for a while." How could she admit to the girl that when the revelation finally came from her lover's lips, it had made him seem even more irresistibly dangerous and exciting! She felt her cheeks begin to flush. Perhaps she did have some remnant of conscience, after all.

She looked at Rachel intently. "You came in here because he was hurting me, didn't you?"

Rachel nodded, and Corrine stared at her with wonder. "And yet I've treated you so badly—even accused you of being in love with Gerald when I knew it wasn't so. Why did you do it?"

"I don't know. You sounded so sad that I couldn't bear it."

To Rachel's obvious surprise, Corrine reached over and

took her hand. "That was a very kind thing you did." Her eyes began to fill with tears. "How I wish I were like you."

"Like *me?*"

"Like you. Clean. Pure."

Rachel hesitated for a moment, then touched Corrine's arm. "I'm not so innocent as you think me. My thoughts are so murderous that they sometimes frighten me."

"Your *thoughts?*" Releasing Rachel's hand, Corrine put her fist up to her mouth. "I wish that were my only sin. What a horrid wretch I've become!"

"I watched you with that child this morning," Rachel said simply. "And you're being kind to me right now."

"Two acts of goodness in my whole life," Corrine murmured. "Weighed against more horrible, selfish actions than I can count." Suddenly she felt drained, crushed by the terrible burden of her own awareness. Her hands began to tremble, and she rose unsteadily to her feet. "I'm going to bed."

"Is there anything I can do for you, ma'am?"

At the foot of the stairs, Corrine looked back over her shoulder. "Can you stop me from dreaming?"

"From dreaming?"

"The thoughts that scream out at me in the night. Can you make them go away?"

"Uh . . . no, ma'am."

Corrine gave her a wan smile. "Then there's nothing you can do for me." She turned and walked halfway up the staircase, then stopped. "On second thought, you can fetch me another bottle of brandy. The one in my dresser is nearly empty."

"But what if Mr. Moore comes back?" Rachel asked.

"Then I'd advise you to keep out of his way."

167

~

The swinging doors to the Waterman's Arms Tavern creaked violently on their hinges behind Gerald as he stalked across the floor to his usual table. His card-playing partners wouldn't arrive for a couple of hours yet, but his mind was not on them. He motioned to the lone saloon maid to bring him a drink, then ignored her when she came over to set a glass of gin in front of him.

I'm sick of Corrine and her whining! he thought as he took a huge gulp and let it burn the back of his throat. *And now she's feeling guilty, of all things. Next thing she'll be telling me she doesn't want to take money from Adam Burke!*

He frowned bitterly. What had happened to the old days when he had been fascinated with Corrine's beauty and her total self-absorption? Like a sponge she had soaked up his efforts to refine her manners and set out with a vengeance to snare any unsuspecting rich bloke that he pointed out to her.

Now she was no fun at all anymore—no fun at all!

And Rachel. Chaste, innocent Rachel, who bewitched him with her unawareness of her own beauty. He knew why she had dashed into the middle of their argument with her tray, of course. Some sense of duty caused her to protect Corrine, who certainly wouldn't have done the same for her. Rachel was getting less easy to control now, and one day she would succeed in finding another place to go.

He took another gulp of the gin. Corrine would behave now. He had seen the terror on her face when he threatened to ruin her looks. He would do it, too. His lips curled up into a smirk. *Then she would be a perfect match for that Burke fellow. And I could teach Rachel to take her place.*

He just had to make sure Rachel was fully aware of the consequences of leaving him.

~

Celia Gibbs let out a curse as her leather slipper caught on a nail protruding from the stoop of the Waterman's Arms. She bent down to inspect the damage and cursed again. She considered going back to Madame Germant's and waiting there for customers. She took great stock in omens, and the jagged hole in the toe of her slipper seemed to forewarn of disaster.

But business was slow at seven o'clock in the evening, and she was eager to make as much money as possible. Ever since seeing *Lilly's Love* from the penny seats in the Pavilion last year, she was determined to be an actress. She spent every Sunday afternoon knocking on stage doors on Alie and Leman Streets, begging for readings and befriending stagehands, customers—anyone connected with the theatre. She was only seventeen, and with her honey-colored hair and striking eyes, people were forever telling her that she would be wonderful on the stage. The dream sustained her; she would do anything—even sell herself, body and soul—to see it come true.

And it would come true. One day she would have enough money to quit working for Madame Germant. Then she would pursue the dream until it became a reality.

Now, however, she had expenses to take care of. Madame took half her earnings, and a good part of her money had to be spent on maintaining an adequate wardrobe. Not to entice customers, for as long as she wore a smile and a come-hither look in her eyes, they didn't seem to care what she wore. Her theatre acquaintances were more difficult to impress.

The inside of the tavern was dimly lit and smelled of cigars and gin. A low murmur of voices came from the dozen or so customers standing at the bar or seated at gaming tables. They would become raucous as the night came on and the saloon filled with workers fresh from their shifts at the shipyards.

Only one barmaid was at work now, a hefty brunette with sagging flesh under her chin. With such meager competition, Celia knew that all eyes were turned to her as she stepped confidently over to the bar, then turned to watch the room with her elbows propped on the counter behind her.

She didn't have to wait long.

"'Ey, Celia." A man with a Cockney accent and one sunken eye walked over, clutching a glass of stout. "Why don't we go for a walk, love?"

Her angular face filled with disgust. "I've got no time to waste on the likes of you—you ain't even got a quid to your name, I'll wager!"

The Cockney's pride was wounded, and he narrowed his good eye at her. "I've got half a quid—that oughta be more'n enough for yer." He spat on the floor at her feet, then disappeared back into the haze of smoke.

Celia had opened her mouth to shout something back at him when she froze. There, sitting alone at a table just twelve feet away, was that man. He was holding a glass of gin and watching her with his pale eyes, and a chill ran down her spine when he raised an eyebrow and smiled.

~

"Can you see them?"

Adam blinked into the darkness surrounding his four-poster bed, trying to identify the sound that had jarred him from his sleep. When the cobwebs cleared from his thoughts, he realized that he was the one who had spoken.

He didn't remember ever talking in his sleep before. He could recall the words he had said, but the dream that had prompted them hovered at the edge of his mind, teasing him with bits and pieces of vague scenes. Finally he decided it didn't matter. Turning his pillow over, he rolled to his other side and closed his eyes again.

Just as the drowsiness deepened his breathing, a vision from the dream reappeared. His eyes closed tightly, he wrinkled his forehead and concentrated. In his mind he saw a garden, a deliberately chaotic scattering of flowers in all colors and hues. *My mother's garden,* he thought. *Back in Gloucester . . .*

~

He was walking in the garden, dressed in the uniform of his regiment, a sword sheathed at his left side, his father's silver medal of valor from the Battle of Navarino on his chest. At his right was a woman in an iridescent gown that was even more brilliant than the flowers. He could not see her face, for a light breeze caused her long golden hair to billow about her cheeks. She allowed him to hold her hand, but he was hurt by her silence as he unsuccessfully tried to make her talk to him.

They came to one of the wrought-iron benches at the end of the garden, sheltered by a dogwood tree in full bloom. He helped her to take a seat on the bench, then heard a faint rustling overhead. He craned his neck and peered up into the branches of the dogwood. . . . Its blossoms had transformed into hundreds of white butterflies, moving their wings as if keeping time with a melody that he couldn't hear.

Smiling as he stood before her, he reached for the woman's hand again. She would speak to him once she saw the butterflies. But now he could see her face, and he was speechless, stunned into silence by the luminosity of her emerald eyes. She seemed to understand that he was struggling to find his voice, and lifting her other hand to his scarred cheek, she whispered his name so softly that it felt like a caress.

His heart pounding within his chest, he pointed up at the branches. "Butterflies . . . ," he managed to say.

He watched her take a quick breath and stare upward with an expression filled with awe and delight.

"Can you see them?" he asked. But then the woman and the butterflies vanished.

~

Lying in the stillness of the dark, Adam tried to recall who the woman was. At first he was certain that it was Kathleen because of the golden hair—and because she had visited so many of his dreams over the years. Then he remembered the shining green eyes and the wondrous smile. *Rachel's face when I showed her the robin nestlings.*

Why did I dream about her? he wondered. Yet he found himself closing his eyes again, trying to recapture that picture in his imagination. Perhaps if he lay still enough, the dream would return.

~

Light was fading and the fog was growing denser as Celia Gibbs left the tavern and made her way cautiously across the wet cobblestones of the street. The gaslights had not yet been lit, but dusk was falling quickly, and the shadowed alleyways and dark corners made the girl shudder with apprehension.

Her memory of the fair-haired man with the strange pale

eyes didn't help her to feel more comfortable. After last night, she had sworn that she would never get within a mile of the man, even if she had to give up her dreams of the stage forever. He looked like a gentleman, he did, but when he began to get rough with her, he turned out to be worse than any Cockney workman or sea rat she had ever been with.

Celia's hand went to her neck. Her throat was still tender from the pressure of his fingers when he had gotten nasty. Rachel, he kept calling her. Rachel.

She had told him her name wasn't Rachel, and that had been a mistake. He had gone crazy almost, slapping her around and trying to choke the life out of her. At last he had gone out in a rage, leaving her bruised and battered, but with no permanent injury. She had been lucky, she supposed, considering the wild look in the man's eyes. But she wouldn't make the same mistake again.

She wouldn't let him back in her room, that was certain. She would go back to the house and tell Chan, Madame's Chinese watchman, not to let him in. Chan was more than a match for the likes of him.

At the entrance to an alley just around the corner from Madame's house, Celia felt a sharp pain in her toe. Leaning against the side of the building, she lifted her slipper and peered at her foot. She had stepped on a piece of broken glass, and the shard had lodged in her foot where her slipper was torn. It was bleeding a little, but it wasn't a deep cut, and if she could just get the glass out . . .

She pulled at the shiver of glass with one hand, straining to see in the gathering darkness. And then she heard, just faintly, the sound of footsteps behind her.

~

Gerald followed the girl when she left Waterman's Arms, slipping behind her in the shadows, watching. A haughty little snippet—who did she think she was, ordering him out of her room last night? "You don't know how to treat a lady," she had said, cursing at him and raising the most awful ruckus. *Lady?* The absurd little doxy thought herself a *lady?*

He edged through the darkness behind her, his heart pumping with anticipation. *So the lowborn wench thinks she's too good for Gerald Moore!* he thought. His temples throbbed and his hands curled into fists. Well, he would show her what was good enough for her. He would let her know, once and for all, that he was not a man to be trifled with.

Gerald moved slowly, shadowing her every turn. His sense of excitement mounted with each step. Then suddenly, she stopped. He watched, breathing heavily, as she lifted her foot and examined her slipper. Her back was to the alley. It was all so perfect . . . as if she were waiting for him.

~

When Celia heard the footsteps behind her, she panicked. She forgot about her wounded foot, forgot everything except the need to run. But her breath failed her, and her heart beat so wildly that she thought she might faint. For a moment she was frozen in place, her legs like lead beneath her.

She hesitated too long.

Hands grabbed her from behind and pulled her into the black alley. Too terrified to scream, she flailed her arms and lashed out with her legs, but he was too strong for her. He dragged her deeper into the darkness, and her nostrils filled with the stench of mildew and rotting garbage.

At last she found her voice. She took a deep gulp of the fetid air and tried to scream, but her shriek was cut off as her throat was squeezed.

Celia Gibbs never saw the face of her attacker. But she knew, with a terrible certainty, that her dream of being on the stage would never come true.

~

After a while the girl stopped struggling and went limp in his arms. Letting her drop to the ground with a thud, Gerald bent down to take hold of her forearms and drag her into the far corner of the alley.

The gaslights had been lit. In the dim light reflecting from the street, he could see a jumble of wooden crates against the back wall of the alley. He kicked her lifeless body into the corner and began piling crates on top of the corpse.

They wouldn't find her until she started to smell. Plenty of time for the patrons of Waterman's Arms to forget exactly who had been there that evening. They didn't know his real name anyway. And who was going to care about the death of one common prostitute?

Still, just to be sure, he would have to keep out of sight for a couple of days. He would stay home for a while, then find somewhere else to play cards. He would get away with it; he had no doubt about that. He always did.

Gerald straightened up and wiped his hands on his trousers. He felt better than he had in weeks. But he wished he had been able to see her face in those last moments of her life. Had she realized it was him? He hoped so.

He peered into the darkness at the crates that served as tomb and headstone, then shook his head and smiled sadly. "You shouldn't have made me angry," he said softly, even sympathetically. "You see what happens to women who make me angry. . . ."

10

"A Joseph Price to see you, sir."
Two hundred miles north of London in the farm-
ing village of Treybrook, Humberside, Squire
Malcolm Nowells III wiped his mouth with a napkin and nodded to Ramsey, his butler. "I'll see him in my study." From
the head of the table he directed an apologetic look at his wife,
Louisa. "Excuse me, dear—pressing business."

Louisa glanced at his half-finished plate, then at their
eleven-year-old son. "But little Malcolm's birthday . . ."

"This shouldn't take long," Malcolm said, already pulling
his considerable bulk out of his chair. "How about if I join
you for cake in the conservatory in an hour?" He picked up
his cane from where it hung on the back of his chair and
limped out of the dining room.

He was settled behind his desk in the study when Ramsey
opened the door and ushered a gentleman into the room.
"Mr. Price," he announced with the same air of formality he
used when heralding the presence of all of the Nowellses'
guests. His duty performed, he stepped aside to wait for any
further instructions from his employer.

"That will be all, Ramsey," said Malcolm. He waited until

the butler had closed the door before motioning to a chair. "Please have a seat, Mr. Price."

Joseph Price, a tall, muscular man in his early forties with thick dark hair and a neatly trimmed beard, nodded and walked over to the chair. "I'm used to dealing with Mr. Fawcett," he remarked as he sat down, "but I received word from him this morning that you wished to speak with me directly." Though his clothes were the tweeds of a country dweller, his elocution and manners spoke of an educated background.

Malcolm straightened his bad leg and leaned forward, resting his elbows upon the desk. "I have great trust in Fawcett— he was my grandfather's solicitor, as well as my late father's."

"Please accept my regrets—"

"Yes, thank you," interrupted Malcolm, waving aside his condolences. "Fawcett tells me you've found out something."

"About the woman, you mean."

"No, about how many silk hats Lord Palmerston has in his dressing room!"

Joseph Price smiled benignly. "That was a rather obvious question," he said with aplomb. "Forgive me. As for Mrs. Hammond, I've got some rather interesting news."

Malcolm's eyebrows lifted. "Yes?"

"It seems she travels with a man. They settle in larger towns so that they can remain anonymous. Then she manages to be introduced to someone wealthy enough to make life easier for her—and married enough to be vulnerable to blackmail later on down the road."

When Malcolm did not respond, Price continued, "I've traced her back to Manchester, Shrewsbury, and Rotherham so far. Fortunately, she feels secure enough to use the same name. Whether it's her real one, I cannot tell yet."

"Of course she feels secure." Malcolm's frown was bitter. "Her victims aren't able to publicize her notoriety or tell the authorities without calling attention to their own indiscretions. Did any of the other men . . ."

"Take their own lives?" Joseph shook his head. "None of the three in the towns I've mentioned. I don't know about other places yet."

"How did you get this information?"

"Mainly servants, Squire Nowells. Most are eager to supplement their wages . . . and more than willing to talk about their employers."

Giving a snort of indignation, Malcolm said, "I imagine some are. I'm certain *my* servants would be more discreet, however."

Joseph gave him another smile. "Be sure to give your son my best wishes on his birthday. And let me express my dismay at the riding accident nine years ago, which cost you the partial use of your right leg."

"Ramsey!" Malcolm pounded his desk in frustration.

"Rest assured, your butler is tight-lipped. He barely spoke to me except to ask for my hat."

"Then who . . . ?"

"It doesn't matter. Nothing of a scandalous nature was offered—not that I would have listened."

"You're rather insufferable." Malcolm glared at the man. "You should learn your place if you wish to stay in my employ."

~

Joseph Price picked up an onyx paperweight from the desk and turned it over in his hands. That was the trouble with

179

gentry, he thought. They were too used to having people bow and scrape in front of them.

"My place is where I choose to be," he said. "If you no longer require my services, you have only to say the word."

Squire Nowells made some sputtering noises, then sighed and held up a hand. "I need your services," he said meekly. "But I must say I'm not accustomed to doing business with your type. Do you always insult the people you work for?"

"I wasn't aware that I had insulted you. If you feel that I have, then I apologize. Now, do you want to know about the man Mrs. Hammond travels with?"

"You have his name?" asked Malcolm, perking up immediately.

"Found it out four days ago, after several false leads. Your solicitor's instructions were to come with a report when I came across something significant."

Malcolm nodded. "That's extremely significant. Who is this cad?"

"He presented three different identities to the landlords in the three cities I mentioned."

"Then how . . . ?"

"How did I find his name?" Joseph smiled and sat back in the chair. "I reasoned that a scoundrel such as this man would be more than familiar with the gaming and liquor establishments in the towns. I found circles of men who had gambled with him. Gin is a sure way to loosen lips. He used the name Gerald Moore in Rotherham and Shrewsbury. In Manchester I traced the same name to a tailor's shop he frequented."

For the first time since Joseph Price had walked into the room, Malcolm Nowells smiled. "Fawcett was right—you're worth every penny of the exorbitant sum I'm paying you. And do you know where he and the woman are now?"

"I have an idea they headed for London after your father's tragic death."

"How do you deduce that?"

"This Mrs. Hammond is an extraordinarily beautiful woman, I've been told countless times. That's been working in my favor during this whole investigation, for quite a few train attendants and stationmasters have recalled seeing a woman whose description matches hers."

"London would make sense. It would be easy to remain anonymous there. Do you think you can find them?"

"I'll find them," Joseph assured him. "But it's not going to be easy." His eyes became questioning. "In fact, I should have left for the city as soon as I found out about Mr. Moore. I'm wasting valuable time here."

"I had a reason for requesting that you see me when you came up with something solid." Nowells seemed to be studying Price carefully. "There's something you and I need to discuss."

Joseph lifted his eyebrows. "Something that Mr. Fawcett couldn't tell me?"

"Fawcett's a good man, as I've said, but his ideas and mine on how to handle the situation when you find the woman differ."

"Meaning . . ."

"I don't want the authorities involved."

Joseph Price was an intelligent man, a man who prided himself on integrity and honor. He chose his cases carefully and held himself accountable to the morals instilled in him by his father.

His career as a detective had, in fact, initially grown out of his strong moral sense and his desire to help others. After teaching for a few years, he had traveled around, picking up odd jobs when he was low on funds. He had been serving as a gardener on an estate in Stockport when his employer expressed a longing to find his wayward son. Joseph felt sorry for the man and set out to try and reconcile the family. He quickly discovered that he had a knack for tracking people down. It took him only three months to find the son and another week to convince the prodigal to go home to his family.

The grateful father had numerous contacts among the upper class, and news of Joseph's skill spread. Before long he was never at a loss for clients. He loved the freedom and sense of adventure his occupation afforded, and he considered himself the luckiest man alive.

Price was not in any sense religious, but he had never done anything that conflicted with his own high standards. He knew what the gleam in Squire Nowell's eyes meant, and he didn't like the idea one bit.

"I'm not an assassin, sir," Joseph declared flatly. "If that's been your purpose all along, then you're to be disappointed."

Malcolm Nowells III drew himself up in his chair. "My father was a decent man who made the mistake of listening to the flattery of a beautiful woman. I will not rest until she and her lover are punished."

"Then perhaps you should be contacting Scotland Yard."

"Why? So those two vultures can bring further humiliation to my family with a public trial? Have you any idea how much sensation a case like this would cause in the whole of Great Britain?"

"I can understand your desire for revenge, but—"

182

"Justice!"

"All right, justice. But I've seen the inside of several prisons in my line of work, and they aren't pleasant places to spend the rest of one's life."

A weary sigh escaped Malcolm's lips. "There is another reason I don't want the authorities involved. My mother was devastated when my father killed himself. Not only did she lose a husband of thirty-five years, but she discovered he was being whispered about by her 'friends.' They pretended to believe my story about Father's being depressed for months before he died, but Mother wasn't fooled. Now she doesn't want to leave the house. Just sits in her room all day."

He regarded Joseph with pleading eyes. "Don't you see? Mother couldn't live through the gossip this would stir up again, and I'm not ready to lose another parent."

Joseph was quiet for a long time. He had killed once before, but only in self-defense when a trio of thieves attacked him on the road to Birmingham. While he took no pleasure in killing one of the men and gravely injuring the others, it had not interfered with his sleep afterwards. Criminals like that would have ended up killing some innocent person one day, if they hadn't already. But to take two lives deliberately—and one of them a woman?

"I can't do it," he finally said. "As much as I sympathize with your family, I just can't. Perhaps you should pay me what you owe me so far and get someone more . . . experienced to look for them in London."

Malcolm nodded gravely and reached into his vest pocket for a key. Wincing at the pain in his knee, he bent down to unlock his bottom desk drawer, then took out a fat envelope and tossed it on his desk towards his visitor. "One hundred pounds."

"Mr. Fawcett has already given me two payments, so you don't owe me near that amount."

"This is a bonus," said Malcolm. "In addition to what I already owe you. Plus that amount again if you're successful."

The implications suddenly dawned upon Joseph. "You mean if I kill these people."

Malcolm nodded.

Hesitating for a moment, Joseph picked up the envelope, counted out ten five-pound notes, and put them in his pocket. Gerald Moore was a snake. He deserved to be stamped out before he struck again. He tossed the envelope back on the desk. "I won't kill a woman," he insisted. "But I'll bring her back here, then you can do with her what you will. I'm sure you can find someone around here who would like to earn that other fifty pounds."

11

THE silence between Corrine and Rachel as they sat in opposite seats in the bouncing carriage became a living thing, a third presence that filled every inch of the space between them.

Not until the carriage reached Mile End Road did Corrine speak, but she dared not meet Rachel's eyes. "I suppose you know that Gerald came back." With her thumb she traced the patterns of the beads on her purse.

Rachel cleared her throat. "I heard him this morning."

"You know I had no choice."

"I know."

"Anyway, he promised never to hurt me again," Corrine said softly, still moving her thumb along the beads. *As long as I do as he says.* She said nothing else until the carriage pulled up in front of Adam Burke's gate, but when the driver came around and held up a hand to help her to the ground, she shook her head.

"I'm not getting out here."

Rachel looked up from gathering her sketchbook and pencils. "Ma'am?"

"I've been worried about little Anna all day. What if she won't eat for anyone else?"

"But Mr. Gerald . . ."

Corrine stared across at the house, her expression uncertain. Surely that Irish woman could give her a bottle just as well. She couldn't go about trying to save every pitiful child in London. But just as she was about ready to change her mind, her lips tightened. "He doesn't have to know about it. I won't be gone long. I can come back here afterwards for a visit, then we'll ride back together."

"What will I tell Mr. Burke? After all, he's expecting you to come with me."

Again Corrine felt uncertain, but only for a second. She smiled at Rachel and, with a voice filled with irony, answered, "You can tell him that the kindhearted Mrs. Hammond is visiting orphans. That should impress him."

~

Lucy, looking very grown-up in a honeysuckle-pink calico dress, stood where her mother had positioned her in front of the marble fireplace in Adam Burke's drawing room. The girl held a bouquet of white rose buds from the conservatory, their stems wrapped with long trailing ribbons.

Shortly after Rachel had taken a seat in a comfortable wing-back chair, Adam and Bernice asked if she minded their placing chairs on each side. Having never drawn in front of an audience before, she felt nervous at first; but she kept her hands from trembling by concentrating on Lucy and the sketchbook in her lap.

"Those are her eyes, all right!" exclaimed Bernice minutes later when Rachel had penciled in the girl's last eyelash with short, feathery strokes. She put a hand up to her mouth. "I'm sorry, Rachel!"

186

"It won't disturb me if you want to talk," Rachel told her. Now that she had gotten off to a good start, her mind seemed to relax and allow her hands to take over.

"I'm curious," Adam said as he leaned closer to watch, "do all portrait artists start with the eyes?"

"I don't know, sir. It just seems the right place to begin."

He nodded. "That makes sense. After all, they're the most expressive parts of our faces. I would imagine you'd want to get them right before starting anything else."

"I've heard it said that the eyes are the windows to our souls," Rachel said quietly.

Adam smiled. "I've heard that, too."

"It's going to be a beautiful picture," Bernice said with pride. "Thank you again for doing this."

"Oh, I should be thanking you for the opportunity. I've never had a chance to work with a live model before," Rachel explained.

"But then how—," Lucy began.

"Lucy, don't talk," her mother admonished. "You can't be twisting your face all up when Rachel's trying to draw you." She turned to Rachel and asked, "How can you draw without a real-live person or at least a picture to look at? Surely you had models in your art classes."

"I usually just draw from the picture in my mind. And I've never even seen another artist work, much less had any lessons."

"So who taught you to draw?" Adam asked.

Lifting the point of her pencil for a second, Rachel shook her head. "I've just always known how. When I lived at the orphanage, I used to take bits of coal and draw on any flat stones I could find."

"Then it was God who taught you," Bernice said with conviction.

"And he's obviously a good teacher," agreed Adam.

Rachel felt a lump come to the back of her throat. "Thank you," she whispered. Their kindness could be overwhelming at times. She knew she would save the memory of this day, like one of her sketches, to be taken out and savored during the lonely times.

~

Adam watched, fascinated as Rachel sketched in Lucy's nose and mouth. The girl was talented, there was no doubt. Talented and lovely . . .

He pushed the thought aside and tried to focus on other things. "How long have you lived with Mrs. Hammond?"

"Six years," Rachel replied.

"It was kind of her to go back to see about one of the children." Though he had been pleasantly surprised to find that Corrine hadn't come along with Rachel after all, he now felt a bit guilty and wondered if he had misjudged the woman. Or was it a ploy to make him think more highly of her?

Whatever Corrine Hammond's motives, he was still glad that Rachel had come alone. He couldn't stop thinking about her. There was a sadness behind those lovely green eyes, but also an intelligence that was obvious in spite of her bashfulness.

He watched the smooth, confident strokes of Rachel's pencil. A lock of honey-colored hair had worked its way out of the chignon at the nape of her neck, and it bounced slightly every time she looked up at Lucy. *She really is a beautiful girl,* he told himself. *And I doubt if she even knows it.*

He wondered how old she was. Sitting there with her brow

wrinkled in concentration, she didn't seem so young, so incredibly far from his own age. But almost immediately he reprimanded himself. He didn't have the right to think that way about any woman, especially one so lovely and talented. His heart suddenly felt heavy in his chest.

"I've got some work to finish," he said, abruptly getting to his feet.

Bernice's round face filled with dismay. "You're leaving? But Mr. Adam—you said you wanted to watch."

"I'm looking forward to seeing the finished project." He noticed that Rachel's pencil had stopped moving and wondered if he had hurt her feelings. "It looks lovely so far," he added kindly. With that, he turned and left the room.

~

"Rachel, do I have to keep smiling?" asked Lucy through stretched lips and closed teeth. "My whole face is startin' to ache."

Rachel looked up from the sketchbook, where she had just put the finishing touches on the girl's collar. "Oh, Lucy! I forgot to tell you that I'm finished with your face!"

Bernice chuckled. "Well, you *told* us you never used a live model before."

Lucy didn't look amused. "I feel like a dead one—and I don't think I'll ever be able to smile again. Can't I take a peek at my picture?"

"I'll show you when I'm finished with the bodice of your dress," Rachel said.

Fifteen minutes later, she walked over to the fireplace and held the sketchbook for Lucy to see. She was rewarded immediately when the girl's face lit up.

189

"I look like a princess!"

Rachel couldn't resist teasing her. "I thought you couldn't smile anymore."

Lucy grinned even more widely in response. As Rachel turned to go back to her chair, Lucy leaned forward and took a quick glance at the grandfather clock in the corner. "It's been over an hour now. When you finish drawin' my dress and shoes, can I sit down?"

"You've stood for longer than that in the kitchen," Bernice admonished.

"But I was working. It's harder to stand still like this."

Rachel smiled at the girl. "Just a bit longer and you can sit down."

"What about the fireplace? Are you goin' to draw that, too?"

"I think it would look nice. But I won't need you to stand in front of it once I get it outlined."

"Then how long will it take after that?"

"Not long at all, I think. Fireplaces are probably easier to draw than people."

"And they don't complain nearly as much." Bernice directed a pointed look to her daughter. She then turned to Rachel. "What about you? Surely you're worn out. Why don't you stop for some tea once you've finished with Lucy?"

Rachel nodded, feeling the strain of the last hour. "Some tea would be nice."

"I'll bring it here," said the cook, already on her feet.

She was back fifteen minutes later with a tray. Rachel had put her pencils down on the carpet next to her chair, and Lucy was holding the sketchbook up to admire her portrait.

190

"Let's sit here at the sofa, like proper ladies," Bernice told them.

Rachel took a place at the opposite end of the sofa from Lucy, allowing Bernice to sit in the middle. "Am I keeping you from cooking supper?" Rachel asked, realizing that the cook probably hadn't known how long the portrait would take.

"Not at all," Bernice answered. She leaned forward to fill the three cups at the tea table in front of her. "The bread was baked Monday, and I started a mutton stew right after lunch. Dora's stirring it every once in a while."

"Mr. Adam doesn't eat fancy when he's got no company," Lucy said, biting into a chocolate biscuit.

"Likes his meals simple, he does," agreed her mother. She poured milk into Rachel's cup of tea and handed it to her. "By the way, we'll have to show him Lucy's picture. I know he'd like to see it."

Rachel wasn't so sure about that. "You don't mean *now,* do you? I'm not finished—besides, he's probably busy."

~

Bernice watched the girl's cup rattle against its saucer at the mention of Mr. Adam's name, and she caught the slight reddening of Rachel's cheeks. How strange. Surely she wasn't frightened of him.

Come to think of it, Mr. Adam had been acting strangely, too—getting up and dashing off like he did, almost like he was nervous. But why would a fine gentleman like Mr. Adam be nervous around a shy little servant girl like Rachel? Unless . . .

Her smile widened. Mr. Adam needed a wife, someone to love, even if he pretended otherwise. Why not Rachel? Even

191

though there was an age gap of about twelve years, Rachel was more mature than some of the older women Bernice had known. And *certainly* more mature than his former fiancée had been, that shallow-brained Kathleen Hardgrove. But knowing Mr. Adam, he would probably need a little prodding in the right direction.

She drained her cup, then set it down on the tray. "Lucy, bring the cups and things to the kitchen when you two are finished. We'll give Rachel some privacy while she sketches the fireplace."

Rachel's eyes darted around the huge room. "I really don't mind the company."

Getting up from the sofa, Bernice shook her head. "We've got work to do. You don't need us here in the way."

"But you just said the stew's already in the pot!" protested Lucy.

"I've decided we need some spiced yams to go with it." Ignoring the ache in her hips from sitting for so long, Bernice bent over to pat Rachel's shoulder. "You're a lovely girl," she said. "And more people know it than just us here."

When she was able to speak, Rachel stammered, "Why . . . thank you, Bernice. You've been so—"

"No need to go on about it," the cook interrupted brusquely. She straightened her back and left the room before the girls could see the tears on her eyelashes.

Bernice walked quickly down the hall and stopped at Adam's study. *You're a sentimental, interfering old fool,* she told herself. Yet she lifted a hand to knock softly at his door.

"Yes?"

Bernice opened the door and stuck her head inside. "Mind if I have a word with you, sir?"

"Of course not." Adam looked up from his desk. "Is the portrait finished?"

"Almost."

"Won't you have a seat?"

"I've sat long enough," she told him as she stood just inside his door. "I just wanted to ask you something, then I'll leave you alone."

Adam lifted the pen he was holding from his ledger and gave her a crooked smile. "Ask away, then."

"Have I been a good servant to you?"

He looked puzzled. "The best! I think you already know that, though." Tilting his head in mock suspicion, he said, "Are you about to ask for a raise, Bernice?"

"My salary's always been more than adequate," she replied. "What I came to ask is a favor."

"All right—what can I do for you?"

"Go watch that girl finish the picture."

"Rachel?"

Hands on her generous hips, Bernice nodded. "I think you hurt her feelings when you walked out a while ago."

Adam's expression filled with concern. "You think so? But I had things to do in here. I certainly didn't intend to be rude."

"Things that couldn't wait?" she gently chided.

"Well, probably not, but . . ."

Bernice walked over to the chair opposite Adam's desk and sat down. "Can I speak plain with you?"

"You always do."

She folded her arms. "I talk with other folks like myself every market day—cooks, maids, footmen, the like. Most of them complain about how their employers treat them." Smiling affectionately across at Adam, she said, "You always expect us to get our work done, but you ain't ever looked down on us for being servants. And I thank our Lord for that."

He winked at her. "Well, God created us all in his image, didn't he?"

"He did, indeed. And some he created more lovely than others."

Adam raised an eyebrow. "Meaning?"

"Rachel. Forgive me for bein' so bold, but I noticed how you looked at her in the room there. I've never seen you take notice of a woman like that since—well, sir, since Miss Kathleen."

The pen clattered from his fingers to the top of his desk, and he snatched it up again. "I was interested in watching her sketch, Bernice. That's all."

Bernice's expression was skeptical now. "Would you be telling me the whole truth, sir?"

"Of course. Why would I lie to you?"

"Maybe it's yourself you're lyin' to, Mr. Adam."

~

Adam stared at Bernice, and she stared back. Lying to himself? What on earth could she mean?

Then the truth hit him with a force that nearly took his breath away. "Bernice, I can't believe what you're implying," he said tersely. "She's just a child."

"She's nineteen years old, Mr. Adam—almost twenty."

"Why, I'm old enough to be her father!"

Undaunted, the cook sat back in her chair and fixed him with a glare. "And how many twelve-year-old boys do you know that's got children?"

He shook his head, wondering for the hundredth time why

Bernice seemed to feel it necessary to mother him. Her preoc-
cupation with his well-being could be so irritating at times! He
let out his breath. "There's no sense in even discussing this. I
don't know how you claim I was looking at the girl, but
you're mistaken. Besides, I hardly know her."

"Then you don't think she's lovely?"

"All right," he sighed with exasperation. "She's lovely."

Bernice grinned triumphantly. "And wasn't that *you* pacing
the whole house this morning, waitin' for her to show up?"

"I don't know what you mean," Adam said through
clenched teeth as he began to tap the end of his pen on the
desk.

"Don't tell me you were waitin' for Mrs. Hammond!"

Adam flashed an incredulous glance at Bernice. "I really have
a lot of work to do here, Bernice. Is that *all* you wanted?"

"Well then, sir," she huffed, pulling herself out of her chair.
"I suppose I'm bein' dismissed!"

"I suppose you are!" he shot back.

He had never spoken to her in such a harsh tone, and he
watched uneasily as she walked through the doorway into the
hall. "Bernice!" he called out just as the door clicked shut.

He was about to get up from his desk, but then the door
opened again, and the cook stuck her head inside. Her face was
ruddier than usual, and he wondered if he had made her cry.

"Sir?"

Adam sighed again. "You're right. I was looking forward to
seeing her."

A look of understanding replaced the hurt in her eyes, and
she stepped back in the room. "Why were you too proud to
admit it?" she asked gently. "Is it because she's a servant?"

The barb hit home. "You know that's not the reason."

Silence hung between them. Bernice finally spoke—as usual, cutting right to the core of the matter. "Rachel's different from the rest. I could tell the first time I met her. Can't you tell?"

Adam glanced down at the smeared blob of ink on the blank page of his ledger where he'd written her name earlier and scribbled over it. "She deserves better."

"Better than you?" She shook her head. "Someone like you is just what she deserves, sir. And I do believe she cares about you."

He gave a deep sigh, stroking his right cheek. "Then what she's feeling for me is pity. I'm not going to take advantage of that."

"Won't you at least come out and see her?"

"Send for me when the portrait's finished. I'll come then."

"All right," Bernice said, her shoulders slumped with resignation. "I'll send Lucy 'round to fetch you in a bit."

Before she could leave again, Adam put down his pen. "Bernice?"

She turned around to face him. "Yes, sir?"

"Do you really think she was hurt when I left the room?"

Giving him another sad smile, she answered, "I'd say it was both of you that was hurt."

~

After Bernice left, Adam tried to concentrate on his work, but his thoughts would not stop returning to Rachel. Finally he closed his ledger. It wasn't polite for him to hide in here after asking her to come. The least he could do was to be courteous. With a sigh, he got up from his chair.

On his way to the drawing room, Adam stopped at a wall

mirror in the hall to adjust his tie. When he had first moved into this house, he wouldn't allow Mrs. Fowler, his house-keeper, to hang any mirrors except in the servants' private rooms. After he became a Christian and began to study his Bible, he realized that vanity was a sin not only of the very beautiful but of the not-so-beautiful as well.

Still, he wondered if he would ever get used to the face that stared back at him. He touched the network of jagged wounds on the leathery skin and watched his reflection as a tear coursed down the craters of his right cheek. What woman would want to be close to him?

He almost changed his mind and headed back for the study, but then he told himself that he was being ridiculous. The girl didn't care what he looked like one way or the other. After all, she most likely had dozens of suitors. However, she was a guest in his home, doing a favor for one of his servants—and he would show her that he had manners.

The door leading to the drawing room was open. Stepping inside, he wondered where everyone had gone. He heard the rustling of paper then and realized that the wing-back chair was still occupied. "Rachel?" he said softly, not wishing to startle her.

"Oh, Mr. Burke," she answered, turning so that he could see her face.

He went over to the chair on her right and set it closer. "Bernice tells me you're almost finished."

"I'm working on the fireplace right now."

"May I see it?"

Rachel handed him the sketchbook. Sitting up in his chair, Adam held the book out where he could examine it. "Incredible!" he exclaimed. Lucy's image smiled at him from in front of the half-finished fireplace, her eyes filled with the joy of wearing a new dress and being the center of attention. "I really believe this is better than the portrait you made of little Margaret. Although her portrait was very good," he hastened to add.

"Thank you," she said with a shy smile. "I think this one's better, too."

"And you say this is the first time you've used a model?"

"It turned out to be much easier than relying on memory."

"I should imagine." Handing the sketchbook back to her, he said, "Well, don't let me disturb you. I'll just sit here and watch if you don't mind."

~

Rachel wondered if he could hear her heart beating, for it had inexplicably started pounding in her ears the minute Mr. Burke had spoken her name. And now that he was sitting there beside her, it threatened to drown out all other sounds. *Concentrate on the fireplace,* she told herself as she put her pencil back to shading another silver vein in the marble.

"I heard the robins out back this morning," he was saying. "I believe the parents have been kept quite busy delivering bugs and grubs."

A picture of Mr. Burke and herself with their heads together peering into the nest flashed into her mind, and she found her face growing warm. "I'm glad they're getting enough to eat," she said, hoping he hadn't noticed the color that was surely in her cheeks.

"Speaking of food—are you hungry?"

In spite of being flustered, Rachel had to press her lips closed to suppress a smile. "No, sir. Thank you."

Adam folded his arms and studied her through narrowed eyelids. "What do you find so funny?"

"Nothing, sir." The struggle grew even harder, but she managed to keep her pencil busy.

Puzzled, he watched her at work for a full minute, then chuckled. "I've been sitting here going back over our conversation. We were talking about bugs and grubs, and then I asked you if you wanted to eat."

Rachel covered her mouth to keep from laughing.

"What's wrong with bugs and grubs? Surely you don't mean to tell me you've never eaten a grub?"

Turning serious eyes upon him, she said, "Not knowingly, sir."

He began to laugh, and Rachel joined in. Finally he wiped his eyes, gave her an appreciative look, and said, "Let me try again. Have you had tea?"

"Thank you, yes," she said, smiling before looking back down at the sketchbook again. "Bernice brought us tea and biscuits a little while ago."

"And then they left you here all alone?"

"They had some cooking to finish."

"But I thought she . . ."

Adam didn't finish his sentence, and Rachel wouldn't intrude upon his thoughts by asking him to. He was a private man, Adam was, and he deserved his solitude.

Adam. Since when had she started thinking of him as Adam? She would never call him that, of course; it would be improper. But she thought of him so often that it seemed silly to refer to him as Mr. Burke in her mind. Still, she was only a servant, and he a fine man. She would speak with the proper respect.

She glanced over at him as she etched another vein in the

marble fireplace. He seemed so deep in thought. *And I imagine they are deep thoughts, too—far deeper than my simple mind could ever comprehend.* But it would be fun to try. What would they talk about, just the two of them, if they had evenings together in front of this fireplace?

"Would it disturb you if we talked some more?"

She jumped at the sound of his voice, startled that his question ran so similar to her thoughts. "Not at all," she choked. "I'd enjoy some conversation."

"Good. I picked out a dozen books for you to look at— they're all favorites of mine. I'll have to remember to load them in your carriage when you leave. Have you read *Pilgrim's Progress?*"

"By John Bunyan?" She nodded. "It was one of the books we learned to read with at the orphanage school." Hastily she added, "I'd like to read it again, though. I fear I was too young to understand it the first time."

"Then I hope you can enjoy it this time."

"I'm sure I shall," said Rachel. "Thank you very much."

A silence stretched between them for a few seconds, the only sound being the lead of the pencil raking softly against the paper. "Did you go with Mrs. Morgan and Mrs. Hammond to the children's home again yesterday?" he finally asked.

"Yes, sir." Rachel recalled the young ones gathered around her for a story and the child on Corrine's lap. "We had a pleasant visit."

He nodded. "The Morgans join me for dinner every Friday night. I imagine Mrs. Morgan will have nothing but praise for the help you've given."

"Not just me, sir." She told him how Corrine had persuaded

the little girl to take some food. "I believe the child would have starved had it not been for her."

Had she imagined the puzzled look that crossed his face? He seemed confused by her story, almost as if he didn't believe her.

"May I ask you something, Rachel?"

"Yes, sir," she replied, turning her pencil sideways to shade the mantelpiece.

"Mrs. Hammond—how does she treat you?"

The pencil froze in Rachel's hand. "Treat me?"

"Yes. Is she good to you?"

If he had asked her that question just two days ago, she might have responded to the concern in his voice and poured out her heart to him about the years of near-slave labor and verbal abuse she'd had to endure—not to mention having to take part in her employers' horrid schemes.

But now she couldn't. Some things were best kept inside, especially when there was nothing to be gained by telling them. And now she realized how vulnerable Corrine really was. Gerald would keep pressuring her to move faster in her pursuit of Mr. Burke, but it was becoming increasingly obvious that Mr. Burke did not care for her. The relief that came over his face earlier when he saw that Corrine wasn't at the door had been all too conspicuous. *It's not going to make Mr. Gerald happy when their plan fails. He'll blame her for not trying hard enough.* What would he do to Corrine then?

Two days earlier she wouldn't have cared. But a bond had been formed between them yesterday—a tenuous one at best, but strong enough to keep Rachel from betraying her mistress. She had no such loyalty for Gerald Moore. What kept her lips closed about him now was the fear of what would happen if

Mr. Burke decided to inform the police. Gerald was too cunning to be easily caught, and she feared his revenge more than anything in the world.

"Mrs. Hammond treats me fine," Rachel finally said.

"That's good to hear." He sounded relieved. "Forgive my prying, but there's . . . there's a sadness about you sometimes. I worried that you were being mistreated."

Worried about me? Her pulse started pounding in her ears again, and she had to erase a stray pencil mark she had accidentally made on the page.

Adam leaned closer. "You're almost finished, aren't you?"

"Almost, sir." She couldn't help the pride that she felt as she tilted the portrait for his inspection. "What do you think?"

"What do I think?" His eyes were on her now, and his voice dropped to a whisper. "Beautiful is what I think."

Rachel's heart jumped in her chest. Why was he looking at her like that?

An awkward silence fell over the room. Rachel tried hard to focus on her work, but she was uncomfortably aware of Adam's eyes on her as she put the finishing touches on the mantelpiece.

After a while he cleared his throat. "You know, I'd like to have it framed for Bernice and Jack if they'll allow me. Do you know anyone who does good work?"

Pleased to have a distraction from the perplexing thoughts dancing around in her mind as well as an opportunity to return Mr. Solomon's kindness, she told Adam about the elderly man and his small gallery. "He says that the right frame is almost as important as the painting itself."

"Do you think he would come here and speak with me if I paid for his time? After his shop closes, I mean."

Rachel nodded. "I believe he would, sir. He's a very kind man."

"Then I'll send a message to him first thing tomorrow morning."

She was finished, and she brushed the stray bits of rubber from the paper. "Do you mind if we show Bernice and Lucy?"

He took the sketchbook from her hands and held it out in front of himself to study. After a full minute he smiled, lowering the portrait. "I'll even fetch Jack out of the yard. I want to watch their faces when they see what you've done!"

12

"CAN'T you go any faster?" Corrine called out to the driver of the hired chaise.

The man simply shrugged his shoulders and pointed to the road ahead, saying something in an accent too thick to understand.

Blooming Frenchmen ought to stay in France! Corrine thought, chewing nervously on a fingernail. She glanced over her shoulder at the sun, hovering just above the steeple of Christ Church, two blocks away in Spitalfields. *I shouldn't have stayed so long—now I won't have time to visit with Mr. Burke.*

A smile came to her lips in spite of her worries about the lateness of the hour. Anna hadn't wanted her to leave. After she had coaxed the child to take some milk—this time from a cup—and a little bread, the child had leaned her head against Corrine's bosom and put her thin arms up around her neck.

She couldn't just walk away and leave her like that, so she had decided to rock the child until she fell asleep. Anna must have sensed Corrine's anxiety, for every time Corrine thought the little girl was asleep and made an attempt to ease her into Mrs. O'Reilly's arms, she would wake up and cling even tighter.

Anna had finally drifted off to sleep, but now Corrine pictured the child waking up in a crib later and looking for her through the iron bars. *I hope she won't cry,* she thought, while knowing that she probably would. *She won't understand that I can't stay there. All she'll know is that I'm gone, just like her mother.*

Gerald's cruel words about her own daughter echoed in her mind, and Corrine tried desperately to rationalize her own pain and guilt. *My sister Mary was more of a mother to her than I was,* she reasoned. *Perhaps Jenny didn't even realize I was gone.* Deep down, Corrine knew it wasn't true. She had seen the pain in little Anna, and she knew she had done the same thing to her own tiny daughter. But her own wounds went too deep; she couldn't bear to let her thoughts take her in that direction for very long.

Think about Adam Burke, she told herself. Gerald was right—her attention hadn't been totally focused on the man. That had to change, for Gerald would be furious if their plans didn't turn out profitably.

Thirty minutes later, the chaise pulled into Adam's carriage drive. As the driver helped her to the ground, Corrine noticed the clouds that reddened the sky where the sun was just visible on the horizon. Perhaps this would work out after all; surely he would feel compelled to ask her to stay for supper. And since this wasn't Sunday, all the servants, including Rachel, would eat in the kitchen while she would have Adam to herself.

Instructing the driver to wait out front, she brushed the dust from her silk shawl, then squared her shoulders and walked down the cobbled footpath to the front door.

The maid Irene—or was it Marie?—led her to Adam's drawing room, where Rachel, Bernice and her family, and Adam were seated. The conversation ceased as they turned their heads toward Corrine.

A pain stabbed her heart—they had looked so content a moment ago, laughing as if they were truly enjoying one another's company. How long had it been since she had felt that way about being with people? Had she ever felt that way at all? She had gotten just a taste of it yesterday when Penelope and Mrs. O'Reilly watched with amazement on their faces as Anna drank from the bottle. And last night, letting down her guard long enough to share her feelings with Rachel—that had been nice, in a way, even though Gerald had made her feel so wretched.

"You're just in time to see Lucy's portrait," Adam said.

Corrine put on her most feminine smile. "I'm so glad." Jack was holding the sketchbook on his knees, and he stood to hand it to her. "Why, thank you," she said sweetly, taking the chair Adam had fetched. She looked down at the portrait, and this time her smile was genuine.

"Why, Rachel, this is beautiful . . . the best you've ever done!" she cried.

"Thank you, ma'am."

She looked up at Lucy, seated between her mother and father on the sofa. "And what a pretty model she had to work with, too!"

While the girl blushed, Bernice gave Corrine a grudging smile. "Thank you for sayin' that, Mrs. Hammond."

"How was the child you visited?" Adam asked after Corrine had handed the sketch back over to Jack.

Her smile faltered for just a second. "Much better. It seems she won't eat for anyone but me, though."

"Then you plan to go there every day?"

She shrugged and met Rachel's eyes. "I suppose I'll have to. She's such a thin little one—we can't let her starve."

Just days ago Corrine would have gladly used the sympathy evident on everyone's faces to make herself look like a heroine, a compassionate rescuer of children. Now, however, a lump had settled in the pit of her stomach. She folded her hands in her lap and tried not to think about the fact that Anna was probably waking up about now, crying for her . . . or about how she was going to hide future trips to the orphanage from Gerald.

From the corner of her eye, she saw Bernice studying her with a mixture of admiration and suspicion. Corrine had known instinctively from that first Sunday dinner that the cook didn't like her—and it hadn't troubled her for even a second. Now she found herself wondering what the woman was thinking . . . and wondering why she cared so much.

"That is kind of you," Bernice finally said in a low voice.

Corrine looked over at her, surprised at the surge of gratitude those words caused in her heart. "Thank you, Bernice."

Bernice nodded, getting to her feet and taking the sketchbook from her husband. "Well, I've got things to do in the kitchen." She turned to Rachel and put a hand on her shoulder. "I can't tell you how happy you've made me today."

At her mother's signal, Lucy got up and followed her parents out of the room, first thanking Rachel for the portrait. "You made me look like a fine lady," she told her with a self-conscious smile.

"Would you like to stay for supper?" Adam asked Corrine after Bernice's family had left. He darted a glance at Rachel. "It's not very fancy tonight, but Bernice always cooks more than enough."

"How did you know I was starving?" Corrine gushed softly, clasping her hands together.

Rachel abruptly realized that she should be with the other servants. She had no cause to expect anything different, but nonetheless she had felt a stab of pain when Mr. Burke offered Corrine the invitation. Perhaps he was beginning to care for her after all. "I'll go help in the kitchen," she murmured, rising from her chair.

Adam came to his feet in an instant. "But won't you have supper with us, Rachel?"

She didn't have to look at her mistress to know the message she would be sending with her gray eyes. "Really, sir, I don't mind eating with the others."

"Oh, but we insist," he said with a hopeful, crooked smile. "Don't we, Mrs. Hammond? I mean, Corrine?"

"Yes, of course we do," Corrine replied lightheartedly but with a noticeable lack of conviction.

"Then it's all settled," declared Adam.

The next thing Rachel knew, the man was offering one elbow to her and the other to Corrine, then ushering them down the hall to the dining room.

Regardless of the fact that she and Corrine had gotten closer yesterday, Rachel knew that her mistress would vent her fury on the way home again. She wished she had thought to slip out of the room when Bernice and her family had left. But it was too late for that now. Adam Burke had her hand pressed to his side, and she had no choice but to walk with him.

~

A fragment of sallow April moon hung over the chilled night air. In the moving carriage, silence stretched between Corrine and Rachel. Corrine sent occasional glances in Rachel's direction. The servant girl across from her just sat staring at her hands in her lap as if ashamed to look at her mistress.

He's absolutely smitten with her, Corrine thought, drawing her shawl tighter around her shoulders. Not that Adam Burke's actions had made it obvious. He had been the perfect gentleman during dinner, dividing his attention equally between both of his guests. But she had noticed the way his eyes lit up every time he looked at Rachel.

Then to top it off, he had carried a carton of books out to their carriage to lend to the girl. He had never asked if Corrine would be interested in reading any of them. Did he think she was illiterate?

Corrine wondered how long this had been going on. She had never noticed the man paying much attention to Rachel before, but perhaps she had been too sure of herself to even consider that he might be interested in someone else.

Her pride was wounded at the idea that he might choose a servant over her. Corrine lifted her eyes to glare at the girl but found herself strangely touched by the misery on her face. She remembered how Rachel had come into the room while Gerald was hurting her. It was a risky thing to do; he could easily have turned on her.

It dawned on Corrine why Rachel looked so miserable now. *She knows Adam doesn't care for me, and she's wondering if I know it!*

The girl had not had enough experience with men to recognize the adoration that had been in Adam Burke's eyes, but Corrine had seen it. *I wonder how she feels about him?*

She straightened in her seat. No matter how Rachel felt, this was a disastrous turn of events. How could she tell Gerald that the possibility of profiting from Mr. Burke was most likely nonexistent? She remembered the pressure of Gerald's hand on her face yesterday. What would he do if he found out?

The remorse that had crept into her thoughts yesterday came back with even more intensity, and she began to regret having ever met Gerald Moore.

"Rachel, are you cold?" she asked suddenly.

"No, ma'am," answered the girl, but her arms were hugged to her sides now.

"Why didn't you bring a shawl? Well, I suppose you didn't realize we'd be out so late." Corrine slid over in her seat and motioned for the girl to cross over and sit beside her. "We'll share mine."

~

When they arrived home, Corrine was surprised to see Gerald still in the house at this late hour. He wasn't even dressed in his evening clothes. "Aren't you going out?" She lifted her face to accept the kiss he brushed against her cheek.

Gerald shook his head. "After our . . . disagreement yesterday, I realized that I've been neglecting you. I haven't been spending enough time at home lately."

He was lying, she could tell at once. How many other times had his flattery been laced with lies and she had been too self-absorbed to realize it? Something must have gone wrong at his gambling place. Had he lost all their money?

Corrine knew better than to ask. For years she had been aware of his violent past, but she had never thought he would lash out and hurt her. Now she feared his temper more than anything.

After ordering Rachel to bring him something to eat and

some wine, Gerald looked at Corrine and smiled. "You've been gone for hours—I take it to be a good sign."

Corrine had years of practice forming her lips into smiles that she didn't feel inside. She offered such a smile to him now. "Well, the man just insisted that I stay for supper!"

"Really!" Avarice shone from Gerald's eyes as he rubbed his hands together. "And what did you and the gentleman find to talk about?"

Corrine lifted her chin haughtily. "Why, he talked about *me,* of course."

He looked pleased with her answer. "I believe we're about to strike it rich soon, love!"

"Well, he seems rather cautious with his money," she countered quickly. She didn't want Gerald *too* optimistic—he was pressuring her enough as it was. While she realized it would be impossible to deceive him indefinitely into thinking that Adam had romantic feelings for her, she certainly wasn't going to come out with the truth until it was absolutely necessary. *I wish Adam Burke would just leave town!* she thought. Then Gerald would have to find someone else to target, and her problems would be over.

Or would they?

~

Downstairs in the kitchen, Rachel warmed up slices of yesterday's roast beef and wondered at the expression that had been in Mr. Burke's eyes all during supper. Just the memory of how he had looked at her made her heartbeat quicken. Had Corrine noticed?

She wondered what those looks meant. Was it his way of showing Corrine that he wasn't interested in her? Yet his eyes had held the same expression earlier, when she had been alone with him as she finished Lucy's portrait. That couldn't have been for Corrine's benefit.

She shook her head and scolded herself for having such lofty pretensions. After all, Mr. Burke was a kind man, and she was still just a servant. He was just being friendly because she drew Lucy's portrait.

Nevertheless, a picture of his warm brown eyes kept returning to her mind, and she knew that tonight when her head touched the pillow, she would close her eyes and think about the way he had looked at her.

~

"Sorry, mate. Never heard the name before," said the saloon keeper at The Gilded Mermaid.

Joseph Price wasn't too surprised. After all, this was the first place he had looked since arriving in London that morning and procuring lodging. "Would you recall seeing a gentleman with light blond features, rather thin lips, and a mustache? He would have only been a customer for the past six weeks or so."

Again, the man shook his head. "I hope you find the bloke so he can claim his money, but we get sailors from all ports here. After a while, all their faces look alike."

Joseph thanked the saloon keeper, left the address of his rooming house, and asked that he be contacted if Gerald Moore should come into the establishment. "It's worth a fiver to me," he added.

By the time Joseph's footsteps rang against the stones leading to the front door of his Butler Street rooming house, darkness had blanketed the city for hours. He had made inquiries to several other establishments and was now in need of some

213

sleep. *Ten years ago, I would have made do with a nap now and then until I found who I was looking for,* he thought wryly. *My age is catching up with me.*

He would have to settle down one day, he realized. He was in good physical condition for a man of forty-two, but time had a way of slipping up on a person. And as much as he loved his occupation, sometimes in the still hours of the night in yet another strange town, he wondered what his life would have been like if he had chosen a wife and family instead of wanderings. He would die one day, and then what would remain of the life he had lived?

It's not too late to settle down, he told himself, knowing that it would probably never happen.

From his waistcoat pocket he was fishing out the key that the proprietress of the house had reluctantly lent him, when a man's voice startled him.

"Mr. Price, I assume?"

Joseph squinted and stepped closer to the shadowy eaves of the porch. The voice probably belonged to one of the saloon keepers whose memory had been jarred by the offer of five quid. "Who wants to know?" When his eyes had adjusted to the blackness, he realized that two men were standing by the front door. One, apparently the one who had spoken, appeared to be in his mid to late fifties, while the other was much younger, possibly still in his twenties.

"My name is August Berrington," said the older man. He extended his hand. "Inspector Berrington, Scotland Yard."

Joseph shook the man's hand. How had Scotland Yard learned of his presence in London? And more to the point, why had two of its men come to call? "I must say you have me at a loss, Inspector."

"Then we must explain ourselves." The inspector introduced Mr. Green, the younger man, and asked Joseph if he would mind accompanying them in their carriage to a café on Regent Street that stayed open for most of the night. "We're interested in the questions you've been asking in the gin houses today."

The café, located on the ground floor of an inn called The Sycamore House, still had customers at its tables from the theatre crowds. The three men took a corner table, ordered sandwiches and coffee, and made small talk until the waiter returned with their food. Here in the light, Joseph was able to study the men seated across from him. Inspector Berrington was a stocky, square-shouldered man, his face dominated by a thick gray mustache. Mr. Green, trim and well dressed, wore wire-rimmed eyeglasses. He seemed to be nervously anxious to please his superior.

When the waiter had left them to themselves, Inspector Berrington launched into an immediate explanation of their visit. "We've had men in saloons all over London today, and lo and behold, it turns out that someone else is making inquiries about a person who matches the physical description of the man we're looking for."

"You don't say?" said Joseph, trying to hide his surprise. In all of his searching for Gerald Moore and Corrine Hammond, he had never had a clue that Scotland Yard was on their trail as well. He had taken for granted that, like Squire Nowells, none of the victims or their families had wanted to involve the authorities because of the publicity involved.

"And why are you looking for this person?" He took a swallow of his coffee. "Assuming that we're indeed talking about the same man."

215

The inspector directed a significant glance to his young assistant, then cleared his throat. "You left your name and address with barkeeps all over town, Mr. Price, which is how we found you. Never mind our purposes. I'd be interested in knowing why you're searching for a man named Gerald Moore. That was the name you gave, wasn't it?"

"You didn't answer my question, Inspector Berrington. Why do you think we're on the same trail?"

"We have no name for our suspect," the inspector explained, "but the physical description exactly matches the man you're looking for. Obviously, we're wondering if he's the same person."

"I don't know if I can answer that," Joseph said. "Not without knowing what your suspect has done."

Leaning back and crossing his arms, Inspector Berrington nodded at his assistant. "Mr. Green will tell you that."

The younger man sat up straight, eager to do his part with the investigation. "In the Limehouse parish this morning, a boy scavenging in an alley came upon a woman's body. She had been dead less than twenty-four hours." He swallowed and continued. "She was a prostitute from an establishment on Narrow Street. A man with blond hair, blue eyes, and a mustache had given her some trouble recently. And they were both seen in the Waterman's Arms Tavern last evening."

Joseph had to sit silently for a minute and digest this information. Could Gerald Moore be a murderer, too? Surely a man who would extort money from people had very little respect for human life. But murder? "Why the secrecy?" he asked at length. "Why haven't you posted the suspect's description?"

"We may be forced to do that soon," Berrington answered.

"But right now we'd rather give the suspect the illusion that his crime has not yet been discovered. If he panics and leaves the city, we may never find him."

"How do you know he hasn't left already?"

"Instincts . . . and an educated guess. The woman was buried under a huge pile of crates in the back of an alley. He didn't want her body to be discovered for a while. Someone who planned to leave town immediately wouldn't go to all that trouble."

Joseph nodded. "Otherwise, he would have wanted to leave the scene as quickly as possible. So you aren't telling anyone why you're looking for this person?"

"No, not yet." The inspector studied Joseph's face with tired, knowing eyes. "We gave a phony reason . . . just as you did."

"I beg your pardon?"

"We know your reputation, Mr. Price. You've let it be known that this Mr. Moore you're looking for has come into some money. Why would someone hire a detective of your caliber to find an heir when they usually turn up sooner or later?"

Before Joseph could answer, Berrington went on. "Now we don't think you're looking for Moore because of the murdered woman, because you've obviously come from out of town to find him. And how could you possibly know about a crime that we just discovered ourselves this morning?"

Joseph gave a reluctant nod. "You're right, of course. My reasons for seeking Mr. Moore have nothing to do with the woman's murder. And I'm not convinced we're looking for the same man."

"That's entirely possible," agreed the inspector. "But your

inquiries have given us a possible name for our suspect when we hadn't one before. You can understand our eagerness to know everything we can about Gerald Moore."

Joseph toyed with the handle of his coffee cup and wondered what the ethical response would be. If indeed Moore were out there murdering women, then certainly he needed to be caught. But his orders not to involve the law had to be considered, too. If he shared what little information he had with Scotland Yard, there was a distinct possibility that they would find Moore before he did.

But how will I feel if it turns out that he killed that woman and I've not helped ensure that he's caught as soon as possible? He thought about his two sisters, Carolyn and Frances. What if a killer were loose in Bristol? Would he not want the police to have every clue available to find the culprit before he murdered again?

Sighing, he ran his fingers through his thick brown hair and looked up at Inspector Berrington. "I still doubt that we're looking for the same man, but I'm going to tell you what I know about the personal habits of Gerald Moore. The reason I'm looking for him has nothing to do with the murdered woman, so I'd rather keep that to myself to protect the privacy of my client's family. If you find Moore, I'm sure you'll determine whether or not he's your killer." To himself he added, *But if I find him first, I'll whisk him out from under your very noses.*

13

THERE'S a Mr. Solomon to see you, sir." Irene
announced Thursday morning at the library door.
Adam set his newspaper on the carpet beside his
chair and got to his feet. "Already?" He had only sent Jack
with the message an hour ago, asking the art dealer to call at
his convenience. "Please show him in. And ask Bernice if
she'll send Lucy's portrait in here."

A genial-looking man with gray hair and spectacles came
into the room at the maid's bidding. If Mr. Solomon was startled at Adam's appearance, he didn't show it. He shook
Adam's outstretched hand before easing himself down in a
chair.

"I wasn't expecting to see you today," Adam told his visitor, feeling guilty at asking an elderly man to take a carriage
ride across town to see him. He hadn't thought to ask Rachel
how old Solomon was. "There certainly was no rush."

Mr. Solomon chuckled, his eyes crinkling at the corners
behind his spectacles. "I haff been training my grandson Levi
to take my place. I'm planning ahead to the time when I'm no
longer able to work, you see. When I received your message, I
decided that it was a perfect time to test the boy's mettle."

"Aren't you worried? A boy running a business alone . . ."

The man laughed again. "My wife tells me I must stop referring to Levi as a boy. You see, he is twenty-three—" He paused, his forehead drawn in concentration for a couple of seconds. "Twenty-*four* years old, and with a wife and child already. My! Time slows down for no one, does it not."

"No, it doesn't," Adam agreed. He smiled at the man. He could see why Rachel liked this Mr. Solomon so much.

"Tell me, Mr. Burke, how did you come to know about my shop?"

"Miss Rachel Jones told me about you. She was here yesterday and sketched a portrait of my cook's daughter." Irene came back through the door as if on cue, the sketchbook in her hands. As Adam instructed, she handed it to the elderly man and left the room.

"Miss Jones said we should keep the sketch in the book until it's ready to be framed, so the paper won't crease," said Adam. "Perhaps I should order another book for her so that she won't have to stop sketching."

Mr. Solomon nodded and lifted the heavy cardboard cover. "That is a good idea." A broad smile came to his face. "And you say Miss Jones drew this?"

"Yes, sir."

"I haff been asking her to let me see some of her work." He looked up at Adam for a second with an expression of pure delight. "I had a *feeling* that the young lady was talented!"

"Do you know her very well?"

The man shook his head, squinting as he studied the portrait. "I know nothing about dear Miss Jones's personal life, only that she loves art. On market days she comes to my shop—always hurrying, but never in too much of a hurry to chat with an old man."

Adam became even more interested. He leaned forward intently. "Why do you think she wouldn't show you her work?"

"I don't know." Mr. Solomon gently closed the cover to Rachel's sketchbook. "Perhaps she thinks because they are penciled sketches, they are inferior. I sell mostly paintings, you see."

"Isn't there a market for sketches?"

Mr. Solomon smiled. "My friend, there is a market for everything in London. But most people want oils or watercolors to hang on their walls."

Leaning back in his chair again, Adam crossed his arms and thought. After a long and sleepless night, he had come to the painful conclusion that he was letting his heart run away with him as far as the girl was concerned. She probably thought him a fool at supper last night, the way his eyes had constantly drifted in her direction.

But what could be wrong with aiding someone blessed with such a talent? He could well afford to do so, and Rachel didn't need to know that he was even involved. *It would be the Christian thing to do,* he told himself. "Do you think Miss Jones would be interested in oils or watercolors if I bought some? The paints, I mean, and canvases and whatever else she would need."

Pursing his lips, the man gave his host a quizzical look. "If *you* bought them for the young lady?"

"Anonymously, of course," said Adam. An idea came to him then. "Perhaps you wouldn't mind letting her think that they're a gift from you. I'd be in your debt."

"She admires the paintings every time she comes in my shop—I think she is fascinated by the colors. But the oils would not do her any good, my friend. She wouldn't know how to use them."

Adam tapped himself lightly on the forehead. "Of course! She needs lessons for that, doesn't she?"

"Most definitely," replied Mr. Solomon, pushing his spectacles up on the bridge of his nose. "She is good, but one can go only so far with talent alone. She must learn technique."

"Can you recommend a teacher?"

"I most certainly can. He studied in Paris for two years and is now an associate at the Royal Gallery. The young man is a most promising young talent."

"Who is he?"

The old man's smile became angelic. "My other grandson, Reuben Solomon. Would you like to meet him?"

Adam laughed out loud. The man was crafty, too! "I'll take your word for that, Mr. Solomon. Would you mind telling Miss Jones for me?"

"But why do you not want her to know the lessons and paints are from you?" asked the elderly man. "Because Reuben is still a student, he will charge you a reasonable price . . . but you may still expect to spend a tidy sum. The giver of a gift of such magnitude should be recognized."

"Because I don't want to burden her . . . to make her feel unduly grateful to me."

For the first time, the man's old eyes seemed to take notice of Adam's scars. "You don't wish that she should be *burdened* with feelings of gratitude?" he echoed gently. "Since when did gratitude become something to be feared? Perhaps the young lady would *like* to know that the lessons are from you."

Adam shook his head. "I'll pay extra if you'll deliver the news to her and keep my secret. Do you have her address?"

"I'm afraid I haff not."

"I've got it written down in my study," said Adam, getting to his feet. "Her employer sends messages to me occasionally. If you'd be so kind as to wait here, I'll go get it." He stopped just short of the door and looked back at Mr. Solomon. "I seem to have forgotten my manners—may I send for some tea?"

The old man waved a hand in the air. "I would enjoy nothing better, my friend, but perhaps some other time. The clouds were becoming dark while I was on my way here. I do not wish to be caught in a storm."

Adam nodded. "I'll hurry with the address then."

Smiling, Mr. Solomon added, "Even more important than the rain, I must go back and make sure that Levi has not given away my Delacroix for twenty pounds."

~

Corrine was standing in front of the mirror over the dining room table when Gerald walked into the room, clad in a gray morning coat and trousers. "Why are you getting dressed in here?" he yawned.

"I didn't want to disturb you." Giving him a slightly nervous smile, she set her pot of rouge on the table. "You're up rather early, aren't you?"

"I don't know. What time is it?"

"Ten o'clock."

He yawned again, walked over, and kissed her on the lips. "That early? Well, I suppose staying home at night has its merits. I'll probably need a nap later, though."

He jerked his head at a noise down in the kitchen. "Is Rachel making breakfast?"

Corrine nodded, straightening the ribbon at the collar of her dress. "It should be ready soon."

Gerald reached over and picked up a bottle of perfume from the table. He lifted the stopper, waved it in front of his nose and smiled. "This has an enchanting aroma. Where are you going?"

Corrine answered quickly, "Why, to pay a call on Adam Burke."

His eyebrows lifted. "Really? He's invited you to visit?"

"Of course," she replied airily. "Didn't I tell you last night?"

"No, you didn't."

"Are you sure? Oh, well, he did. And that's where I'm going."

Smiling, Gerald set the perfume bottle back on the table, came up behind her, and put his arms around her waist. "I'm pleased that you're listening to me," he said, nuzzling her shoulder. "You'll thank me, too, when Burke 'lends' you enough money to pay your debts until your 'estate' is settled. Then perhaps we'll go to Paris before we find another sheep waiting to be fleeced."

Corrine watched in the mirror as Gerald kissed her neck, and she felt a repulsion she had never felt around him before. It was all she could do to keep from pushing him away. Fortunately, he gave her shoulders one final squeeze, then stepped back.

"Paris would be nice," she said, picking up her hairbrush. *But I'll never see it,* she thought darkly. *You've been promising to take me there for eight years, but you always manage to find another "sheep" right away.*

Gerald leaned against the wall next to the mirror and studied her face. "Is something wrong?"

224

"Wrong?" Corrine winced as she pulled her brush through a tangled curl. "What could be wrong?"

"I don't know. You're not worrying about that brat in the orphanage, are you?"

Corrine shrugged. "Not at all."

"That's good." Then he folded his arms and cocked his head. "Are you sure?"

"Absolutely," she assured him. "Like you said, I just let that minister confuse me for a little while, and I wasn't thinking straight."

"I'm glad to hear you've come to your senses. Besides, you can still see the child every Tuesday. I never heard of anybody starving to death when there's food about. She doesn't need you." He frowned at the door leading to the kitchen stairway. "Of course, *I* may starve if Rachel doesn't come in here soon with something to eat. What's taking her so long?"

"She had to get dressed, too. We're leaving right after breakfast."

"Why are you taking her with you? The idea is to spend time *alone* with the man."

"You forget what kind of man Adam Burke is. He thinks I'm a good Christian lady—one who wouldn't travel about town unescorted." Giving him a reassuring wink, she added, "Besides, Rachel knows she must disappear as soon as possible. She'll visit with the other servants."

~

After a debate on whether to put up the hood in light of the approaching storm, Corrine gave directions to the driver.

"We're not really going to Mr. Burke's?" Rachel asked.

"I'm sorry—I couldn't tell you before. I was afraid something in your face would show in front of Gerald."

The carriage started moving, and Rachel spread her open palms on each side of her seat to steady herself. "Miss Corrine," she said, biting her lip, "are you sure he believed you?"

"Why, of course he did. Why wouldn't he?"

Rachel craned her neck to look back at the house, getting smaller with each beat of the horse's hooves on the stones. "I don't know, ma'am. Perhaps I'm making things up in my mind, but the way he looked at you when he walked us to the door seemed . . . strange."

Giving a sigh of exasperation, Corrine glanced over her shoulder. From the worried look on the girl's face, she half expected to see Gerald standing in the street watching them. "You're just more afraid of him since he threatened us," she said when she'd turned back around. "Gerald never goes out in the daytime. Besides, he's probably back in bed and sound asleep right now."

Rachel nodded, but she didn't look convinced. When the carriage was a block away from Sydney Street, which they would normally take to go to Mr. Burke's, Rachel leaned forward and put a hand on Corrine's knee.

"Ma'am . . . please tell the driver to turn up ahead."

"But, Rachel, this is silly!"

"Please!"

She's never been this insistent before, Corrine thought. *Is it because she wants to see Adam?*

Perhaps Rachel was just as smitten with him as he obviously was with her. But even if that were so, surely she wouldn't make up all of this just to be able to see him again. And Rachel had never been one to lie.

"Driver!" She called twice before the man slowed the horse and turned to look at her. "Turn here at Sydney Street." She pointed to the right. "We want to take Bow Road."

With a shrug the man flicked his whip and reined the horse to take the right turn. "I still think this is ridiculous!" Corrine snorted. Yet she was taken aback at the great relief that washed over the girl's face.

"Thank you, ma'am," Rachel breathed, settling back in her seat.

"What am I supposed to tell Adam Burke—that we just decided to pop in?"

"We did it once be—"

"I know that," Corrine snapped impatiently. "But it isn't proper for a lady to make a habit of it. He'll think I'm too forward."

Rachel looked as if she feared her mistress would change her mind. "But what's more important, ma'am? What Mr. Burke thinks, or what Mr. Gerald will do if he finds out you went to the orphanage?"

Corrine resigned herself to looking like a fool in front of Adam Burke, but she was still convinced that Rachel's imagination was playing tricks on her. She was an artist, after all, and artists were prone to flights of fancy.

Twenty minutes later, the chaise came to a halt in Adam's carriage drive. "All right, Rachel," Corrine sighed as she waited for the driver to tie off the reins. "I hope you're happy! Now I don't want to stay here long—I'm still determined to see if Anna is all right."

Just as the driver was helping them both to the ground, the

ringing of a horse's hooves sounded, coming up the cobbled road. It wasn't unusual to hear horses and carriages anywhere in London, but Rachel glanced anxiously in the direction of the sound.

"Ma'am!" she cried, grabbing Corrine by the arm.

Corrine's back was to the road. When she turned around, a hired tilbury was just passing their carriage. Gerald, still in his morning coat, smiled and tipped his hat from his seat beside the driver.

For a long time neither woman could speak. They watched the tilbury disappear down the road.

"Where did he get a carriage so fast?" Corrine finally whispered, a hand up to her throat.

"I don't know," Rachel breathed. She was light-headed from her heart hammering rapidly in her chest. "But what if he had followed us to the children's home?"

Corrine shuddered. "I don't want to think about it." Turning to look Rachel in the eyes, she put a hand on her shoulder. "That's twice you've saved me from his temper."

"It's all right, Missus."

"No, it's not. I've called you stupid since the first day you came to live with us." She swallowed. "You're not stupid at all—it's your wits that saved me."

Uncomfortable with so much gratitude, Rachel shifted on one foot and glanced towards Mr. Burke's lawn. "Bernice's Jack is coming this way."

Corrine dropped her hand from Rachel's shoulder. "Oh, dear. . . . I suppose we *have* to stay here now."

Rachel's eyes widened. "You weren't thinking about—"

"Going on to the orphanage? I was considering it. Don't you think Gerald's on his way home now?"

"I don't know, ma'am. But I wouldn't care to risk it."

"But what if Anna won't eat?"

"What if Mr. Gerald comes back this way?"

Corrine put a hand up to her cheek and looked back towards the road. "Anna will think . . ."

Giving a wave to the approaching gardener, Rachel said gently, "You got her to take some food for two days now. If she won't eat today, she won't starve, and you can find a way to see her tomorrow."

"Tomorrow?" Corrine echoed sadly, blinking her eyes. "I suppose so." At the sound of Jack's footsteps on the gravel, she turned on her heel. "Good morning, Jack," she said brightly. "Is Mr. Burke in?"

~

Joseph Price held a finger on one of the advertisements for rentals in the *London Daily News* spread out on the library table. The sheet of stationery in front of him was covered with addresses.

It'll take me a week to check out all of these, he thought glumly, surveying the stack of last month's newspapers. *Not to mention combing the saloons at night. They knew what they were doing when they chose the biggest city in the world!*

At least he had a description of the man and a name. *Let's hope he feels safe enough to use his real name again.*

He folded the newspaper and reached for another, trying to ignore the rumbling in his stomach. So great had been his haste to leave his room and get back to work that he had slipped out of the boardinghouse before his new landlady had breakfast laid out. *She likely wonders if I'm still up there asleep right now,* he thought wryly, *and if her new boarder is a layabout.*

Food and sleep were necessary to Joseph, but right now his single-minded determination to beat Scotland Yard to catch Gerald Moore—and Corrine Hammond—took precedence over everything.

~

Thirty minutes after Mr. Solomon's departure, Adam had just walked into the kitchen from the garden when Lucy spoke to him. "Marie's lookin' for you, Mr. Adam. You've got some visitors in the front parlor."

"Did she say who they are?"

"Mrs. Hammond and Rachel," replied the girl.

Adam looked down at his fingernails. He had not been able to resist digging up an earthworm from the underside of one of the planters—an experiment to see if the ever hungry robin nestlings would eat from his hand when the parents were out foraging for food. The experiment had succeeded, and now he had to step over to the basin and clean his hands.

"Where's your mother?" he asked as Lucy handed him a towel.

"Papa made her go lie down after breakfast was cleared."

He stopped wiping his hands and looked at her, concerned. "Is it her rheumatism?"

"Yes, sir. The dampness in the air and all."

"Shall I send for a doctor?"

"She wouldn't let Papa. Irene's comin' in here to help me with lunch, and Mummy says she'll be up before time to cook supper."

"Tell her not to worry about supper," he said, handing the girl the towel. "Just some bread and cheese or whatever you've got cold will do fine."

"Beggin' your pardon, sir, but you know she won't—"

Adam sighed. "Yes, I know. I'll just have to tell your papa to lay down the law to her."

Her face doubtful, the girl nodded. "All right, sir, but she don't always listen to Papa . . . not where her kitchen is concerned."

"Then *I'll* go up and talk with her after lunch. Just let me know when she's awake."

~

Adam made his way up the steps leading to the rest of the house, hoping that he didn't smell of dirt and earthworms. His heart had jumped in his chest at the mention of Rachel's name, but he was determined not to take advantage of the girl's obvious pity for him. *I let myself get carried away yesterday. It won't happen again.*

By the time he reached the open door to the front parlor, he had convinced himself that a restrained politeness was the best way to handle the situation. *For both of them,* he thought. During last night's supper, he had realized that his instincts about Corrine Hammond were still on the mark . . . although there had been a sense of futility about her flirtations that had puzzled him.

"Good morning, ladies," he said, pretending not to see Corrine's daintily lifted hand as he took a chair across from the ones they were seated in. "What brings you out on such a foreboding day?"

"How foolish you must think me!" Corrine bubbled. "But we were out for a ride and suddenly realized that a storm was almost upon us." As if on cue, a peal of thunder rattled the windows on either side of her chair. Seconds later, sheets of rain hammered loudly against the glass.

While still intending to remain aloof, Adam knew that he couldn't very well send them out into the deluge. "Is your driver taken care of?" he asked, standing and walking over to peer out the window.

"I believe your man Jack offered him shelter."

"Then why don't we go to my library?" he offered, finally allowing himself to glance at Rachel for the first time since he walked into the room. *My word . . . she looks stunning!* he told himself before forcing his eyes away. The yellow dress she wore enhanced the golden streaks in her hair, and he wondered if she even knew it. "We shouldn't be so close to the windows."

"If you're positive that we aren't intruding," Corrine murmured. "Because I certainly don't want to be a pest."

You don't say. Another clap of thunder rattled the windows again, and Adam led the women to the library. This time he did not offer an arm to either of them.

14

WELL, I'm certainly glad the rain didn't last long," Corrine sniffed as the wheels of their carriage splashed through glimmering rain puddles in the streets, carrying them away from Adam Burke's cold hospitality. "He didn't even invite us to stay for lunch!"

"Perhaps he was ill," Rachel said quietly. She wished her mistress would stop talking about Adam, for she didn't even want to think about the way he had received them with such obvious reluctance. While he hadn't been actually *rude*, it had been plain to see that he had more important things to do than entertain them through a rainstorm.

He didn't even say a word to me, she thought. She had no right to expect him to, of course. After all, servants were generally expected to be seen and not heard when acting as traveling companions for their employers. But he had been so kind yesterday when he watched her sketch and later at supper with Corrine. Did he think she was too forward yesterday . . . acting above her station?

One good thing came out of his behavior today. She was absolutely convinced that Adam Burke was not likely to be beguiled by Corrine's charms. Rachel didn't have to feel guilty every time she delivered a message to his house or chatted with Bernice and Lucy.

She glanced across at Corrine, careful to avoid any show of sympathy on her face. Yet, she admitted, she was growing fond of her missus. While she was relieved that Corrine wouldn't be taking money from Adam, she knew that Corrine's failure was going to put her in an awful spot with Gerald.

~

"Why, Miss Rachel Jones!" beamed Mr. Solomon two hours later, as the door of his shop closed behind her, causing the bell over it to send out one last tinkle. "I was going to call upon you tomorrow—now you haff saved an old man the trouble."

"You were?" Rachel set her basket down just inside the door and made her way over to her friend. "Why?"

He pointed to a huge trunk in the back of the gallery. "You see? I must find places to put more paintings." After glancing out the shop window, he lowered his voice. "From the estate of a certain member of Parliament who passed on last year. He did not leave enough money to satisfy his eldest son, who wishes to continue a life of wanton idleness."

He threw up his hands, his voice rising with indignation. "So the worthless boy wants to sell paintings that haff been in his family for years. He is selling some of the carpets and furniture, too, I have heard." As if suddenly remembering that Rachel had asked him a question, he said, "There is some good news I must tell you, Miss Jones. First, would you like some tea? Levi is upstairs making a pot."

"No, thank you." Rachel stifled her impatience to hear Mr.

Solomon's news. He would get around to it when he was ready.

"What are you doing, marketing in the afternoon?" he asked. "You haff always before shopped in the mornings."

"I had somewhere to go this morning with my missus." She shifted on one foot. "I'll have to be leaving soon."

"Oh, then you must forgive an old man's chattering! The good news I have to tell you is this. My gifted grandson I told you about—Reuben—is doing well in his studies, and he would like to train and inspire other lovers of art while he is trying to make a name for himself." Clasping his hands together at his chest, he exclaimed, "I have the portrait you made of the young girl here, to frame. I showed it to Reuben, and he would like you to be his first student!"

"*Me?* I'm honored. But I can't possibly afford . . ."

He waved away her protest. "Afford nothing! Reuben would first like to find out if he has the aptitude for teaching before committing himself to other pupils. You would be doing him a great favor by allowing him to teach you."

Rachel couldn't believe her ears. How many times had she stood in front of a painting, following the patterns of brush strokes and looking for any hints on how such a thing was done. "But how can I possibly accept such a generous offer?"

"But don't you see? Reuben will benefit from this, too. So many artists have not the temperament for teaching others—it is good that my grandson finds out before accepting any money from someone he may have to disappoint." He smiled. "But you will not be disappointed, my dear Miss Jones," he hastened to add. "He will teach you to use the oils and canvas just like the masters."

"Just like the masters?"

"Who knows? You may be selling your paintings in your old friend's gallery one day."

An incredulous smile on her face, Rachel reached for the man's hands. "My salary is small, but it'll help pay for the paints. This is so overwhelming!"

Mr. Solomon squeezed her hands. "The paints are included, my young friend." Seeing that Rachel was about to argue, he lifted a finger. "You must respect my age and not argue."

"I . . . I don't know what to say." Rachel remembered suddenly that Corrine and Gerald were waiting for her to prepare supper. "I'll come back and talk with you more as soon as I can," she said, smiling. "But I've got to go now. Thank you so much for your kindness—and please thank Reuben also!"

The old man returned Rachel's wave as she started for the door. "I will do that, Miss Jones."

Rachel lifted her basket, then stopped and turned around. "Sunday afternoons are the only times I have off. Will your grandson mind?"

Mr. Solomon chuckled. "We are Jews, my young friend. He will not mind."

~

What's wrong with me? Corrine wondered, pacing the kitchen. For the second time she lifted the lid to the pastry crock and peered inside, as if she might have overlooked a seed cake or torte the first time. Finding it still empty, she reached on the cupboard shelf above it for a much smaller crock. She took the crock and a spoon over to the table.

There was no sound coming from above the kitchen stairs, but just to make sure, Corrine eased over to them and listened. Gerald had been napping when she and Rachel returned from

Adam Burke's and was apparently still doing so. *I hope he sleeps all day,* she thought darkly. *In fact . . . I hope he never wakes up!*

Seating herself at the table, she opened the sugar crock and plunged the spoon inside. She brought the heaping spoon up to her mouth, closed her lips around the white powder, and allowed it to melt on her tongue.

How was she going to tell Gerald they were wasting their time? She had never failed before, partly because he was a genius at finding just the proper gentleman for her to pursue. What if he decided to leave her? As much as she now wished for such a thing, she knew Gerald would take every last penny with him.

Then what would she do? The only thing of value she owned was her treasured strand of pearls, and now that she realized how villainous Gerald could be, she feared that he might force her to dig them out of their hiding place and hand them over before he left.

I'd have to get a job then, she mused. But she had become accustomed to the soft life. She doubted that she could still work as hard as she did at the dairy back in Leawick. And the thought of standing in front of a machine in a textile mill or factory for ten to twelve hours every day was a horrid one. She would have no money for rent, no place to live.

Another possible profession came to Corrine's mind. She had seen those women, brazenly walking the streets along the river or standing near lampposts, lifting their skirts to reveal their ankles to any man who seemed a likely prospect. She shuddered in revulsion.

Corrine Hammond was no fool. She recognized the parallels between what those women did for a living and what she had been doing for the past eight years. She had always told herself that it wasn't the same, but deep down she knew that it was.

She took another spoonful of the sugar and closed her eyes. How did her life get to be such a mess?

Seconds later, she had just replaced the lid to the sugar crock and put it on its shelf when she heard the back door open. Rachel appeared at the head of the kitchen stairs with her basket. "Oh, hello, ma'am," she said with just a bit of her old shyness. Glancing back over her shoulder, she closed the door and lowered her voice. "I've got half a dozen seed cakes for you."

"Thank you." Corrine appraised the girl coming down the steps, wondering why her cheeks were glowing. Why, she had been rather pale and downcast this morning after their visit with Adam Burke.

At the foot of the stairs, Rachel walked over to set her basket on the table. Then she stood bashfully eyeing her mistress as if trying to decide whether to say something.

Ever impatient, Corrine sighed. "All right, Rachel. What is it?"

"Ma'am?"

"Why is your face all lit up like a Christmas candle? Are you going to tell me or keep me standing here guessing?"

Rachel was too excited to let the exasperation in Corrine's voice distress her. "Oh, Miss Corrine, something just happened!" Smiling, she hugged her arms to herself. "I can barely stand to think about it. It's so wonderful!"

"Well, what happened?"

"I'm going to get art lessons—free!"

"Art lessons? But you already know how to draw."

"Only with pencils. And there are still many things I don't

know. Mr. Solomon's grandson Reuben is going to teach me to work with paints!"

"Mr. Solomon?"

"The nice man who owns the shop next to Katrina's bakery." Hesitating briefly, she said, "I . . . I sometimes go there and look at the paintings when the marketing's done."

Corrine shook her head wearily and pulled out a chair for herself. "Sit down, Rachel." When they were seated across from each other, she reached into the basket for a seed cake wrapped in brown paper, then pushed the basket aside. "Now, why would this Mr. Solomon's grandson offer you free lessons?"

"Because he needs to give lessons to help support himself, but he wants to see if he has the temperament first."

Likely story! Corrine pressed her lips together. "Rachel, that doesn't make any sense. You're too young and naive to realize this, but there are lots of people out there who make a living by cheating others." *You should know,* came a voice in her head, but she shook the thought from her mind.

Rachel looked unsure for only a moment, then her expression changed to one of determination. "But how can he cheat me when the lessons are free?"

Shrugging her shoulders, Corrine pinched off a corner of the seed cake and popped it into her mouth. A light came on in her eyes. "The supplies. He'll have you use plenty of expensive paints and such, then bill you for double or even triple their worth."

"No, ma'am. The supplies are included."

"Then the young man hopes to win your affections."

Rachel clamped a hand over her mouth to stifle a giggle.

239

"I'm sorry, ma'am," she said, her face a mixture of shock and amusement. "It's just that we've never even met."

"What about this Mr. Solomon? Perhaps he wishes to curry favor so you'll be grateful enough to become his mistress."

"Mr. Solomon?" Rachel's eyes grew wide. "But he's very old. And happily married, too."

"Well, no man is too old to make a fool of himself," Corrine snorted. "I've seen plenty of old men with young mistresses."

Shaking her head, the girl insisted, "Not Mr. Solomon, ma'am. He's not like that."

Corrine had a strong feeling there was more to this than the obvious, and she was determined to find out what it was. "Then tell me everything he said to you."

"Well, I can't remember it all, ma'am," answered Rachel. "I became rather flustered when he started talking about the lessons. But he did say he was planning to come here tomorrow and tell me about it . . . before I showed up at his shop, that is."

"So you've given the man this address?"

Rachel's brows drew together as she thought this over. "No, I don't recall ever doing that."

I knew it! Corrine thought, her gray eyes glowing triumphantly. "Then how was he going to find his way here?"

"I don't know." She held up a hand. "Wait a minute—Mr. Solomon mentioned the portrait I made of Lucy. Mr. Burke must have already asked him to frame it and must have given him this address."

"Excuse me?"

"Mr. Burke asked yesterday, after I finished Lucy's portrait, if I knew someone who would do a good job framing it, and I recommended Mr. Solomon."

Corrine nodded. "I see. Then Adam has obviously already spoken with the old man. And he does indeed have my address because he sent that message about the charities here that time."

"But why would he find it necessary to give the address to Mr. Solomon?"

Corrine frowned. *I was right last night when I thought Adam Burke was smitten with her,* she mused. *And he still is, even though he put on that ridiculous act this morning.* A bitter smile turned up the corners of her mouth. She would have laughed out loud had her conclusion not added to her sense of impending doom. "Adam Burke. He has arranged to pay for these lessons."

"Mr. Burke? But that can't be. Mr. Solomon didn't even mention him."

"Of course he didn't," sighed Corrine. "Mr. Burke is a tediously honorable man who doesn't want you to feel beholden to him. So he instructed your Mr. Solomon to keep that part quiet."

Rachel shook her head. "Begging your pardon, ma'am, but why would Mr. Burke do that? Pay for the lessons, I mean."

Corrine knew that the bewilderment on the girl's face was genuine. She felt a twinge of envy at the innocence in those wide green eyes and the freshness that radiated from her expression. *You'll do all right in this world, Rachel Jones. There's a man out there who loves you, whether or not he is aware of it.* "Can't you guess why?" she finally asked.

"No, ma'am."

She sighed again. "Because he's in love with you . . . or is close to becoming so."

~

Rachel must have heard wrong. "In . . . what?"

"Oh, come now," Corrine said wearily. "Surely you've noticed the way he looks at you."

Rachel couldn't deny that she had seen something in his eyes yesterday and even the day before when they had looked at the robins together. She would have never gone so far as to presume that it meant anything other than a charitable warmth, however. "But this morning—"

"This morning he was *just* as obvious by his avoidance of you. No doubt he's in a battle with himself over his feelings. After all, you *are* just a servant and much younger than he is."

"That just can't be possible," Rachel murmured half to herself.

"And the scars," Corrine continued, as Rachel hadn't spoken. "That may have something to do with it, too. He may be afraid that you find him repulsive."

"Repulsive?" Rachel looked up with a start. "Why would he be afraid of that?"

Corrine seemed genuinely surprised. "He's got mirrors, hasn't he? I know you have this fascination with faces that aren't quite . . . aesthetic, but you can't rightly call him anything but ugly."

Stunned speechless, Rachel could only stare at her mistress. How could Corrine have seen Adam's face so many times and missed the beauty in it? Why, his eyes, though deeply masculine, were the gentlest Rachel had ever seen. She even found the crooked half-smile charming.

There's no use in even hoping that she's right, Rachel thought.

He's never going to be really interested in a servant, no matter how fine a gentleman he is. "I'm sorry, ma'am, but if Mr. Burke *is* paying for my lessons, then it's only because he is a kind and generous man."

"Whatever you say." Corrine reached for another seed cake. "But I'd wager my last pound that the man's in love with you."

"How can you say it like that?" asked Rachel.

"What do you mean?"

"You sound as if you wouldn't mind even if it were true."

Corrine hesitated, then replied, "Because I don't mind." A quick, nervous smile came to her lips then disappeared. "You deserve the chance to get away from here. And I've come to the realization that the man is simply not interested in me, so I'm not going to waste any more time grieving about it."

"But Mr. Moore . . ."

Shifting in her seat, Corrine glanced back up at the stairs. "Now that's another story. How am I going to tell him?"

Rachel reached across the table to put her hand on her mistress's arm. "You mustn't, ma'am—he'll hurt you again!"

"But how long can I pretend that Mr. Burke is interested in me?"

"At least long enough to think of something else."

"That's all I've thought about since yesterday," said Corrine, "and I'm no closer to a solution."

"Then why don't we ask for help?"

Corrine's eyes widened. "Don't even think of such a thing!"

"Why can't we ask Mrs. Morgan? Or maybe even Bernice?"

"Because we just can't!" Corrine lowered her voice, but her

words still came out forcefully. "I don't want to go to prison, Rachel!" Breathing a long sigh, she closed her eyes and began rubbing her forehead. "Not that I don't deserve it and not that part of me wouldn't welcome the chance to do penance for the evils I've done. Maybe that would give me some peace of mind. But . . ." She paused. "Who would see about little Anna? And when would I ever see my—"

Corrine stopped abruptly, and Rachel looked up to see an expression of utter misery in her mistress's eyes. *To see her daughter,* Rachel thought. *She wants to see her daughter again.*

With all her heart Rachel wished she could help Corrine— but they were going to have their hands full just keeping a step ahead of Gerald Moore.

~

In her room upstairs, Bernice sat propped up with pillows at the head of her bed, an open Bible in her lap. When a knock came at the door, she was not surprised to see Adam Burke's face appear in the doorway. She smiled suspiciously at her employer. "First Jack and now you."

Adam pulled out the stool to her dressing table and sat down. "I beg your pardon?"

"Aren't you here to tell me to stay in bed?"

Propping an ankle up on his knee, he leaned back to rest his elbows on the dressing table behind him. "No, I'm not. You're a grown woman, and I wouldn't presume to keep you prisoner up here for the rest of the day. What I *am* going to tell you is that I don't want you to worry about supper."

"But I'm much better now that the rain's dryin' up."

"Well, that's good to hear. Just to be sure, though, I want you to take it easy until you can get back on your feet without hurting." With a stern look, he cut short her attempt to protest. "Even if you have to take a few days off. I daresay we won't starve."

It was useless to argue. Bernice nodded and mumbled her thanks. "But I just know I'll be back to work in the mornin'," she added. "I can't stand to be away from my kitchen for too long."

"Whatever you say. Now, is there anything I can send up to you?"

The cook glanced down at the Bible in her lap. "Got all I need right here, sir. Food for the soul."

Adam smiled. "You're a good woman, Bernice."

Waving away the compliment, she changed the subject. "Lucy tells me that Mrs. Hammond and Rachel came by earlier."

"They did," he replied. "It seems they were almost caught in the rainstorm."

"Well, that's something." Bernice knew she had said too much yesterday when she had lectured him in the study. Mr. Adam was a fair man, but there was a limit to what a servant, even a pampered one, should be allowed to say.

To her surprise, though, he seemed willing to talk. "I'm afraid I was . . . rude," Adam said after a moment's hesitation.

"To Mrs. Hammond?" she asked carefully.

He considered this and then shook his head. "I don't think so. . . . I don't remember. But I wouldn't even look at Rachel. . . . At least I tried not to."

"Why?"

"I thought it was a good idea at the time."

Bernice blinked. "To be rude? That's not like you."

"No, but I let myself act like a lovesick schoolboy last night when she stayed here for supper with Mrs. Hammond."

"I *knew* you had feelings for the girl!" the cook exclaimed. Forgetting her resolve to hold her tongue, she remarked, "So you decided to play coy this morning?"

Adam's face colored. "Only for her sake."

"For her sake or for yours?"

~

Adam shook his head in wonder. Sometimes Bernice was *too* perceptive, and she made him uncomfortable. But he was determined to be honest with her. "All right . . . maybe it was for my own sake. You see, if I let my feelings be known and she reciprocates, I'll never know if it's because of pity—or even because of my money."

"And you think that those are the only reasons a woman would feel affection for you? Pity or greed?"

"Well, it certainly wouldn't be because of this." He touched his cheek and frowned. "No woman in her right—"

"No woman in her right mind would want you, is that it?" asked Bernice. "Well, let me ask you, sir, what if Kathleen would have gotten injured and lost her looks. Would you have loved her in spite of it?"

"Of course," Adam answered immediately, but doubt sprang up in his mind just as quickly. Would he have still loved her? Of course he would have done the right thing and married her, but hadn't her beauty been the thing that he was most proud of? Come to think of it, they had shared little in common besides a mutual admiration of her complexion, her eyes, and her flair for the latest fashions. Had Kathleen's beauty blinded him to her shallowness? *Have I*

*been a shallow fool myself, expecting everyone else to be as enam-
ored of physical beauty as I used to be?*

Bernice was smiling sadly at him as if she understood the
struggle going on inside him. "Are you all right, Mr. Adam?"

He turned to glance at his profile in the dressing table mirror. "This face certainly has complicated my life."

"Maybe God allowed those scars to happen for a purpose,"
she said gently.

"A purpose?" he frowned, turning back to her. "I'm not
sure what you mean."

"Well, look at the apostle Paul. He had some sort of affliction, and he asked the Lord three times to take it away. But
God wouldn't do it, even though Paul was probably the great-
est preacher that ever lived. Do you know what the Lord told
him was the reason why?"

Adam nodded. He had read the account many times, sometimes even wondering why God didn't go ahead and remove
the apostle's affliction. "He told Paul that God's grace was sufficient for him."

"God's grace," Bernice echoed, her voice touched with
awe. "Our Lord knew that Paul would have to keep
dependin' on him because of his physical condition. Paul's
body was only a temporary thing—he ended up dying just like
we're all going to do one day. But it was good for his soul to
walk close to his Father. It made him an even better person.
The soul don't die, Mr. Adam."

"No, it doesn't." He smiled, envying Bernice's ability to
find something in the Bible to apply to every situation. "And
you think these scars can make me into a better person,
Bernice?"

"Yes, sir, if you'll let them; in fact, I think they already have. You've learned the hard way about where the real worth of a person lies . . . and it ain't on the outside. I've got a feeling that Rachel learned that lesson, too, sometime in her life. I've seen the way the girl looks at you, and it seems to me that it's not your brown eyes . . . or your money . . . that she's admiring. It's the Adam Burke that I've known for years that she's longing to get to know better."

Her words made sense and gave him more hope than he had possessed in years. Still, he had been mistaken about someone's feelings for him before. "I'm afraid I'll get hurt again," he admitted in a whisper.

"You'd take that chance with anybody, Mr. Adam. Do you plan to be a hermit for the rest of your life?"

He shook his head. "No, I don't want that. But how can I know for sure about Rachel?"

Bernice glanced down at her open Bible. "It says here that our good Lord gives us wisdom if we ask for it. Pray for some of that wisdom so you can tell how she feels. And get to know her better—that is, if you didn't scare her off this morning!"

"You think I should apologize?"

"That might scare her off, too. Why don't you just invite her for supper tomorrow night with the Morgans?"

Adam snapped his fingers. "I forgot about that! You're not ready to cook for guests. I'll just send . . ."

"Really, sir, please don't spoil my Friday night! It's the only time you let me cook as fancy as I like."

"It won't hurt to skip a week, Bernice. I really must insist that you rest."

Bernice shook her head. "I'm feeling much better. And I have Lucy—and the others will help if I need them."

"Are you sure?"

"Positive." She sighed. "I suppose you'll have to ask Mrs. Hammond, too. I wonder what she thought about your acting like a lovesick schoolboy, as you put it, around her maid last night."

"I don't know," Adam mused, rubbing his chin. "Sometimes I think I've got the woman pegged, and then she surprises me. I can't quite figure her out."

"Me, too," agreed Bernice. "At first when she mentioned going to see that little orphan girl, I just knew it was to get your attention. But she really seems to care about the child."

"Maybe she's got a heart after all." Abruptly changing the subject, he said, "Do you really think this is a good idea—inviting Rachel to dinner?"

"Yes, I do, sir." She winked. "But then, I'm just the cook—what do I know?"

"Apparently more than I do," conceded Adam as he got to his feet and pushed the stool back under the dressing table. He gave the woman an affectionate grin. "Perhaps I should learn to cook."

~

About midnight Rachel reluctantly marked her place with a scrap of paper and closed *Pilgrim's Progress*. Swinging her legs over the side of the bed, she leaned toward her night table and blew out the candle, the second one she had lit since starting the story of Christian on his way to the Celestial City. *I'm going to be worn out in the morning if I don't get some sleep.*

Yet an hour later, she was sitting up and lighting the candle again. Her body cried for sleep, but her mind was restless, jumping from one remarkable incident of the day to another.

Why would he pay for her art lessons, if indeed he did, and

then order Mr. Solomon not to tell her? It just didn't make sense. And Corrine had to be wrong about Adam Burke's affection for her, as much as she wished it were so. Things like that didn't happen to servant girls.

Don't they? another part of her brain seemed to argue. *How many maids are allowed to borrow books? And how many get to take art lessons?* One day she would be a great portrait artist and make enough money to live on her own. *I'll even take the Missus with me if she still wants to leave Mr. Moore.*

Then she remembered Gerald's threat to fix Corrine so that no man would ever look at her if she ever left him. He had said something else, too, Rachel recalled, just before storming out of the house. She had been too concerned with tending to her mistress to let them sink in, but now she remembered his words with unnerving clarity. He had pointed his finger at her and said, "The same goes for you!"

Rachel was certain that sleep would not come anytime soon. Nonetheless, she leaned toward her night table and blew out the candle. *No sense wasting any more candles. My eyes are too tired to read, and I can lie awake in the dark just as well as in the light.* She considered going downstairs and getting a start on tomorrow's work, but remembered that Gerald was staying close to home lately. It wouldn't do to run into him in the dark.

The window was cracked open just a bit to let in some cool night air. She thought she heard the creak of carriage wheels just in front of the house and the slow cadence of iron horse-shoes against stones.

~

Adam's original plan had been just to pass by Corrine Hammond's house in his dogcart. When he saw the attic window suddenly light up, he had reined in his horse, Jupiter, to a spot just across East India Dock Road.

He knew without having to think about it that it was the window to Rachel's room—after all, most attic bedrooms were given to servants, and Corrine spoke of having only one maid at present. *Is she having trouble sleeping, too?* He wondered what Rachel would think if she knew he was right outside the house where she lived.

Staring up at the faint amber glow of the windowpanes, he felt close to her, as if he could sense the turmoil going on in her mind. As long as she kept the candle burning in her room, he was safe from being spotted as he sat there in the dark street. He wished she would go to the window so that he could see her face.

Had Mr. Solomon told her about the lessons yet? They had only arranged the deal that morning, but the old man had seemed eager to tell her as soon as possible. Adam tried to imagine the surprise and joy on her face when she found out, envying Mr. Solomon for being able to witness it. He was happy he could give her this opportunity without causing her to feel obliged to him, but another part of him wished she could know the truth.

It was selfish to think that way. The important thing was that she would be able to advance her talent. Still he could hope that one day, even if it were years from now, she would find out.

Suddenly the window was swallowed up again by the black facade of the house. A stab of pain shot through Adam's heart, and he watched in vain for a moment, hoping the light would come again. When it didn't, he flicked the reins, clucked softly to Jupiter, and headed for home.

15

M Y goodness—you look awful!" Corrine declared
bluntly the next morning as she walked into the
kitchen for a cup of tea.

"I'm sorry, ma'am," murmured Rachel, fetching the pot
from the stove.

Corrine sat down at the table and raked aside some dark
tangles from her cheeks with her fingers. A mischievous smile
came to her lips. "Don't tell me . . . you stayed awake all night
pining for Mr. Burke."

Rachel froze with the teapot in her hand. "Miss Corrine!"

While the maid stood there frowning, Corrine attempted
unsuccessfully to mask her fit of giggles with a cough. "You
should see the indignation on your face right now. It's a relief
to be able to laugh at *something* after the past couple of days."

"I didn't sleep," Rachel admitted sheepishly.

"Nor did I. But I had sense enough to powder the circles
under my eyes."

The girl shrugged her shoulders as she poured Corrine's tea.
"I don't imagine it matters how I look, Missus, as long as I get
my work done."

"Ah, but that's where you're wrong," she said, spooning
sugar into her cup. "While you were in here banging pots

around, one of Adam's servants was just at the back door with a note from you-know-who."

Rachel set the teapot on the table and tried not to look too interested as her mistress brought a folded paper from the pocket of her wrapper. Yawning, Corrine slowly unfolded it, then looked up at her.

"Oh, pour yourself some tea and sit down," she scolded lightly. "You make me nervous standing there holding your breath."

"Thank you, ma'am," Rachel said, already on the way to the cupboard for a cup.

Seconds later, when she was seated, Corrine handed the letter to her and smiled. "You may as well read it for yourself. I accepted the invitation for both of us, by the way."

Rachel unfolded the sheet of vellum writing paper, immediately recognizing Mr. Burke's even script, and read silently:

Dear Mrs. Hammond:

Would you and Miss Jones be so kind as to have dinner with me this evening? Reverend and Mrs. Morgan will be there as well.

Please give your reply to my footman, Hershall. If you desire, he can pick you up with my carriage at six o'clock, or whatever time is convenient for you.

Yours very truly,
Adam Burke

"As liberal as the man is about the treatment of servants," Corrine remarked as Rachel set the letter down on the table, "he cannot stray too far from the bounds of propriety. But I'm sure you realize the invitation is for your sake."

"For my sake?"

Corrine yawned again. "No doubt he grieved all day and night about ignoring you yesterday morning. Men in love are so predictable!" When Rachel blushed and started to protest, she cut her off. "We went over all of this last night, and I'm not in the mood to do it again. But I do think you should get a nap today so you won't frighten the man."

Rachel gave her a grateful look—a nap would be nice. Then she remembered the list of chores waiting for her attention. "But the downstairs floors—"

"Can wait till next week—or even the next. We never have company, so what does it matter?"

"Oh, thank you, ma'am!" the girl cried. "I'll get them done as soon as possible, to be sure."

Corrine shrugged. "Now, pour me some more tea. And you'd better get started with breakfast. I heard Gerald stirring upstairs just before I came in here." She sighed and lowered her voice. "I wish he would go back to staying out all night and sleeping all day. No doubt he'll be ecstatic over this invitation to dinner."

Rachel nodded, unsure of what to say. While she was pretty certain that her mistress was beginning to see Gerald for what he was, she had seen them fight and make up enough times to be wary of speaking her mind freely. One of the things that kept her awake last night was the fear that she had already said too much.

"Actually," Corrine went on thoughtfully after draining her cup of tea, "it's a godsend."

"Ma'am?"

"The invitation. I'm positive that he won't follow us this

time—not when we have proof here in writing of where we're going."

Rachel's mouth flew open. "You're not planning . . ."

"To see Anna? Of course I am, after I drop you off at Adam's."

"But Hershall will be driving!"

"Hmmm . . ." Corrine pursed her lips. "Well, Adam supports the orphanage. Surely he'll allow me to borrow his carriage and driver for a little while. If not, I'll just send for one myself. I think it'll be—"

The sound of footsteps upstairs silenced her, and seconds later a voice called through the door at the top of the stairs, "How about some breakfast up here!"

~

"Actually, the house belongs to my husband's sister," explained Mrs. Graham, perched on the edge of her chair in the front parlor of her Park Lane home. "She's spending a year in Italy with some friends of the family and asked us to lease it for her." She patted her white chignon. "This is so exciting—someone unaware that he's about to become wealthy!"

Joseph Price took a sip of his tea and smiled at the elderly woman. "That's what I like about my job—surprising people."

"I can imagine! The only thing is, my husband will not be home until quite late tonight. And I don't know the name of the tenant."

"Aren't there any papers you can look through? Rent receipts?"

Mrs. Graham laughed, "My dear Mr. Price, I wouldn't know where to begin to look. And anyway, Charles is quite touchy about his desk and ledgers."

Setting his cup and saucer on the side table next to his chair, Joseph thanked her for the tea and stood. "I have some other landlords to look up in the meantime. May I return in the morning if I don't get any leads?"

"Well, not *too* early. We're usually finished with breakfast by nine."

"Thank you. And by the way, in the off chance that you should hear from this tenant, please don't mention our conversation. It wouldn't do to give people false hopes."

The woman was obviously delighted to be in on a secret. She put a conspiratorial finger up to her lips. "Not a word."

~

Occasionally checking the list of rentals in his pocket, Joseph called upon a dozen other landlords. He was fortunate to find every one of them at home or at his office, save one, but that one had a wife who knew her husband's business matter better than Mrs. Graham had. He was unfortunate in the fact that none had ever heard of Gerald Moore or Corrine Hammond. Even more discouraging, two of the landlords mentioned that an investigator from Scotland Yard had been around earlier, asking about Moore.

The morning newspaper had mentioned nothing about the slain woman, but the authorities couldn't keep news such as this quiet for much longer. Scotland Yard's search would be intense.

Unless he found a lead soon, he just might be beaten in the race to find Moore. The idea left a bitter taste in his mouth. He tried to console himself with the notion that at least justice would be served. It was a weak consolation at best, for he was becoming obsessed with the desire to capture Gerald Moore.

Whether he would be capable of carrying out Squire Nowell's desire for immediate justice, he was still unsure. He would decide that when Moore was in his grasp.

He was under less pressure to capture Corrine Hammond right away because, so far, it didn't seem that Scotland Yard even knew of her existence, much less her past activities. Once he had taken care of her lover—one way or the other—he would take her back to Treybrook and let the squire decide what to do with her.

~

Gerald smiled broadly across the breakfast table and waved Adam Burke's supper invitation at Corrine. "You've done it again, you little temptress! How could I ever have doubted you?"

Corrine arched her eyebrows and sent him a cunning smile, expertly keeping any trace of hatred out of her expression. *He only cares about me when he thinks money's on the way,* she thought. *Why didn't I see that years ago?*

"In fact," he continued as he speared a piece of bacon with his fork, "I believe I'm going to take a little walk after breakfast and buy my darling some roses . . . a dozen!"

"Roses would be nice," Corrine answered. *Anything to get you out of my sight for a while.*

~

At six-thirty that evening, as soon as Adam Burke's carriage stopped in front of his house, Rachel started protesting to Corrine again. "But, ma'am, it isn't proper for me to be calling on Mr. Burke alone."

"Now, now, Rachel," Corrine soothed. "Stop whining and

let poor Hershall help you get down. I'll be back shortly, and besides, the Morgans are probably already here."

"But what if they aren't?" Rachel glanced across the yard at Adam's house. "Can't I go with you to the orphanage?"

"And waste the time I spent arranging those beautiful curls of yours? Absolutely not!" She turned to the servant, patiently waiting at the side of the carriage. "Please escort Miss Jones to Mr. Burke," she said, "and be so kind as to ask him if you may deliver me on an errand of mercy."

Realizing the futility of arguing the matter, Rachel turned and gave her trembling hand to Hershall. "Don't worry, Miss," he whispered after her feet were on the ground. "Mr. Adam don't bite."

The servant's effort to cheer her up didn't work. *Adam will think the missus and I are scheming!* she told herself as she followed the man across the lawn. *Especially the way I'm dressed.* She wished she hadn't allowed Corrine to talk her into curling her hair and wearing the green dress, the one that enhanced the emerald color of her eyes.

Marie answered the door and walked with both of them to the drawing room, chatting gaily about Lucy's portrait. "You look lovely, Rachel," she said as she led her over to an over-stuffed couch and took her shawl.

Adam came through the door seconds later, wearing a gray broadcloth suit and straightening his tie. He smiled and greeted Rachel, then raised his eyebrows at Marie.

"Mrs. Hammond's still outside," the maid said.

"She wants me to drive her to the orphanage," explained Hershall. "She asks your permission."

Confusion briefly crossed his face, but Adam gave Hershall his consent. After the servants had left, he walked over to the other end of the couch and sat down. "Is it cold outside?" he asked gently, as if sensing Rachel's shyness.

"Cold?" came her wavering answer. "No, sir."

"I take it that your mistress went to see the child?"

"She's worried that the little girl might not eat."

"How thoughtful," said Adam, sincere with his praise, but not looking too disappointed at her absence. "Perhaps she'll join us later?"

"Yes, sir—I believe she will."

"Well, good! Meantime, if the Morgans get here soon, perhaps we'll have time for a game of whist before dinner."

"Yes, sir."

Adam tried not to let any amusement show on his face. The girl sat there clutching her hands together in her lap, only looking up when spoken to. She would no doubt be more comfortable in the kitchen helping to prepare the meal than seated here beside him.

"Have you had the chance to look through any of the books yet?"

At this, her shyness seemed to ease a bit. Rachel nodded and smiled. "Thank you again for lending them to me. I read a bit of *Pilgrim's Progress* last night."

So that's what you were doing with your light on, he thought. He couldn't resist saying, "I find that reading is helpful when I have trouble falling asleep, don't you?"

She darted a quick, questioning glance toward him, then dropped her eyes to her hands again. "Sometimes."

Marie came into the room again, pausing just inside the door. "Mr. Adam, here's a note from Reverend Morgan," she said. She brought an envelope over to him and then left the room again, sending a quick smile in Rachel's direction on the way.

Adam opened the envelope and read the message. "I'm afraid Penelope is under the weather."

"Oh, dear—I hope she's not seriously ill!"

He shook his head. "I don't think so. I believe it's a touch of morning sickness . . . in the evening, rather."

Rachel's expression turned from shyness to wonder. "Do you mean she's expecting a baby?"

"I'm sorry—didn't you know?"

"No, sir."

"She only found out recently. I'm sure she would have told you and Mrs. Hammond before long. I remember how she suffered this affliction while carrying Margaret. I hope you don't think . . ."

"Think what, sir?"

He cleared his throat. "That I planned it this way. This evening, I mean."

Rachel could feel her cheeks burning again. *He's disappointed that I'm the only one here.* She wished that Corrine hadn't left with Mr. Burke's carriage; otherwise, she could offer to go back home. "I'm sorry," she finally said, fighting against the tears that threatened to spill from her eyes any minute.

"Sorry?"

"The evening isn't turning out as you intended." She felt miserable for having caused him so much trouble. The memory of how he had ignored her yesterday morning came back then, and she straightened her shoulders and forced herself to look him in the eyes. *It's not my fault that I'm the only one who showed up,* she told herself, lifting her chin, *and I'm tired of cowering!* "If you don't mind, Mr. Burke, I'll wait with Bernice and Lucy until Mrs. Hammond returns," she said with as much dignity as she could muster. "I'm sure there are things I can help out with in the kitchen."

To her surprise, he looked hurt. "You'd rather visit with them?"

"Wouldn't you rather I did?"

"No," he said quickly. "I'd rather you stayed with me. That is, if you want to."

A strange tension filled the room, surrounding them. Rachel wondered if Mr. Burke was aware of it, too, or if she was the only one who sensed it. "But you just said you didn't plan . . ."

"I didn't want you to think I *arranged* for this to happen." A crooked smile came across Adam's lips. "But of course you wouldn't think that. After all, how could I know that Mrs. Hammond wasn't planning to stay—or that Penelope would be sick?"

"You couldn't," she answered.

He grinned. "Exactly! So why don't we just enjoy each other's company?"

Suddenly lightheaded, Rachel managed a smile. "Yes, sir."

"Would you like to see the conservatory?" he offered suddenly.

"That would be nice."

"Good!" Rising, he turned to take her hand and help her from the couch. He did not let go then, but led her down the hall past the dining room and library to a sitting room in the east wing of the house. Adam opened a set of French doors on the far wall of the room. "We'll have our Sunday meetings in here next month, when it's a bit less humid."

He ushered her into a room with low brick walls on three

262

sides and windows glazing up to the level of the eaves. Rachel saw the outlines of dense greenery in the evening dusk, and she felt enveloped by the musky smell of soil and damp leaves.

"Stay here," Adam said, letting go of her hand and taking a couple of steps away. A match flared, and a second later a lantern filled a good portion of the conservatory with light.

"This is Jack's favorite part of the house. In fact, I'm surprised we didn't come upon him just now." With one hand he held the lantern; with the other, he took her hand again and guided her around the room, pointing out exotic plants and ferns, lilies and jasmine, stephanotis and gardenias, artfully arranged in brass and china planters and hanging pots. "Careful," he warned. "The tiles are slick in some places."

"It must be lovely in the daytime," she murmured, looking around. In truth, she was barely able to take in the sights. The sensation of his hand holding hers was all that she could absorb.

"Just wait until those roses are in full bloom. It's like walking into a perfumery."

"I can't imagine." She turned her head in the direction he was pointing and banged her forehead abruptly against a hanging pot of ivy. "Oh!" she cried, more from surprise than pain.

Dropping her hand, Adam immediately reached up to steady the swinging pot. "How stupid of me not to warn you about that!" He turned to her then, holding up the lantern to see her face. "Are you all right?" he asked, his brow furrowed with concern.

"Yes, sir." She was embarrassed at her clumsiness and wished the incident could just be forgotten. Moving her hand from the place above her brow, she straightened. "Really I am."

Unconvinced, Adam stepped closer and studied her forehead. "I don't see a knot, but perhaps we should let Bernice look at it."

Rachel couldn't help but smile. "Perhaps you should be inspecting the pot instead. Sometimes a hard head is convenient."

He laughed. "You're the last person I'd call hardheaded. Let's get into some better light and make sure."

Taking her hand again, he led her back through the French doors and into the sitting room. A huge coal-oil lamp burned brightly on a corner table. He extinguished the lantern and set it aside, drew a stool next to the lamp, and had her sit down on it. "I thought earlier we would all come in here to play whist," he said, frowning as he gently probed her forehead with his fingers. "I'm glad the lamp was already lit—it's a beast to fool with."

"My head really feels fine."

"That's good." Relief crossed his face and he smiled. "But if you should feel even the slightest nausea or have trouble seeing, you must let me know right away so I can send for a doctor."

"Yes, sir—thank you."

Dropping to one knee beside her, he lifted his hand as if to take hers again, then put his hand back at his side. "Would you do something for me, Rachel?" he said, watching her face anxiously.

"Sir?"

His voice dropped to almost a whisper. "Would you stop calling me *sir?*"

Rachel's heart hammered forcefully in her chest. "I don't

think I can," she breathed, overwhelmed by the warmth in his brown eyes.

"Why can't you?"

"Because I'm . . ." Her words trailed off, and she could only shrug her shoulders.

"Because you're a servant?"

She nodded.

He smiled gently. "But you're not *my* servant."

She thought she heard footsteps coming down the hall . . . or was it her own pulse pounding in her ears? A modest young lady should coyly lower her eyes, she knew, and not stare into his without so much as blinking, but she was unable to turn away. "It's become such a habit," she finally explained.

His eyes were crinkling at the corners now. "You mean like covering your mouth when you yawn?"

"Yes, sir." Rachel returned his smile. "I mean, yes."

"There you go! We'll work on the 'Mr. Burke' habit some other time. I can't go expecting too much from an injured lady, can I?"

A sudden sound at the entrance to the hallway caused them both to look up. Lucy stood there, shifting from one foot to the other and studying the carpet under her feet.

"Yes, Lucy?"

"Mum says dinner is ready," she mumbled before disappearing through the doorway.

Adam got to his feet and held out a hand to Rachel. "Shall we?"

~

"What do you mean, she's not here?" exclaimed Corrine, her eyes frantically scanning the cribs in the orphanage nursery.

Mrs. O'Reilly stood there wringing her hands. "Her mother came for her yesterday, ma'am. Said she had some family in the country willin' to help out, whereas they wouldn't before. You know how—"

"But she had no right to!"

Taking Corrine's elbow, the Irish woman gently but firmly guided her away from the children's curious stares, out into the hall. When she had closed the door behind them, she said, "She was her *mother*, Mrs. Hammond. You should have seen little Anna when she saw her face."

Corrine fumbled in her purse for a handkerchief and blew her nose. "But *I'm* the one who got her to eat!" she cried with a trembling voice.

"Yes, ma'am, you likely saved her life. You were good to the child when she needed someone. I think little Anna will remember you."

Helplessly, Corrine raised her hands and then let them drop to her side. "I'll never see her again!"

Mrs. O'Reilly's eyes became moist, and she wiped them with her fingers before speaking. "Ma'am," she began, with a voice full of compassion, "you were only with the child two— no, three times."

"What does that matter?"

The woman hesitated for a second. "Mrs. Hammond, perhaps there's somethin' else that's troubling you? Maybe somethin' that's just too hard to think about?"

In spite of her misery, indignation managed to rise in Corrine's chest. How dare this woman lecture her on how she was supposed to feel! She glared at the Irish woman and snapped, "Well, I certainly appreciate your words of wisdom. I'll let you get back to changing diapers now!"

Corrine turned on her heel and headed for the staircase. Already she felt remorse for shouting at Mrs. O'Reilly when she was just trying to help, but she was too full of grief and loss to turn around and apologize.

~

After his fifth game of solitaire, Gerald brushed the cards away with the back of his hand—a dozen or more fell to the carpet underneath the Pembroke table, but he made no effort to pick them up.

Boring, boring, boring! He walked from the sitting room into the dining room and took another bottle of gin out of the sideboard. Not bothering with a glass, he drank several gulps straight from the bottle. The liquor scorched the length of his throat on its way down, but he paid it no mind.

He wiped his mouth on the back of his frock-coat sleeve. The newspaper lay open on the table. Again, there had been no mention of the girl he had killed. He should have been relieved, but he felt betrayed, somehow . . . as if he weren't important enough to make the news. He pointed a wavering finger at the paper. "I'm tired of reading about von Bismark and Western provinces and Mr. Lincoln!" he sneered. "Why don't you find out what's going on right under your noses!"

Suddenly he realized that it was his own voice filling the room. *Get hold of yourself!* he thought, setting the bottle back on the sideboard. He had to get out of the house. It had been three days since the girl had disappeared—surely it would be safe for him to go to another saloon. Anywhere he would choose to go, he could always count on there being blokes ready to lose money to him at cards—or to take money, depending on how his luck went.

267

16

I told Bernice to keep the meal simple tonight," Adam said. He eyed the spread of fish, deviled kidneys, chops, and various vegetable dishes they had barely touched. "She didn't listen, of course. I hope you enjoyed the trout. Irene's brother-in-law caught it in the Lea just this morning."

"It was delicious," answered Rachel. "And so is this custard. But I'm sorry Bernice is ailing."

"She insists that she's fine now. Still, I'm going to have to keep an eye on her when the weather's damp."

"You treat everyone here so well."

"I hope so," he replied, smiling. "They've been good to me, too."

Rachel could hardly believe she was sitting adjacent to Adam Burke, carrying on a conversation like old friends. He had a way of making her feel at ease. He had teased her about blushing when Lucy came upon them in the sitting room. And it had seemed so natural that they should laugh together when Marie and Dora left the dining room after seeing to their place settings; the sisters had sent covert glances to each other the whole time.

"I was so surprised when I heard about your Sunday services here," continued Rachel. "How many people care about seeing that their servants go to church?"

Adam shrugged, but it was obvious that he was pleased at her words. "You're making me out to be a saint, Miss Jones."

He was watching her, studying her face again, and, she thought, trying hard *not* to. Rachel busied herself with her dessert and pretended not to notice.

To her relief he finally said something. "Speaking of our church services, what do you think of them?"

Why did everyone ask her that question? She tried to remember what she had told Penelope Morgan when the minister's wife had asked the same question, but she couldn't. At least she could tell him part of the truth. "Reverend Morgan and his family are so nice," she answered while staring at the pattern on her custard spoon. "And I enjoy the meals when everyone's gathered in here."

"And the service?"

"You are kind to invite us," she answered after taking a deep breath. "I'm sometimes confused by what the Reverend says, though."

"It would distress him to hear that," said Adam, drawing his brows together. "He tries to speak with such clarity."

Rachel turned alarmed eyes towards him. "I'm sorry—I didn't mean to sound so ungrateful!"

"You didn't . . ."

"Of course, he speaks with clarity," she continued quickly. "I'm just too dense to understand some things. But I'm positive that with time I shall understand, too, just like everyone else."

Adam laughed. "You know, I believe that's the most you've ever said to me at one time!"

"Sir? I mean, I beg your pardon?"

His eyes were still smiling. "You don't strike me as being

dense at all . . . and you don't have to be afraid to speak your mind. Would you mind telling me what it is you don't understand?"

Rachel put down her spoon and sighed. "I'm confused about whether God wants us to be born again or to be sheep, or both."

~

Adam watched Rachel and, without thinking, smiled at her honesty—and her intensity. Suddenly an angry expression flashed across her face—an expression he had never seen.

"I didn't say that to amuse you, Mr. Burke."

She's certainly got spirit under that bashfulness! Adam forced the smile away. "I'm sorry. Please don't be offended—you just have a charming way of putting things. You're referring to the two sermons that you heard, yes?"

She sat up straighter in her chair. "Yes."

"Well, you're right when you ask if God wants us to be both. Born again *and* sheep, that is. The reason you're confused is that you know they're both physically impossible."

Rachel nodded.

"Well, let's start with the 'born again' part." He leaned forward at the table. For several seconds Adam was quiet. *Lord, forgive me for not even thinking to ask her earlier if she understood the gospel,* he prayed silently. *Please give me clarity of words now.* "We're all born with sinful natures—do you understand that?"

"Everyone?"

"Even our dear Queen Victoria herself, bless her soul. I'm sure you've experienced it growing up in an orphanage. Did any of the children tell lies, or perhaps fight or steal?"

"Many of them." She hesitated before adding, "Myself included. It was the only way to survive."

Her candor was refreshing. "Certainly the adults in charge didn't teach the children to do these things. Why do you think they happened?"

"I would think it was because we were orphans and poor."

"Let me assure you that my sister and brother and I got into the same kinds of mischief, and we grew up with money *and* parents. There's something inside of us that naturally wants to do wrong."

"And that's our sin nature?"

He nodded. "Inherited from our great-great-grandfather Adam. The problem is, God is so holy that he can't fellowship with us because of our sin."

"But I thought God loved everybody."

"He does, Rachel. That's why he offered his only Son, the most cherished being in heaven, as a sacrifice for our sins. And Jesus went to the cross willingly, too, because he knew it was the only way."

"But why?" Rachel shook her head. "Couldn't God just have forgiven everybody without his Son having to die?"

"But then the penalty for our sin wouldn't have been paid. See, in the Bible it's written that the wages of sin is death. Back before Jesus' death on the cross, people would sacrifice a spotless animal, usually a lamb, as payment for their sins. But God promised them that one day he would send a perfect offering as a onetime sacrifice for sin."

She was quiet as she considered those last words. Adam inferred from her silence that he had confused her even more. "I've botched it all up—I wish Robert were here!"

Rachel covered his hand with her own. "No, it's good of you to explain this to me. May I ask you something else?"

"Ask anything," he said, flattered that she still trusted him to explain things to her and awed by the featherlight touch of her hand upon his.

"If Jesus died for everybody, then why isn't everybody forgiven?"

"That's a good question. We all have forgiveness offered to us, if we will just confess our sin and accept Jesus as our Savior. It's a *gift*, forgiveness, but God doesn't force it upon anyone—that's not his nature. By the way," he added, "when we accept Jesus, that's when we become born again."

"Born again," she echoed faintly. "It sounds like becoming a different person."

"Exactly! Our sin natures are cleansed somehow with the blood that Jesus shed on the cross. Then when God looks at us, he only sees the innocence of his own Son. Just as Jesus rose from the dead, we're given eternal life as God's children."

"But what if we commit sins after we're born again?"

Adam smiled and nodded. "We most *definitely* sin afterwards. Saint Paul called himself the chief of sinners. We still ask for forgiveness, even as children of God, because our sins grieve him so. But because of Christ's sacrifice, God forgives our sins—and loves us more than we can imagine."

Rachel suddenly looked down and saw that her hand was covering Adam's. Obviously embarrassed, she started to pull it away. "Please don't," he said simply, quietly, . . . and she left it where it lay. The blush on her cheeks subsided, and her expression became intent.

"Then, as you explain it, it's possible for *me* to be born again?"

The question had come from her lips with such longing and hopefulness that Adam found himself remembering how he had been affected the same way right before he became a Christian. He hadn't wanted to spend another minute without Jesus in his life—and what a difference it had made!

"Absolutely," he answered, his voice thick with emotion. "Would you like to do that right now?"

"Here?"

"I don't see why not."

She nodded slowly and lowered her eyes. "Please tell me what to say."

"There are no magic words, Rachel. Just ask Jesus in your own way to forgive your sins and be your Savior."

~

Rachel took a deep breath. She wanted to do this—more than anything in the world. But she was a little afraid, too. Afraid of making a mistake. Afraid, somehow, that it wouldn't work, that her sins were too great to be forgiven. But if she didn't try, she would never know.

For a moment she was silent. Then she began to pray. "Dear Jesus, I repent of my sins and ask your forgiveness," she said quietly. "If you'll have me, I want to be yours more than anything."

When she finally looked up, she was unable to speak.

Adam was quiet too. His hand clasped hers, and his face was turned toward her. Finally he smiled and whispered, "I forgot to tell you about the sheep."

She smiled back. "I think I understand that."

"You do?"

"Jesus is my good shepherd now, so I'm one of his sheep."

He let out a joyous laugh and squeezed her hand. "Do you feel any different?"

"Why, I don't know." Her thoughts turned to panic at his question. This whole evening had been so overwhelming from the start that she had no way to gauge if the euphoria she felt inside had to do with her spiritual birth or her proximity to Adam. "I'm glad to know that I'm not an orphan anymore," she said even as the realization dawned on her. "I've got a heavenly Father now—that's nice. Should I feel anything else?"

Adam shook his head. "I shouldn't have asked you that. Now you'll worry. You just looked so . . . so radiant after you prayed, as if you could take wings and fly. When I responded to Christ's call, it took me a couple of days to realize that the empty place that had become such a part of my life was gone."

The empty place? She was startled to hear that someone else had lived with that hollow ache, that longing for something that couldn't even be defined, that had been a big part of her life. Ever since she could remember, she had felt incomplete, as if she were the only person alive who wasn't whole. It made her sad to think of Adam feeling that way, too, even if it had been in the past.

"When I have a chance to be alone and think," she told him, "I'm sure my thoughts will be easier to sort out. I'm happy, but besides that, I don't know exactly what I'm feeling now."

He was gazing at her with such intensity that she lost all sense of everything else in the room, of even the pressure of his hand upon hers. After a few seconds he cleared his throat. "I know what *I'm* feeling right now."

Rachel's lips began to tremble. *Was Corrine right?*

~

"Please thank Mr. Burke for the use of his carriage," Corrine intoned lifelessly to Hershall as he helped her to the ground in front of the house on East India Dock Road. Her voice was raspy, her eyes swollen and red.

"Shall I get the door for you?" the servant asked.

"No . . . thank you." In the darkness she turned to drag herself up the front walk, still holding a handkerchief to her cheek. The brandy in her upstairs bedroom was waiting for her, and she intended to numb her senses and sleep for as long as possible.

Only when she turned the knob to the front door did she remember that Gerald had been staying home evenings. *I don't care!* she told herself, swinging open the door. Yet she felt immeasurable relief to discover that the house was empty.

~

Following a trail of gaslights down Narrow Street, Gerald kicked the loose pebbles at his feet and cursed his luck, cursed England and the Parliament, and cursed the two men who had come into Salty's Spirits asking around for a Gerald Moore. Just when he had a straight flush and twenty quid on the table, he had overheard the saloon keeper repeating a question one of the strangers, an older man with a bushy mustache, had just asked him.

Fortunately Salty, or whatever his name actually was, was hard of hearing. He had leaned over the bar and barked out, "Who you say? Gerald Moore?" loudly enough for everyone in close proximity to hear.

"Nature calls," Gerald had whispered to his startled card

partners before slipping away, abandoning his twenty pounds on the table. He couldn't remember what name he had given them when they had started up the game, but he was certain he hadn't used his own. Still, it was unnerving to know that someone was looking for him.

Maybe they found the girl, he thought. But how would the police, if that's who those men were, connect the murder of a prostitute to *him?* He cursed again at the thought of having to stay home for no telling how long. But they couldn't find him if he didn't go anywhere.

A brief worry crossed his mind. He had used his real name when he leased the house! But he dismissed the thought immediately. Even if they were on his trail, Scotland Yard would never think to connect the rental records from several weeks ago, especially on such a dignified street, with the murder of a prostitute.

"Hey, mister—want to have some fun?" came a listless voice next to a broken gaslight on the corner near Wharf Road.

Scowling at the woman, who looked pockmarked and unwashed even in the foggy darkness, Gerald spat out a vile oath at her and kept walking. He could hear her footsteps behind him as she sought a safer corner.

It's no use! he told himself, frowning bitterly. For whatever reason he was being sought, it was just a matter of time before he was discovered. The two men in the saloon had worn serious, determined looks. Here were men not likely to leave any stone unturned in the search.

He was closer than ever to being flat broke. The thought of the twenty pounds he had left on the table in Salty's brought another curse to his lips. He had never before risked that much on one hand, but having to stay away from gambling for a couple of nights had made him careless.

We've got to get out of London, he told himself as he turned up the walkway to the house, *as soon as possible!* But how could they relocate without money? Corrine would just have to move faster with Burke. She could do it—she had done it before.

A table lamp was burning in the sitting room when he walked inside, and Gerald assumed he must have left it on earlier. Then a noise drifted down through the ceiling. *Corrine?* He squinted at the mantle clock. What was she doing home at nine-thirty?

~

Corrine was sitting on the side of her bed with a glass of brandy in her hand, and she was startled when Gerald appeared at the door. "I didn't hear you come in," Corrine said, slurring her words faintly.

He walked over to stand in front of her. "How long have you been home?" he demanded, taking in the crimson splotches on her face and red-rimmed eyes. "And what happened to you?"

This was Corrine's second glass of brandy, and her mind was beginning to grow dull around the edges. But she knew she had to come up with an explanation at once. *Why didn't I have sense enough to go back to Adam's after I left the orphanage!* she silently berated herself.

Gerald folded his arms across his chest and frowned. "Corrine?"

"Adam's cook served some oysters that must have been bad," she lied. "I got sick!"

278

"You got sick?"

"I'm just now feeling bet—"

"I can't believe it!" he cut in. The veins were showing at his temples now. "How could you get sick?"

"Well, I wasn't the only one." Her muddled thoughts racing, she took a swallow of brandy and contrived a grin on her face. "You should have seen Adam Burke—I didn't think the man could look any uglier, but I was wrong!"

"That's just wonderful!" he growled. "Wonderful!" He bent down and grabbed both of her shoulders, his contorted face only inches from hers. "I need you to get some money from the man, and you both get sick!"

Fear cut through Corrine's brandy-induced fog. She had to pacify him somehow. The story about becoming ill might not have been the best one she could have told on the spur of the moment, but she was stuck with it now. Trying to keep her voice calm, she declared, "But Gerald, before Adam got sick he told me that he loved me!"

"What?"

"The Morgans were over an hour late, so Adam asked me to take a walk outside with him to look at the stars. He kissed me as soon as we were alone!"

Gerald let go of her shoulders and the corners of his lips curled up into a smile. "I knew you could do it!" he exclaimed, pounding his fist into his other hand. "The money's as good as in our pockets!"

Relieved, Corrine returned his smile and handed him her glass of brandy to share. While she still had the problem of Adam Burke not being infatuated with her, the immediate crisis had been taken care of. "I believe you could say that," she murmured, wishing Gerald would find something to do and leave her alone. The liquor hadn't dulled the pain in her heart, but it had made her sleepy.

But Gerald wasn't finished. A suspicious glint came into his eyes. "Did Rachel and the Morgans get sick?"

Rachel! Panic seized Corrine again. Was Rachel even home yet? "The preacher got a little queasy," she said quickly. "But I don't think his wife tried the oysters. As for Rachel, she was eating in the kitchen with the other servants, and I didn't see her when Adam had his man drive me home. She may still be there, exchanging recipes with Bernice or whatever it is they find to talk about." She waved a hand in the air. "I don't think they had oysters, though—surely we would have heard if they had gotten sick, too."

Gerald finally seemed satisfied with Corrine's explanation. Taking another swallow of brandy, he said, "Do you think tomorrow's too soon to ask Burke to lend you some money?"

"Tomorrow?"

"A couple of men were asking around for me tonight. I'm afraid we'll need to leave London as soon as possible."

~

"I love you, Rachel," Adam whispered, his hand still clasping hers on the tabletop. His earlier resolve to move slowly, until he could be sure about her feelings toward him, had vanished, and he found a strange and wonderful sense of freedom as the words left his lips.

"But you hardly know me, Mr. Burke."

"Adam. Please call me Adam."

"All right, Adam. How can you say—"

"That I love you?" His lips crooked into a smile. "You're right—we haven't known each other for long. But I've always loved you, Rachel, even before I met you. I've been waiting for you all of my life. I thought I loved someone else a long time ago, but it was nothing like what I'm feeling now."

Rachel put her left hand up to her heart. "This is all so much."

He nodded sympathetically. "I know. I should have waited until you were used to being around me. But I'm glad I told you, Rachel. I hope one day you'll feel the same way about me."

A fleeting expression—a look of longing, Adam thought—passed over Rachel's face, then she lowered her eyes. For a long time she said nothing. At last she murmured, "I shall never forget this evening."

"Nor shall I," he returned. "And one day you're going to love me, too, Rachel. I know I'm not pleasant to look at, but I'll treat you so well that . . ."

Rachel's eyes turned back to him with horror. "Not pleasant to look at?" she whispered forcefully.

"I'm sorry—that wasn't a bid for sympathy. I just wanted you to know that there's more to me than just these scars."

"Your scars are nothing ugly to me, Mr. . . . ." She leaned closer, her expression intent. "Adam. Your kindness makes you . . . well, beautiful." Timidly but deliberately, she removed her hand from his and reached up to touch the right side of his face.

Adam took her hand again and, closing his eyes, moved it over to his smooth left cheek. She felt wetness on her fingers and realized that it was his tears.

"I think I should take you home now," he whispered at length. The longing to get up from his chair and gather her in his arms was almost overwhelming, but he fought against it.

He would not take advantage of any tenderness she might feel for him. *She's likely confused enough right now as it is.*

"Yes." She tilted her head slightly. "Did you say *you* were going to take me home?"

"I don't mind taking the carriage out after dark—in fact, I go for a ride once or twice a week." He put her fingers to his lips just for a second, then lowered his voice. "Will you think about what I told you?"

Rachel smiled. "I'll think of nothing else."

When they had walked through the drawing room and he had fetched her shawl, Rachel remembered her mistress at the orphanage. "Miss Corrine has your carriage, remember?"

Adam shook his head. "I heard Hershall's voice coming from the hall a little while ago. Your Mrs. Hammond must have decided to go on home."

"Oh, dear—I hope she's all right."

"Why don't I go find Hershall and make sure?" he offered, leading her to a chair.

When he was gone, Rachel tried to figure out why Corrine would have gone home without her. Surely that would be risky, since Gerald thought they were having dinner with Adam together.

Seconds later Adam returned, his expression filled with concern. "He says that Mrs. Hammond was crying when she came out of the orphanage. Do you think something's happened to the child she was visiting?"

Rachel remembered how emotional her mistress had become the other times she'd gone to see Anna. She was certain that Corrine's tears also had something to do with her own abandoned child, but she couldn't say this to Adam.

"Sometimes the child's situation—not having a mother and all—makes her sad," she explained.

"Perhaps we should see about her when we get there."

"That won't be necessary," she hastily assured him. She certainly couldn't have him coming in the house with Gerald there—not that she wouldn't have minded exposing Gerald and his insidious plot. But she didn't want Adam to know that she had been dishonest about her personal life. What would he think of her if he knew she had participated with the scheme, however reluctantly? "Miss Corrine likes to be alone when she's feeling low."

~

The horse led them slowly through the quiet, darkened streets of East London. Adam wished that the trip would take hours. To his joy, Rachel had given him a bashful nod when he had asked her if she wouldn't mind riding in the dogcart so they could sit together and talk.

They had hardly said a word but held hands and smiled at each other occasionally. His heart filled to almost bursting, Adam had to restrain himself from blurting out a proposal every time he looked at the girl beside him. *Thank you, Lord, for sending her into my life.*

~

This has to be a dream, thought Rachel as Adam gave her hand a squeeze. What had she done to deserve such happiness? And what would happen tomorrow and the day after? Would he still profess to love her?

So much had happened that evening. Only when the horse came to a stop in front of the house did she remember her conversation with Mr. Solomon about the art lessons. With that memory came the almost certain knowledge that Adam had arranged them.

The question was on the tip of Rachel's tongue. She knew that Adam would tell her the truth if she asked him directly, but she decided against it and closed her mouth. *If he wants to keep it a secret, for whatever reason, then I'll not spoil it.*

"Please don't get out," she said, putting a hand on his sleeve before he could start to tie off the reins.

"But I'll walk you to the door."

Rachel was already slipping down from the seat. "I'll need to see about Mrs. Hammond myself." On the ground now, she smiled up at him. "Thank you for a lovely evening."

As soon as she entered the house, Rachel noticed Gerald's silk bowler hat and evening coat hanging from the hall tree and wondered how her mistress had explained coming home early. There were no sounds coming from upstairs, so perhaps there hadn't been a fight.

As quietly as possible she hurried up the stairs and to her room. When she had changed into her nightgown and was about to climb into bed, she remembered that she was a Christian now and wondered if she should get on her knees and pray before going to sleep. Adam hadn't mentioned that being necessary, but perhaps it would please God if she did.

Easing down to the floor, Rachel rested her elbows on her mattress and closed her eyes. *Thank you for allowing me to be your child,* she prayed. *And thank you for this evening with Adam—please watch over him.* She was about to get into bed when another petition came to mind. *Please protect Miss Corrine—and help both of us get away from Mr. Gerald.*

As she pulled the blanket up to her shoulders, she reflected on Adam's question: "How do you feel?" In the quiet of her room she waited, sure that if she was still long enough she would know.

For how long she lay like that, barely daring to breathe for fear of missing something, she could not imagine. But by the time her eyelids were beginning to get heavy, she sensed a freeing of her soul, as if an immense burden had been taken away. Rachel smiled in the darkness. She still couldn't decide if the new calmness inside her was because she'd been born again or because of Adam . . . but she hoped it would stay forever.

17

A T the stove the next morning, Rachel heard her mistress's footsteps on the kitchen stairs. "Oh, hello, ma'am. Are you all right?"

"Yes," Corrine answered. But as she came down the steps, Rachel could see that her eyes were swollen.

"Did Mr. Gerald . . . hurt you?"

Corrine shook her head. "But I wanted to talk with you before he wakes. He's so unpredictable these days that I never know where or when he's going to show up."

Rachel set a mug of steaming tea on the table and pulled out a chair. "Why don't you sit then, Missus. Would you like anything to eat?"

"Later." Corrine sat down and took a sip of the tea. "It's good. Now come sit down." After the girl took the chair next to her, Corrine first glanced at the top of the stairs and said, "If Gerald asks, you must tell him that I had supper with Adam Burke yesterday."

"Does he think—"

"He believes I went to Adam's for dinner as planned, then I took sick on some oysters. I'm just telling you this in case he gets suspicious."

"Yes, ma'am." Rachel felt a pang of regret at the possibility of having to lie again. *I'll just have to stay away from Mr. Moore as much as possible,* she thought. *Then perhaps he won't ask.* Already she was in the habit of listening for his voice outside any room she planned to enter and of peeking through key-holes or cracks in the doors for any sign of him.

Just for a little while longer, she told herself. She would study hard at her art lessons, even if that meant working up in her room for hours after her chores were done. Once her paintings were good enough, surely Mr. Solomon would help her to sell them.

Then I'll leave this house—rent a room somewhere and take Corrine with me if she wants to come. We'll warn Mr. Moore that we intend to send for the police if he comes around.

Deep in thought, she forgot that Corrine was even in the same room. *And who knows? Maybe one day Adam will ask me—*

"Rachel?"

At the sound of Corrine's voice, Rachel snapped back to reality. "Sorry, ma'am. Would you like some more tea?"

Corrine's face wore a frown. Her eyes were looking at Rachel, yet they seemed to look through her at the same time, to something in the distance. "Anna was gone yesterday."

"Oh, dear! You mean she . . . died?"

"Her mother came back and got her. I didn't get to say good-bye."

Rachel let out a sigh of relief. "I'm so sorry, ma'am. But at least you know she's all right."

"Yes," she said woodenly. "She's all right."

At a loss as to how to console the woman, Rachel thought of the one thing that always seemed to work for Corrine. "Let me fetch you a pastry," she offered, starting to push away from the table.

Corrine shook her head. "They're all gone. I couldn't sleep last night, and I finished them off."

"Then when I go to market, I'll stop by—"

"Perhaps you'd best not. Gerald will be furious if I gain any weight." She leaned closer, and her voice became a whisper. "He says we're to leave London soon."

Rachel felt her heart lurch in her chest. "Leave London!"

"Sh-h-h!" Corrine sent a fearful glance at the stairs. "He says someone is looking for him. Perhaps the family of that girl back in Holdenby—the one he set his hounds on."

It was too good to be true after all! The art lessons were about to be snatched away from her, possibly even before she could begin them. Worse than that was the likelihood of never seeing Adam again. She swallowed around the lump in her throat and whispered, "When?"

"As soon as I can . . . borrow some money from Mr. Burke." She shook her head. "I know the man feels nothing for me, but perhaps his generosity will compel him to lend me some anyway."

"But you can't do that—not to Adam!"

Corrine's eyebrows shot up. "Adam? When did you start calling him that?"

"He asked me to."

"What happened last night, Rachel?" asked Corrine, her voice softening.

Rachel blushed. She couldn't tell Corrine—or anyone.

"He told you he loved you, didn't he?"

Rachel looked down at her hands. "Yes, ma'am."

"Then that's wonderful for you! It means you can get away from Gerald." Corrine reached out to touch her shoulder. "And from me."

How can I if we're going to leave? Rachel thought. She turned hopeless eyes toward her mistress. How could it be that she had gone to sleep last night with so much joy and hope for the future welling up inside of her and awakened to the same futility that had darkened her life for years?

Though her heart was dead now, she could still feel sympathy for Corrine's obvious misery. "Don't say it that way," she said softly. "You're good to me."

"Only lately." Corrine's face looked years older now. "If only I hadn't been so self-centered, perhaps we could have been friends."

"We are friends, ma'am."

Corrine wiped her eyes with the back of her hand. "Thank you for saying that. Anyway, even though I'll miss you, I'm happy that you'll be getting away from all of this."

"I don't see how. Now that we're leaving London . . ." Rachel shook her head helplessly.

"You have to tell Adam what's happening." Corrine's expression suddenly filled with determination. "Let him help you! I know it's proper to wait for a proposal and such nonsense, but you haven't got time."

"I can't do that! What if he's not planning . . ."

"To propose? I can assure you that when men like Adam fall in love, they think about marriage." Corrine swallowed. "I only wish I had found a man like him years ago, before I met Thomas . . . or Gerald. Anyway, even if he's not ready for that, at least he can help you find a safe place to stay until Gerald and I leave town."

A chill climbed up Rachel's spine at the thought of going to Adam with her hand out. Worse yet, she would have to confess her part in Corrine's duplicity. "Then you're still going with Mr. Moore?"

"I *have* to—don't you see? He won't allow me to leave him alive. And if I don't get some money from somewhere . . ."

"Then tell Adam the truth—perhaps he'll *give* you enough money to make Mr. Moore happy."

"The truth?" she sighed. "That my lover and I have to go away because he killed someone a long time ago, and now people are looking for him?" A bitter smile came to her lips. "Then I could explain that we need enough money to set ourselves up in another town where we can find another wealthy man that I can extort . . . or perhaps 'borrow' money from."

Rachel felt torn between the two people who mattered most to her. While she couldn't sit by and let the man she loved be deceived into giving money away on the pretext of a loan, she also knew the danger Corrine faced by incurring Gerald's wrath. "There's got to be another way!"

Corrine closed her eyes. When she opened them again, there was resigned acceptance of the inevitable in them. "There is another way," she said flatly. "I can sell my pearls, and tell Gerald the money came from Adam."

"Won't Mr. Moore ask about them?"

She shrugged. "Hopefully, he won't miss them until we're in another place, and I have to dress up to meet some other man. Then I'll pretend to look for them and get upset. He'll think they were lifted from my satchel on the train or something."

"What if he doesn't believe you?"

"Don't worry. I've become an expert at lying."

Before Rachel could comment, Corrine turned to her and said, "Wait and go to market after Gerald wakes up. While we're finishing breakfast, slip upstairs and get the necklace from my felt slippers in the back of my wardrobe. You can put them in your apron pocket. Then take them out and try to sell them."

"To whom, ma'am?"

"Your friend with the art gallery can tell you that, I'm sure. I'd sell them myself when Gerald's expecting me to go to Adam's this afternoon—but who knows if he'll follow? If you can bring back some money in the bottom of your market basket this morning, then I promise my visit with Adam will just be a social call. I won't ask for a shilling."

"May I go with you?"

"Don't you trust me?"

"Yes, ma'am, I do." Rachel replied earnestly. "But I don't want to stay here alone with Mr. Moore."

"Of course. I forgot about that," Corrine nodded. "There's another reason you'll have to go with me. Once Gerald knows I have the money, he'll expect all of us to leave—probably tomorrow."

Rachel put a hand up to her throat. "Tomorrow?"

"Which is why you've got to ask Adam for help *today*. Unless you want to spend the rest of your life following Gerald and me all over England."

"I just don't know if I can ask him," Rachel said. But a shudder racked her at the thought of living in the same house as Gerald, even for one more day.

"Don't, then," Corrine sighed. "I'll just send you to the kitchen to visit Bernice and then tell him your predicament myself. Then he can bow out gracefully if his affection for you isn't genuine, and you won't have to worry about whether he felt pressured into anything." When Rachel started to protest, she lifted a hand. "I'm still your mistress, dear girl. We'll do it my way."

"Then let's ask him to help both of us! If Mr. Moore has to leave town in a hurry, maybe there's somewhere we can hide until he's gone."

Temptation was evident on Corrine's face, but she shook her head sadly. "You don't know how obsessed he can be. I would be looking over my shoulder for the rest of my life! In fact, you run that very risk yourself."

"It's worth the risk to me," Rachel said quickly.

"Then let's just concern ourselves with delivering you from this situation." Pushing out her chair, Corrine stood, then surprised Rachel by leaning down to plant a kiss on her forehead. "If I can do something noble in my life, then perhaps my life will have meant something."

Rachel got up and threw her arms around her mistress's shoulders. "Oh, Missus—your life means something to me. And to God!"

"That would be nice to believe," said Corrine, gently disentangling herself from the girl's arms. "But it's too late to expect anything from God."

"No, ma'am! Adam told me—"

Both jerked their heads towards the top of the stairs at the sudden noise. "Gerald's awake," whispered Corrine. "You'd best start breakfast. And remember what I told you about the pearls!"

~

"And when did you say Mr. Moore answered the advertisement for your sister's house?" Joseph Price asked Mr. Eugene Graham.

Standing in the spacious foyer of his home, the elderly man drew his brows together. "Middle of February or first of March. It's recorded in my ledger if you need the exact date."

"That won't be necessary, but thank you for offering. I would be grateful for directions to the house, though. I'm still not familiar with the city."

"My pleasure." Mr. Graham lifted his bushy gray eyebrows. "My wife says that Mr. Moore has an inheritance coming?"

"Yes. From a distant cousin he kindly gave assistance to several years ago."

"That's good," the man nodded. "I like to see people like that rewarded."

Joseph smiled. "My feelings exactly."

~

"I think you should change into the blue silk instead," Gerald remarked, bending slightly to scan the dresses in Corrine's wardrobe. "Didn't you say it was Burke's favorite?"

"Yes," Corrine answered absently. For the seventh or eighth time, she glanced at the clock on her mantel and wondered if Rachel was having any success with selling the pearls.

"How much do you think you can 'borrow' from the man?"

She held her brush poised against her shoulder. "How much?" Forcing lightness into her voice was a struggle considering the heaviness of her heart. "I'm not sure. We haven't known each other for very long. Two hundred pounds?"

Gerald frowned and turned to watch her reflection in the mirror. "Don't you think he's good for five hundred?"

"Five hundred? I can certainly ask for that much, but there's no guarantee that I'll get it."

"That's the *last* time I pick out a religious milksop!" Gerald said bitterly, pounding his fist into his hand. "If only you had slept with the man, we'd have a chance at much more!"

Corrine winced inwardly at how casually Gerald could talk about prostituting the woman he professed to love, but she managed to keep her expression serene. "Are we really leaving in the morning?"

"Just as soon as we can get our clothes packed. Did you tell Rachel?"

"Yes. I'll get her to start packing when she gets back from market."

"Why did you send her? We don't need food if we're not going to be here."

"We'll need supper tonight, as well as a hamper to take on the train."

Gerald nodded. "Good idea—I didn't think about that." His face paled when a knock sounded from downstairs. "Are you expecting anybody?"

"No." Corrine set down her brush and stood. Her knees felt like water. "I'll go see who it is."

As she left the room and started down the stairs, an idea began forming in Corrine's mind. Perhaps there was a way out after all!

If the police are hunting for him because of that poor girl back in Holdenby, then they're not looking for me! Another knock sounded, and she glanced back at her bedroom door. *I didn't even know him when that happened!* All she had to do was open the door and let them in. Gerald certainly couldn't stalk her if he were in prison . . . or better yet, dangling from the end of a noose!

Quickening her steps, she crossed the sitting room and hall

to the front door and swung it open. All her hopes died at the sight of Jack, Adam Burke's gardener, standing there.

The big man snatched his cap from his head. "Beggin' your pardon, ma'am," his deep voice boomed. "Got a letter for Miss Rachel here."

Corrine was so crushed that she didn't even thank the man when he handed her the envelope. "All right," she mumbled and pushed the door closed.

Even in her depression, she knew beyond a shadow of a doubt that the envelope would spell trouble. She had to hide it. But when she walked into the sitting room, she found Gerald standing at the foot of the stairs.

"Why would Rachel be getting a letter?" he asked, suspiciously eyeing the envelope in her hand.

"You heard him?"

"The bloke didn't exactly whisper, whoever he was." He held out a hand. "Come on, let's see it."

Corrine's hand tightened, crinkling the paper. "But it's for Rachel."

Gerald laughed. "So?"

"I don't think we should—" She let out a startled cry as he snatched the paper from her hand.

"Calm down," he said as he tore open the envelope. "Let's see what our snow princess has been up to."

Something inside warned Corrine to turn and flee for her life, but her legs were barely able to keep from buckling under her as it was. Her heart felt as if it would fail her any minute as she watched Gerald's eyes moving along the page.

He could obviously sense the agony she was going through, for he kept his face free of any expression. He delighted in tormenting others, letting them feel everything was all right—for a little while. How could she ever have found this sadistic man attractive?

"A most interesting letter," he said at last, holding the page out to her. "Perhaps you'd care to read it?"

She took a step backwards. "I don't think . . ."

"Oh, but I insist." The corners of his mouth were curled in a smile, but there was an ominous gleam in his pale blue eyes. "Or would you like me to read it to you?"

Her throat dry, Corrine took the letter from his hands. Adam Burke's handwriting was instantly recognizable.

Dearest Rachel,

I cannot let the morning pass without telling you how much joy is in my heart! When I had consigned myself to a solitary existence, God sent you into my life. I know his hand is in this because he is the giver of perfect gifts. I will never believe that mere coincidence put us alone together yesterday evening; I can see his hand in that as well.

I pray that I did not frighten you with my declaration of love and that the affection you have for me will one day grow into something more. That is my most fervent desire; however, I will be patient and not pressure you to speak of things you may not yet feel.

When I informed Bernice that you have accepted Christ, she was beside herself! What a privilege it was for me to show you the way to the Cross; I shall never forget the look on your face as you prayed. Even now it comes back to my mind like a portrait.

Hershall delivered some documents to the children's home for me this morning. He came back with the news that the child Mrs. Hammond was so attached to is gone and that the good woman was inconsolable last night when she found out. Please give her my condolences. I am ashamed to admit I misjudged her greatly. I hope she will not mind that I took the liberty of sending a message to Penelope Morgan, asking if she could look in on Mrs. Hammond whenever her delicate condition would allow.

I look forward to seeing you again, dear Rachel—as soon as possible.

Yours always,
Adam

Corrine had barely been able to absorb the words on the page as she read, for the heat coming from Gerald's rigid posture was all her senses were capable of registering. With trembling fingers she lowered the page. Unable to look him in the eye, she focused on his mustache. "Gerald, I know this looks—"

The back of Gerald's hand raked across her face so forcefully that she stumbled backward and fell to the floor.

"I should have realized all along that you were lying to me!" he raged, standing over her with eyes bulging and both fists clenched.

"No!" she cried, trying to rise. Her whole face throbbed with pain, and blood trailed down from her nose to her chin. "Please let me explain!"

"Don't you say a word!" Gerald reached down and grabbed her by the collar, yanking her up to her feet. This time he slapped her across the face open-handed, keeping a choking grip on her collar so that she wouldn't fall.

"Please stop!" Corrine lifted her eyes pleadingly into his, shuddering at the murderous expression that scored his face.

Gerald suddenly let go of her collar, and she automatically lifted her arms to protect her face. With her eyes covered, Corrine could not see the blow coming, but when his fist slammed into her stomach, she screamed and doubled over.

~

As she turned down East India Dock Road, Rachel was careful not to let the market basket swing at her side. The basket, with its seventy pounds sterling tucked away under the fruits and cheeses, was in no danger of tipping anyway, for her steps were wooden, and her feet were as heavy as her heart.

How can I let Miss Corrine ask him to take me in like a poor wretched orphan? What would he think of me then? Yet how could she bear to leave London just when she'd gotten a taste of a life that promised such happiness?

The answer came into her fevered mind like a cool drink of water—Mrs. Morgan! While it wouldn't be proper for Rachel to ask Adam to hire her as a maid, hadn't the minister's wife told her that they could afford only one servant, a housekeeper who didn't even live in?

She could offer to work for nothing . . . only her meals. Surely she could convince them that she was a hard worker. And Margaret did seem to like her. In fact, Rachel could now recall Mrs. Morgan complimenting her ease with children during that first meal at Adam's. She would only ask for Sunday afternoons off so that she could pursue her art studies.

The best part of the plan was that Gerald wouldn't know where to look for her. She could slip out of the house after lunch—she still had the note Penelope Morgan had sent her, thanking her for the tiny portrait of her daughter, and the address was included!

For the first time that morning, her steps lightened. She wondered why the idea hadn't occurred to her before when she was desperately knocking on back doors looking for another position. Perhaps God had sent her the idea. She turned into the cobbled walk leading to the back of the house. Would God do something like that?

The only sad part of her plan was that she could see no way to help Corrine get away from Gerald. She thought about the money in her basket. If he was in such a hurry to leave London, why couldn't Corrine take the money and find a place in the city to hide? Seventy pounds seemed like a fortune to Rachel—surely someone could live for years on that much money.

I'll suggest it to her before I leave, she thought, her hand on the back-door latch. The door blurred as her eyes filled with tears. *When it's time to tell her good-bye.*

18

Must be the maid, thought Joseph Price, watching from the seat of his hired wagon as Rachel disappeared around the back of Gerald Moore's house. *Corrine Hammond has dark hair.*

He glanced back in the wagon bed at the two huge wooden trunks he had bought yesterday. Since he couldn't very well parade a bound and gagged woman through the streets of London without the police raising eyebrows, one was to be Mrs. Hammond's traveling berth until they reached the country—and the other Gerald Moore's coffin.

Joseph was not a cruel man, and he didn't relish the idea of locking any woman inside a box for three days. He had packed a jar of water and some fruit inside, and had carved numerous airholes in the top, but he was still uncomfortable with the whole idea. If Mrs. Hammond agreed to be quiet and not try to untie herself, perhaps he could remove the gag and allow her to lie concealed behind the wagon seat when the city was behind them.

Gerald Moore was a different story. Joseph patted the pistol in his coat pocket. Whether he actually had the nerve to shoot an unarmed man, he would soon find out. If he faltered in the end, he would bind and truss Mr. Moore with every inch of rope he could spare. Then he'd give Malcolm Nowells back his fifty pounds of blood money and let him dispose of the vermin himself.

~

At the sound of the back door swinging open on its hinges, Gerald stopped kicking Corrine. Immediately he turned on his heel and hurried to the back of the house without a backward glance at the woman huddled on the floor.

Rachel had just entered the hall. An expression of fear filled her eyes, and she drew back as he approached, clutching her market basket closer to her body.

Gerald eyed the basket she held in front of her like a shield, and his rage burned. He snatched the basket from her hands and flung it against the back parlor wall. The sound of coins raining against the marble floor drew his attention, and he stopped long enough to stare at the overturned contents of the basket.

"Why, what have we here?" he asked, turning a leering smile to the girl as he roughly seized her shoulders. "You've got Adam Burke paying for your services? Here I was sending the wrong woman to get money!"

Rachel's face went white. "No!"

"And how expertly you played the innocent maiden around me, only to go throwing yourself at a freak like him! You should be on the stage, Rachel . . . you're quite an actress!"

"I haven't . . ." Rachel's eyes went to the red stain smeared across Gerald's disheveled shirt. She covered her mouth with her hand. "Where's Mrs. Hammond?" she demanded weakly.

"Dead for all I care! Now come upstairs!"

"Dead?" Rachel tried to pull away from him, but he grabbed her arm and bent it behind her back. "You killed her!" she cried.

Still holding her arm in a painful grip, Gerald put his mouth inches from her ear and whispered, "We don't need her anymore, dearest Rachel. You and I are going to be partners starting right this minute—in *everything!*" Then walking behind her, he pushed her toward the sitting room, forcing more pressure on her arm every time she struggled.

When they reached the bottom of the stairs, Rachel saw her mistress lying on the floor across the room. She lunged toward her. "Corrine!"

"She can't hear you," he snarled, jerking her back to his side. "Now get moving before I break your arm!"

~

Joseph got down from the wagon and tied his horse's reins to a low-hanging branch. He decided to follow the maid's steps to the back—most likely that door was unlocked during the day. He had thought about just knocking at the front door, but it would certainly be less trouble to slip inside and make sure Gerald Moore and Corrine Hammond were indeed there. The element of surprise would be crucial in a situation like this.

When he made it around to the back of the house, he stopped and put his ear to the door. A man's loud but unintelligible voice was coming from somewhere inside. *Must be Moore,* he thought. His blood ran cold then when his ear caught the unmistakable cry of a woman. Quickly Joseph eased the doorknob to the right—it yielded to the pressure of his hand.

~

In the sitting room, Corrine was only able to raise herself to her knees by strength of will. Never had she been in so much pain—her whole face ached, and her side throbbed so badly that she had to take shallow breaths to keep from passing out.

Her heart skipped a beat when she became conscious of Gerald's ranting voice. Was he coming back to do her in? She couldn't take another beating.

The sound of Rachel's fearful cry startled her and, trembling, she turned her head toward the staircase where the two were struggling. *Got to get help!* she thought.

Crawling on her hands and knees, she made it down the hall. Once at the front door, she grabbed the doorknob and pulled herself up. *Can't stop now!* she told herself, though the urge to lie back down was almost overwhelming. Holding her side, she opened the door and fell through the doorway. Then she got to her feet again and staggered to the road.

A young man dressed in the clothes of a laborer was passing by on a horse. He dug his heels into the mount's side and hurried away before Corrine could reach him. Panting and still clutching her side, she tried to wave down a carriage with two startled women passengers, but the driver refused to slow down.

Exhausted, Corrine stumbled to the middle of the road— the next carriage would *have* to stop! While she waited for someone to come along the quiet street, she looked with longing at the horse and wagon tied just a few feet away. But she had never learned to handle a horse, and she was in no condition to start now.

She began to fear that she would lose consciousness right where she stood when the sound of horse's hooves came from behind her. Corrine wheeled around as fast as her fading strength would allow.

A hired hansom cab was turning into the street and began

slowing down as it came her way. Waving an arm, she croaked out, "Help!" and fell to one knee.

"Mrs. Hammond?" A familiar voice called down from the inside of the carriage.

"Penelope!" rasped Corrine as she crumpled to the cobble-stones. She heard the minister's wife instruct the driver to help her into the carriage. Moments later she was inside, propped up in Penelope's arms. Pain racked her whole body now, but at least she wasn't going to die in the middle of the street.

"Must get Adam . . . help Rachel!" she whispered.

"Let's get the police," answered Penelope, white as a sheet. But before she could call to the driver, Corrine grabbed her arm.

"No police! Get Adam now!"

~

"No!" screamed Rachel, wrestling with Gerald at the top of the stairs. Her left arm felt as if daggers were cutting at her nerves, but she determined that she'd rather have him kill her now than drag her into Corrine's bedroom.

"You're going to obey me if I have to beat the stubbornness out of you!" he snarled back. "Don't think you can get away with—"

"Let her go, Moore!" came a deep voice from below.

Still struggling desperately, Rachel caught a glimpse of a dark-haired, bearded man at the foot of the stairs. He was holding a pistol pointed in their direction.

"What the—?" Gerald jerked his head to look down at the intruder, easing his grip on Rachel just a little. She seized the chance and pulled away from him with every ounce of strength she possessed.

305

With the force of Rachel's escape from his arms, Gerald lost his balance. His right foot groped for the step behind him, then he began tumbling down the stairs, flailing his arms and shrieking as he fell.

He landed on his back on the marble floor, within inches of the stranger's boots. For several horrible seconds Gerald lay there with panicked eyes wide open, wheezing and clawing for air. Then his arms dropped to his chest, and he was still.

The tall man put his pistol in his pocket and bent down to touch Gerald's neck. Straightening again, he looked up at the girl on the stairs.

"You all right, miss?"

"I don't . . . know," she breathed. She felt weak, and her teeth chattered as she hugged her arms to her side.

The man stepped over Gerald's body and began coming up the stairs. "Step back a bit," he told her. "You look like you're about to faint."

Rachel obeyed, taking a step backwards. "Are you a policeman?" she managed to ask through trembling lips.

"No, ma'am. Joseph Price is my name." Just five or six steps below the top landing, he pointed to the bedroom door behind Rachel. "Is Mrs. Hammond in there?"

"Mrs. Hammond!" With a strength born of sheer panic, Rachel gathered her skirt and flew down the stairs. She passed the startled Joseph and stepped over Gerald's legs at the bottom.

She let out a cry when she reached where Corrine's body had lain, near the hallway entrance. Smears of blood led a path through the hall to the open front door. Ignoring Joseph's questions as he followed in her wake, she ran outside and peered in every direction.

"She's not dead!" Rachel cried, shielding her eyes against the noon sun. "But where did she go?"

"Do you think she went for the police?" asked Joseph.

"I don't know! She was hurt—there was blood all over her!"

~

Joseph glanced over at his rig on the other side of the road and frowned. Obviously someone had aided Corrine Hammond. She was probably on her way to the hospital now, meaning the police would arrive here at the house any minute.

At least one of the trunks will be put to use, he thought grimly. Malcolm Nowells would require proof of Gerald's death, so he had to get the body out of the house and on its way before anything could happen to prevent it.

As for Mrs. Hammond—he wasn't about to kidnap a woman who could be dying. He thought about the blood on the floor. Surely she would have to stay in London for a while as she recovered from whatever wounds Moore had inflicted. He would deliver Gerald Moore's remains to Mr. Nowells and come back.

"Are you going to be all right?" he asked the maid, who had given up on her search and was taking sluggish steps back toward the house. There was an unnatural pallor about her face, and he wondered again if she were about to faint.

"Yes," she answered, worry etched into her features. Still, after a few seconds she managed to add, "Thank you for coming inside when you did."

He turned and joined her. "I'm glad he didn't hurt you," he said truthfully. His concern returned to business. "Don't you have *any* idea where Mrs. Hammond might have gone?"

307

~

Adam! Rachel thought instantly. But she immediately dismissed the idea. Corrine was too afraid of being caught; and anyway, Adam never went out into the streets during the daylight.

"No, sir."

Joseph sighed. "If there's a blanket you can spare, I'll get Mr. Moore out of the way for you."

She shuddered visibly. With a sidelong gaze she studied the stranger's face, wondering for the first time how he happened to show up at exactly the right time. Did she have the right to allow him to take Gerald's body away, no matter how she wished to have it out of her sights?

"It's all right, ma'am," he assured her, as if sensing her perplexity. "I may not be a policeman, but I might as well bring the body to the proper . . . authorities."

"Please take him then. What did you say your name was?"

"Joseph Price. And what is yours?"

"Rachel Jones."

"Are you Mrs. Hammond's housekeeper?"

"Yes, sir."

The man smiled and followed her through the front door. "I'm sure I'll be seeing you again soon, Miss Jones."

~

Ten minutes later, Joseph Price was sitting in the wagon seat with his prize in one of the trunks behind him. He had done it . . . beaten Scotland Yard's finest detectives! *You're not too old for this job after all!* he told himself.

He would eventually alert Scotland Yard to the fact that

Gerald Moore was dead—after he had delivered the evidence to Squire Nowells. Perhaps he was guilty of interfering with a murder investigation. But the authorities would no doubt be glad that a murderous beast like Moore had gotten what he deserved. And once the body was examined, there would be little doubt that Price was telling the truth about the cause of death.

Joseph was relieved that he hadn't had to kill Moore himself, even if the man was a snake. Half his job was done. Corrine Hammond could wait. Wherever she was now, her maid would no doubt tell her that Moore was dead. That should make her feel safe enough so that she would stay in the city until he could return to find her.

He gave the reins a gentle snap, urging the horses to a trot. He had been paid, and paid well, not to involve the law . . . and that's what he would do. For the time being, Scotland Yard would assume that the Gerald Moore they were looking for had left London. He glanced over his shoulder at the trunk behind him. And they would be right.

~

Just a few more minutes, Penelope Morgan told herself in the swaying carriage. *Don't get sick!* With both arms the minister's wife cradled Corrine's head and shoulders in her lap, and she fought against the nausea that threatened to take over. Taking shallow breaths, she tried to concentrate on bracing the woman through the jarring ride through the streets of East London.

Over the squeaking of the wheels she thought she imagined a sound from Corrine's lips. She bent closer. "Mrs. Hammond?"

"Faster," came the almost inaudible whisper. "Go faster."

Penelope tightened her arms and steeled both herself and the woman against the sharp turn up ahead. "He's going as fast as he can."

Corrine's lips moved again. "Taking too long. Get police instead."

"Sh-h-h," Penelope answered, wishing she had insisted on doing that in the first place. "We're almost there now, so don't try to talk." She lifted a voiceless prayer for Rachel and wondered if the girl was in the hands of whatever monster had so severely beaten Corrine.

Minutes later they pulled up in front of Adam's house. Jack was tending to some shrubbery on the front lawn.

"Get Adam!" she called to him.

The driver had jumped from his seat and was at the side of the carriage now. "What can I do, ma'am?" he asked, his eyes wide.

"Can you carry her inside?"

"Right away!"

~

Rachel wandered from room to room, painfully aware that this was the first time she had ever been in the house alone. She took the food that had tumbled out of her market basket down to the larder, setting aside the apples that had been badly bruised until she could decide what to do with them.

Then she came back up the kitchen stairs and gathered the money she had gotten for Corrine's pearls. The rosewood desk against the wall in the sitting room seemed like a good hiding place until she could give it to her mistress. A raw ache came to the back of her throat. She had no idea where Corrine had disappeared to or if she would ever see her again.

Rachel avoided looking at the bottom of the staircase, where Gerald's body had lain. The fact that she was free of him hadn't fully sunk in yet. Even though she had watched Mr. Price carry him out, she almost expected Gerald to come walking back through that door at any minute.

For the third time she went to the dining room and straightened the chairs. If Corrine did come back, she'd be upset at the bloodstains trailing from the sitting room to the front door. She went down into the kitchen and filled a bucket with water. Taking several rags from the rag-bin and a cup of sand for scouring, she carried it all back up to the sitting room.

It was good to have some hard work to keep her mind occupied. On her knees she scrubbed at the white marble floor with an almost maniacal zeal, following the smeared blood into the hall. She was almost at the front door when, with her head lowered, she grazed the coat stand with her shoulder. The stand began to rock against the floor, and she automatically reached out a hand to steady the swaying wooden pole. Gerald's evening frock coat fell from the rack, landing across her back. With a cry of fright, Rachel grabbed the coat and flung it away from her.

Then the floor beneath her began to grow dark.

~

Adam Burke leaned forward and dug his heels into Jupiter's side. As his steed galloped around omnibuses, coaches, and pedestrians that crowded Haycock Street, Adam became aware for a brief second that everyone within sight was watching. Some were even pointing his way. Whether it was because of the speed of his horse or the scars on his face, he didn't

know—and didn't care. Rachel was in trouble, and that was
the only thing that mattered.

Why didn't I grab my army pistol? he upbraided himself. *Or at
least my sword!*

It was too late to do anything about that now. He would
use whatever weapon he could find to protect her, even his
bare hands. He only prayed that it was not too late!

He rode Jupiter right up to the steps of the house and
jumped from the animal. The front door opened readily, and
he almost tripped over Rachel's body. To his horror there was
blood on the floor nearby. With a cry of anguish, he fell to his
knees.

~

Vaguely aware that whoever had been speaking to her in her
dream was now running his hand through her hair, Rachel
blinked her eyes. "Adam?" she asked cautiously.

"Rachel!" His voice was the most welcome sound her ears
had ever heard. Then the joy in his expression turned to concern. "Where are you hurt?"

Her thoughts were still quite muddled. She had to lie there
for a few seconds before she realized that, aside from a small
ache where she had bumped her head on the floor, she was all
right. "Not hurt," she finally told him. "Mrs. Hammond . . ."

"She's at my house." He helped her to her feet, then put his
arm around her shoulder and led her into the sitting room. "I
left right after Penelope told me you were in trouble," he said
as he eased her into the cushions and sat down beside her, "so
I don't know the extent of her injuries, or even what happened. Who did this?"

"Mr. Moore."

"Mr. Moore? Who . . . ?"

"He lived here," she tried to explain. "He beat her, and then he tried . . ."

Adam's face darkened. "Where is he?" he demanded, starting to get to his feet.

"He's dead," Rachel answered flatly. She put a hand on his arm. "Gone."

"Where?"

"I'm not exactly sure. A man named Mr. Price took his body away. He saved my life."

Adam leaned back on the cushions and rubbed his temples. "I don't understand any of this, Rachel."

He looked so confused that Rachel's heart went out to him. She longed to have him take her in his arms again and tell her that he didn't even want to know what had happened in the past.

But that wasn't going to happen. Besides, she owed him a confession of the secrets she had kept from him. But she first had to know if her mistress was going to live.

"May we first see about Mrs. Hammond?" she asked him. "Then I'll explain."

"Are you strong enough?"

"Yes."

He nodded. "Jack's following with the dogcart—he should be here shortly."

When he turned away and didn't speak for a little while, Rachel thought he was angry. Unsure of what to do, she touched his arm again. He turned his face toward her, and she noticed the tears in his eyes. "Adam?"

Hesitating only for a brief moment, he put his arms around

her and drew her close. "I'm so sorry all of this happened," she whispered, closing her eyes.

"Sorry?" His arms tightened around her. "I was so afraid I'd lose you right after I found you. . . . I'm just thankful to God that you're alive!"

"I have so much to tell you."

"And I think I need to hear it," he said. "But whatever it is, Rachel, it won't make me stop loving you."

19

LUCY was standing on the front porch, looking quite anxious, when Rachel, Adam, and Jack arrived at Adam's house. She rushed out to the drive before Adam could help Rachel from the dogcart. "I was afraid you were dead!" she blurted out to Rachel, her red-rimmed eyes proof of her state of mind.

"I'm fine." Rachel gave the girl a weak smile. Once on the ground, she allowed Adam to put his arm protectively around her shoulders. "How is Mrs. Hammond?"

"I'm not sure. Mum and the doctor are in there with her now. Mrs. Morgan, too."

"Maybe you should make Miss Rachel some strong tea," Jack suggested to his daughter as he climbed down from Jupiter's back.

"I believe we all could use some, Lucy," said Adam. To Rachel, he asked gently, "Are you able to walk?"

"I am." Leaving Jack to tend to the horses, they started for the house. Though concern about the condition of her mistress was uppermost in her mind, Rachel couldn't help but be conscious of Adam's strong arm around her. *Am I able to walk?* With him holding her like that, she almost felt that she could fly.

An older man carrying a black bag and wearing a black suit, whom Adam addressed as Doctor Gilford, stood in the hallway. "Mrs. Hammond's ribs are bruised badly, but none appear to be broken," he said in answer to Adam's inquiry. "Her nose, however, has been broken. She is asleep at the moment, and I'll be back this evening to check on her."

"You don't think she needs to be in a hospital?"

"That isn't necessary; she'll mend much more quickly right where she is. Complete bed rest for at least three weeks. I've given her some laudanum. I almost had to give her another dose to calm her. She was quite concerned about a young lady. . . ." Looking over his spectacles, the doctor seemed to notice Rachel for the first time. He turned to Adam with a questioning look.

"This is Miss Jones," Adam told him, "the young lady Mrs. Hammond was worried about. Would you examine her as well?"

"I'm fine," Rachel protested. "I'd like to stay with my missus, so she won't be alone when she wakes."

"Now, now," Doctor Gilford clucked in mild reproof. "That will be hours from now, and there is already a woman with her. Perhaps you are fine, but let me just make certain that you aren't going to faint ten minutes after I'm gone."

They moved into the drawing room, and after Rachel was persuaded to take a seat on a couch, the doctor sat next to her and peered into her eyes with practiced skill. "Your pupils are not dilated." After taking her pulse, he continued to hold her arm. "Your skin still feels warm," he remarked with a smile. "That is a good sign."

"Are you sure?" asked Adam, hovering over them. "She still looks pale to me."

"Some rest would be good for her, but I see no evidence of anything that should alarm us." Straightening, he gathered up his black bag. "I'll be back this evening. Send for me in the meantime if you need me."

Dr. Gilford had just left when Lucy came into the room with a tray, followed by Penelope Morgan. The minister's wife immediately sat down next to Rachel. "I was so worried about you!" she exclaimed, putting an arm around her. "Mrs. Hammond didn't want me to summon the police until it was too late to do so. I've felt wretched since we arrived here. I was afraid that something would happen to you, and it would be my fault for not going to the police."

"Please don't blame yourself," Rachel told her. "The police couldn't have gotten there any faster than Mr. Price."

"Mr. Price? Who is—"

At a cautious shake of the head from Adam, Mrs. Morgan waited in silence for a wide-eyed Lucy to serve the tea and leave the room. "A man materialized out of nowhere," Adam explained, still looking a bit confused himself. "A stranger, at that. He took Mr. Moore's body away."

Penelope blinked. "I'm sorry, I don't understand. Was Mr. Moore the man who beat Mrs. Hammond so severely?"

Struck dumb at the memory of Gerald's rage, Rachel nodded.

"Then shouldn't we notify the police now? After all, a man is dead."

Panic forced Rachel to find her voice. "It was an accident . . . he fell down the stairs." She reached out to put a hand on the woman's arm. "Please, you mustn't tell the police."

"Can you tell us why, Rachel?" Adam asked. He took a

chair across from the couch and leaned forward intently. "Are you in some kind of trouble?"

Her fingers clasped tensely in her lap, Rachel looked up into Adam's serious brown eyes and wondered if she would ever see the love in them that she had seen just last night. A wave of apprehension swept through her. Had he really said, just a little while ago, that nothing would make him stop loving her? Or would he reject her when he heard the whole story? "I don't know," she answered in a feeble voice, blinking away the tears that stung her eyes. "I just don't know."

Penelope took that as her cue to leave the two of them alone. "I'm going up to tell Bernice that you're safe, if Lucy hasn't already," she said in a quiet voice. "Then I must go home. I'm certain that Robert will want to come back here this evening and see about Mrs. Hammond, so we'll visit with you then."

Adam got up from his chair to escort her from the room. "I can find my way to the door, Adam," Penelope said gently.

"But I want to get someone to drive you home."

"I can ask Jack myself," replied Penelope. "Stay here with Rachel."

When she was gone, Adam came over to sit next to Rachel. "You know, I think I'd like to buy Robert and Penelope a horse and carriage, as a gift when the baby comes," he said. "I don't know why I haven't thought of it before, but it must be such a bother to have to depend upon hired transportation all of the time. Do you think they would like that?"

"Yes," Rachel murmured. *Tell him now,* a voice inside her urged. She could live not a moment longer with the uncertainty of what his reaction would be. Swallowing around the lump in her throat, she said, "Adam, I want to tell you what

I've done." Before he could say a word, she blurted out in detail her part in Corrine's extortion of Squire Nowells and half a dozen other men.

She could not look at Adam when she reached the part about Corrine's most recent deception, Adam himself. "I delivered letters here that I knew were written to ensnare you," she confessed. "It was only a miracle that you weren't duped. You're the first one."

A tense silence enveloped the room for a moment. She sat clutching her skirts miserably, waiting for him to walk out. To her surprise, his fingers gently lifted her chin to face him.

"My God has been known to work a miracle now and then," he smiled. "I'd say that it was a miracle that led me to you."

Had he been listening? "Adam, I lied to you."

"Did you? Tell me Rachel, how old were you when Corrine and this man adopted you?"

"Almost thirteen."

"And you're nineteen now. That makes over six years of being told that you would go to prison if you told anyone what they were doing. You can't be held responsible for that."

Rachel was grateful for the warmth in his tone, but she shook her head. "You're being kind, making excuses for me. But I could have at least left them. At least in the workhouse I wouldn't have had to tell lies and hurt people."

"No, you wouldn't," he agreed, his brown eyes shining at her. "But it would have been a hard choice to leave the only home you knew, however mistreated you were. I understand that."

"I don't want you just to understand. What I want . . ." She swallowed again. "What I need is your forgiveness."

319

"Yes, of course," Adam replied at once. He gathered her hands up in his own. "I forgive you, my dear Rachel Jones. The past is over, so let's concentrate on the future."

He looked at her intently. "But what should be done about Corrine Hammond." Anger tightened his voice. "Perhaps the police should be notified of her past actions."

"Oh, please don't," Rachel pleaded. "She's changed, Adam. You mustn't blame her for this."

"But you don't have to be afraid of her anymore."

"I'm not afraid of her now. She tried to help me get away from Gerald—in fact, that's probably why he beat her."

He didn't look convinced. "What if she tries to extort money from someone else in the future?"

"She's not going to do that."

"How can you tell?" he probed gently.

"I just know," she answered. "You forgave me; can't you forgive her?"

A crooked smile touched his face as he raised her hand to his lips and kissed it. "For you, I could forgive Napoleon," he whispered. "In fact, Mrs. Hammond is welcome to stay here for as long as she needs."

"Thank you, Adam."

"Now what are we going to do about you? We certainly can't send you back to that house alone." He frowned in concentration. "And it wouldn't be proper for you and me to be living here under the same roof."

"No, it wouldn't." Rachel was glad he had been gentleman enough not to ask her to stay. She would have felt like a kept woman, in spite of the innocence of the circumstances.

"There is a very staid boarding establishment for ladies in

the city. I've seen it advertised in the *Times*. The head-
mistress—"

"I haven't enough money to pay for such a place." She
raised her hand to stop the offer that she knew was on his lips.
"And I can't accept your charity, Adam." Then she remembered the idea that had come to her earlier. "This morning I
thought of asking the Morgans to hire me . . . just for room
and board. Do you think they would?"

"You mean, as a servant?"

"That's what I am. It seemed that . . . God put it in my
mind to ask them. Does he do things like that?"

"I believe he does," Adam answered. "But at the risk of
interfering with the work of the Lord, do you mind if I make
a suggestion?"

"A suggestion?"

"Yes. Ask the Morgans. I would feel better about your
being with them, and it's likely that, in her condition,
Penelope could use some help with Margaret." The crooked
smile came back to his face. "But please don't get too comfortable over there."

Rachel's breath caught in her throat. "Don't get too—"

"Comfortable." For the first time since he brought Rachel
back to his house, he looked anxious. "Because as soon as
you'll have me—if you'll have me, that is—I'd like you to be
my wife."

When she couldn't answer, the anxiety on his face
increased. "Would you consider marrying me, Rachel?"

"I'll . . . yes, I'll marry you," she stammered. "I love you."
He gathered her in his arms, and she closed her eyes for his
kiss. A soft, sweet kiss that held the promise of forever.

A little while later, she sat with her head resting against his chest while he stroked her hair and whispered how much he loved her. She marveled at how so much happiness could come to a person who had been so wretched. Not too long ago, in fact, she had cried out to God from the depths of this misery, *Isn't there someplace I can go?*

In his kindness, God had answered that prayer. She would have a place. *A place where I am loved,* she thought with wonder. Lifting a hand to touch her future husband's cheek, she breathed another prayer, this time a prayer of thanks.

~

After a late lunch of soup, bread, and cheese, Adam persuaded Rachel to rest for a while. The ordeal had drained her physically. She agreed, with the condition that someone would inform her when Corrine awakened.

At her employer's request, Marie smiled and led her down the inner hallway to an impressive marble staircase leading up to the spacious landing of the next floor. "Mrs. Hammond's in there," the maid whispered as she pointed to one of several closed doors upstairs.

She walked past it and paused at the door next to Corrine's. It opened up into a cheery boudoir, the walls covered with gilt-trimmed rose wallpaper. The room was furnished with a writing table, a chaise lounge, and an armchair. They went through the boudoir into a dressing room with a washstand, clothes press, another armchair, a large wardrobe, and a mirror. Next came the bedroom itself, offering just a bed and two bedside tables.

"I can't imagine taking a nap in a place so fine," Rachel said softly, reaching out to touch one of the many chintz-covered pillows on the bed. "It's too nice; I wouldn't be able to sleep for fear of wrinkling the covers."

Marie laughed. "These rooms are crying out to be used, dear. Why don't you make yourself at home?"

"The chaise in the other room would suit me better. Do you mind if I rest there?"

"Of course not," she replied.

"And someone will tell me when my missus wakes?"

"The very moment."

~

Marie was true to her word, for Rachel was awakened a while later by a hand on her shoulder. "Mrs. Hammond's asking for you."

Rachel opened her eyes and blinked. She was expecting Marie, but it was Adam's cook beaming down at her. "Bernice!" She jumped up from the chaise lounge to embrace the woman.

"I'm sorry I didn't come down to see you when you got here," Bernice said. "Lucy told me you were fine, and I just couldn't leave your Mrs. Hammond by herself. She's such a frail little thing, really."

"I'm glad you stayed with her. May I see her now?"

"Now's a good time. When the doctor comes back, I'm sure he'll put her to sleep again." Rachel brushed the wrinkles from her dress and followed the cook to Corrine's door.

"I'm going to see about my kitchen now," Bernice whispered. "You go on in. I'll be up later to see about your missus."

Corrine lay motionless, propped up on several pillows. Her nose was swathed with white bandages and her bruised face was shaded a deep purple. Her eyes were the only part of her that moved, following Rachel as she walked into the bed-room.

"Oh, Mrs. Hammond!" she exclaimed, coming over to kneel at the side of the bed.

"Rachel," came a hoarse whisper. Corrine's lips, while part-ed, were stiff and barely moving.

"Are you hurting terribly?" It was a foolish question; Rachel could see that her mistress was in pain.

"Yes," Corrine replied. "But it doesn't matter. You're safe."

"Mr. Gerald told me that he killed you!"

"I was afraid he would do the same to you. How did you get away?"

"It's a long story, ma'am. Perhaps I should tell you when you're better."

Corrine gave an almost imperceptible shake of the head, then winced at the effort. "Does he know where we are?"

Rachel's eyes widened. Hadn't anyone told her? But of course—she had been asleep since Rachel arrived. She didn't want to be the one to tell Corrine, but Corrine needed to know that Gerald couldn't find her and finish the job.

"Mr. Gerald is dead. He can't hurt you anymore."

There was no reaction from the woman in the bed, and for a moment Rachel wondered if she had heard. She was just about to repeat herself when Corrine asked, "Are you sure?"

"I saw him die."

Corrine blinked rapidly, and Rachel saw that her eyes were wet with tears. "I should have died, too," she whispered.

"Oh, no, ma'am. Don't say that!"

"I hurt too many people, just like Gerald. Why didn't God let me die?"

A soft knock at the door prevented Rachel's reply. Dr.

Gilford, accompanied by Bernice, came into the room. "I see my patient is awake," the man said as he carried his black bag over to the bed.

Rachel got to her feet, then stretched closer to whisper in Corrine's ear. "Maybe God has a good reason for letting you live."

20

A week later, Corrine was sitting up in the bed in Adam's guest room. "The soup was delicious."

Bernice smiled and moved the tray to a nearby dresser. "Thank you, ma'am. Now, let's get you back under the covers." Helping the bedridden woman slide back down between the sheets, the cook frowned when Corrine winced. "Are you hurtin' much?"

"My ribs still hurt a bit when I move, but I believe I could manage the stairs. I know it's an inconvenience to bring my meals up here."

Waving her concerns away, Bernice said, "It's no bother at all. And let's wait and try the stairs on Sunday . . . that is, if you're still determined to go to the meetin'."

"I'd like to go very much." For the first time, the thought occurred to her that Adam Burke probably knew about her past by now. He hadn't turned her in to the police, no doubt for Rachel's sake, but would he welcome her at his chapel meetings? She bit her lip and looked up at Bernice. "The only thing is . . ."

"Yes?"

"Do you think I'll be welcome?"

The cook smiled. "You're worried about that? Well,

Mr. Adam asked me this morning if I thought you would need some help with the stairs, come Sunday."

"He did?"

"Indeed he did. We'll have to get one of your pretty dresses ready, and Dora can style your hair for you."

"It won't help, I don't think." Corrine lifted a hand and gingerly touched her swollen nose. "I've been so conceited about my looks—it seems somehow fitting that this should happen to me."

"Now, don't go sayin' things like that," Bernice gently scolded as she stood over her. "The doctor said it'll still take a while for the swelling to go down, but one day it'll be almost as good as new—you'll see. As for it being fitting, you could have died coming here to get help for Rachel, so don't be too hard on yourself!"

Corrine gave her a weak but grateful smile. "Thank you, Bernice."

The cook smiled back. "Well, I'd best be gettin' back."

"Will I see you at suppertime?"

"No doubt you will! You think I trust anyone else around here to see that you get the proper nourishment?"

Corrine breathed a sigh of relief. She had some more questions to ask Bernice about God, and she didn't think she could wait until tomorrow. "Will you read to me again tonight?"

Bernice glanced at her Bible lying at the foot of the bed and nodded. "I'll read all night if you want me to. I've never seen a person so thirsty to hear the Word of God."

When Bernice had left, Corrine closed her eyes and waited for sleep. After the first day, the doctor had left some laudanum in case her bruised ribs caused too much pain, but she had refused every time Bernice or one of the maids offered to give her a dose. *I've numbed my thoughts too many times,* she told herself. *It's time to face the things I've done.*

Some of the scenes from her life that replayed in her mind were far more painful than her physical injuries. But Bernice had said it was a step in the right direction to own up to them. "We can't reconcile with God till we're ready to admit that we're sinners," she had said.

The kindly woman had offered to explain further, but Corrine hadn't been ready then to hear it all. The offer of mercy, of forgiveness for all of the sins she had committed, had been too strange, too wonderful a concept to absorb all at once.

Now she was more than ready. She hoped that the hours would pass quickly until Bernice came back to see her again.

As she had so many times lately, she wondered what Jenny, her daughter, was doing at this moment. And Thomas, her own husband . . . would he still be terribly bitter that she had left, even after all these years?

She was determined to find out, one way or another. Dr. Gilford had said that, since none of her bones were broken, she could ride in a carriage in about two more weeks. She would go to Leawick and see if it was possible to make amends for the hurt she had caused two innocent people.

~

"I thought you'd never get here!" Adam greeted Rachel and the Morgans in the front hallway on Sunday morning.

"Were you missing me, my friend?" Robert teased as he helped the women with their capes. "Or was it Penelope or little Margaret here that you couldn't wait to see?"

Adam patted Robert's giggling daughter on the head, then

reached for Rachel's hand. "I missed all of you, of course."
But his loving smile was for Rachel alone.

Robert and Penelope Morgan had refused to even consider
hiring her as a maid. "Adam has told us that you plan to
marry," Robert told her. "We have an extra bedroom, and
you're to stay as our guest." Still, Rachel made it a point to
give a helping hand to the housekeeper and to entertain
Margaret.

Her first art lesson had been Wednesday morning. Now that
she had much more free time, Reuben Solomon had gracious-
ly agreed to change the day and time of the appointment. He
was a talented artist and a patient teacher, and he told Rachel
that she had great potential.

She was still uncertain whether to tell Adam that she was
aware that he had arranged the lessons. For now, she would let
him enjoy his little secret. She would thank him by working
hard to become the finest artist she could be.

And she had a secret of her own. Her first portrait in oils,
based on her sketch the first day she met him, would be a
painting of the man she loved—scars and all, with the light of
love and compassion shining from his warm brown eyes.

~

Robert's sermon was about the grace of God. Seated in
Adam's most comfortable overstuffed armchair, brought into
the drawing room just for her, Corrine drank it all in. Marie
and Dora had fussed over her, gathering her dark hair in
ringlets at the crown of her head. They had dabbed a little
powder under her eyes to cover the bruises, but they could do
nothing for the swollen bridge of her nose.

It didn't matter. Corrine was barely aware of her appearance or of the fact that she was dressed up for the first time in a week. Closing her eyes, she remembered Bernice's words—the words that finally convinced her that she could be forgiven of her past misdeeds. *"Where sin abounded, grace did much more abound."*

~

After the worship service, Corrine was too physically drained to continue sitting. She allowed Hershall and Jack to help her upstairs, first admonishing Bernice not to follow with a tray. "I'd like you to stay and enjoy your lunch," she told the cook. "Besides, I'm more in need of a nap right now than food." Rachel insisted on escorting them upstairs so that she could turn down Corrine's sheets. After the men had left, she brushed a kiss against her mistress's forehead. "Sleep well," she whispered. "I'll come up later and tell you what happened at lunch."

"Oh?" Corrine smiled weakly. "Some important announcement, perhaps?"

Adam's letter, the one he had sent to her yesterday, was tucked into the sleeve of Rachel's yellow gown. The feel of the fine vellum paper against her arm reminded her how much he loved her. *I've waited for someone like you all of my life,* he had written. *Please give me permission to ask Robert to marry us right away.*

Rachel had sent him a reply that very same hour. She smiled back at Corrine, arranging the comforter around her shoulders. "You'll find out after your nap."

She went back downstairs to find Adam, the Morgans, and the servants waiting just outside the dining room. "I thought you would go ahead and start without me," she said timidly. "I'm sorry to keep you waiting."

"Worth waiting for, Miss!" Jack replied, provoking a round of laughter. Rachel remembered the gardener's standard Sunday morning compliment to Robert Morgan and joined in the laughter. Taking the arm that Adam offered, she walked with him into the dining room.

When the meal was finished and everyone was involved in animated conversation, Adam stood and rapped his dessert spoon on his water goblet. "I have something to tell you." His face glowed.

Rachel felt her cheeks go warm. All eyes turned toward her.

"I believe you are aware that dear Rachel has agreed to marry me. What I would like to ask . . ." He stopped and corrected himself. "What *we* would like to ask all of you, dear friends, is that you attend our wedding as soon as Robert can arrange to marry us."

Hearty cheers rose up from all corners of the table. Rachel looked around at the expressions of warmth and acceptance, and realized that she had a family at last.

"If *when* you plan to get married is dependent upon me," Robert said wryly, "I can marry you in the morning. After all, the chairs are already set up in the drawing room."

"Tomorrow morning is too soon," Adam answered immediately. Then, giving Rachel a look of pure, unabashed love, he added, "I don't think you could have your chapel ready by morning."

A hush fell over the group. Even Rachel was caught by surprise. She, too, had assumed that the wedding would take place here in Adam's home.

"You want to marry in a *church,* Mr. Adam?" Bernice finally asked.

Adam raised an eyebrow. "Why do you all look so surprised? A church is a proper place to have a wedding, isn't it?"

"But, Mr. Adam," Lucy blurted out, "you don't like folks to see—" At the sharp looks from her parents on either side, the girl cut her sentence short and looked down at her hands.

"It's all right, Lucy. I've hidden away in this house long enough. It's time to see what London looks like in the daylight."

Robert beamed at his old friend. "I think it's a wonderful idea! What made you come to this decision?"

"I had a little help," Adam replied, sending a wink to Bernice. Then his tone grew serious, and his hand came up to finger the scars on his cheek. "If this affliction was allowed so that I would draw closer to my God, then I will wear it with honor. And if this lovely young woman—" he smiled gently at Rachel—"can accept me as I am, then I must accept myself as well. Perhaps when people realize that I'm not ashamed, they will see a picture of a man who has found God's grace to be truly sufficient."

A silence filled the room again, save for a few sniffles. Adam turned to Rachel, his face lit with the crooked smile that she had come to love. "That is, if anyone even notices me. I suspect that all eyes will be on the beautiful woman at my side."

More 19th-century romantic fiction by Tyndale House . . .